STOLEN FLAME

THE SEVEN CHAMBERS SERIES

D.W. MARSHALL

WICKED MOON PRESSING

Paperback ISBN: 978-0-9968729-5-9

Cover design by D.W. Marshall

Editing and Interior Layout by The Authors' Assistant authorsassistant.com

Printed in the United States

To my family for their laughter and love.

1

CARD ME, PLEASE

*T*omorrow can't come soon enough. It's 9:15 and I'm already in bed. I can't even begin to calm myself down. For starters, I'm turning the fabulous two-one! I can finally give a big "eff you" to every doorman and bartender in Vegas who sent me on my way when my fake ID didn't pass the test. I dare them all to card me after tonight. As a matter of fact, I may just punch a hole in my license and wear it as a necklace. Take that, Mr. Can I See Your ID Please. I want to wear a sign around my neck that says: Vivian Travis. I'm legal, bitches!

Of course, this plague only befalls me because I look so young. My best friend Maddie has had C cups since I met her in the fricking seventh grade. She never gets carded. Somehow, my less-than-B-cups —that just sounds better than my first-letter-of-the-alphabet cups— are a red flag that screams, "card me."

Maddie always tells me that if I made small efforts to look older it would help. She and I are complete opposites in the looks department. Maddie has blonde hair and striking blue eyes. She's more Sports Illustrated, and I guess I'm Girls Life. My hair is long, straight, and nearly black, making my pale skin seem even fairer. People always compliment me on my steel-gray eyes, but the combination of my skin, eyes, and hair have always made me feel like my ancestors are some breed of wolf. Add that to my runner's body and lack of a desire to wear makeup, and I guess I can see why I appear younger than I am. It's not that I have anything against makeup or a curling iron, I just happen to love sleeping more. My appearance is not worth trading for the extra forty-five minutes I get snuggled underneath my comforter.

The second thing that I'm so jazzed about is that Maddie, her boyfriend, Stevyn, and Liam are taking me for a surprise birthday weekend, and I happen to love surprises. When I was a kid, I would get a thrill at the butterflies attacking my stomach on the first day of school. The higher the drop on a coaster, the better for me. When I asked what we should do for my birthday, I was told by my friends to leave everything up to them. Since then, I have been a bundle of nerves. That's not the only thing that has my stomach in knots, though. It's the weekend with Liam that I'm the most thrilled about. Liam and I have also been friends since seventh grade. He and Maddie are my best friends in the whole world. You rarely see one of us without the other.

The problem is, I've managed to fall in love with him. I've always thought he was a good-looking guy. Okay, that's an understatement. With his dark hair, blue eyes, and perfect body, he could be cast in the role of Superman. Growing up, I always knew he was a great catch for any girl lucky enough to be on his radar. Never me. He's been more like a brother to me, and, we've always been on completely different wavelengths when it comes to relationships. Liam is kind of a ladies' man, and I believe in abstinence. How could we be compatible?

Sex always seems to be a deal-breaker in my relationships. I've yet to meet the guy who shares my beliefs. I don't get why guys think I'm such a freak because I don't want to give up something so sacred to me. I'm sorry, guys, but our third date is not a significant event, nor enough of a commitment for me to give up that part of me. I can only give that to someone once, and I'm not saying it has to be my husband, but I would prefer it be someone I love enough to one day become my husband. Liam could be that person, but I can't expect him to wait for me, and I'm not sure I'm willing to sacrifice my personal beliefs, even if I am in love with him.

About a year ago, something changed. I began confiding in him about my failed dates and relationships, something that I never really did before. Maddie was always my sounding board for that. My failed relationships had been a long-running joke between Liam and me, but one day, I took a leap and sought out a male point of view. It was then that I saw a different side of him. He was supportive and patient and a great listener. He stopped making jokes about my romantic misfortunes. He told me how special I was and how beautiful I was. Really? He would tell me about what he would do if he was with someone like me. Not me exactly, but someone like me.

I could gaze into his baby-blue eyes all night. He made me feel special. Over the course of the last year, Liam altered my view of him. I started to think that maybe with the right woman, someone he could really love, he could be tamed. Now, I'm lost. I'm a bumbling idiot around him. Of course, I haven't said anything to him because I could ruin everything.

Liam's emotional support for me is no different than what he would do for Maddie. If I told him about my changing feelings, things could get awkward fast. Or, worse, if we did try and it didn't work out, we could end up hating each other. Are my new feelings worth risking our friendship?

Unfortunately, Maddie noticed how weird I started acting around Liam. I couldn't lie to her when she asked me what was going on, so I confessed my feelings for our fellow best friend. In true Maddie form, she couldn't wait to jump at that chance to intervene. She had no problem reverting us back to early middle school. She might as well have sent Liam a fucking note: Do you like Vivian? Check yes or no.

I wanted to kill her when she told me she pumped him for information about how he feels about me. Then she came back with the news that he is also into me, and I almost died. Liam "The Hotness" Patrick is into me? Holy crap! That goes a long way to making this weekend one of the most important birthday weekends of my life.

The only details I was given about my birthday weekend were to pack an evening dress, a slutty party dress, and a bikini. No doubt the latter are for Maddie's elaborate plan to ensure that Liam and I are a couple by the time we return home. I openly pray that her plan works as wells as she hopes it does, because the idea of Liam and I as a couple keeps me up most nights. All I want is to be on the receiving end of those sparkling blue eyes and that dazzling, dimpled smile.

So, other than my constant obsession that my best guy friend and the secret object of my desire wants me, the rest of my birthday celebration is a mystery. My brain is working on overdrive tonight. Maybe I should make another sign to hang around my neck declaring my love for Liam. If only I were that brave.

After hours of tossing and turning, I finally drift off into a Liam-filled dream. I've always been a light sleeper, so I rouse when I hear the creak of my door opening. I don't know how long I was out, but my body tells me that the sun isn't up yet. I know my door is open; I can see it's dark in the hallway. Probably Growl. If my door isn't closed all the way, my black lab comes and visits me in the middle of the night. There have been plenty of mornings when I wake up to him hogging most of the bed. I think nothing of it and close my eyes, prepared to let sleep consume me in hopes that I can return to my dream. Liam was just about to grab me in a lover's embrace and kiss me. Suddenly, I feel something slip over my head. I can't see anything.

"What the hell?" I gasp, and right as I'm prepared to scream, I remember the surprise. These fools. Might as well play along. No sense ruining the surprise, especially since they went to the length of staging a kidnapping. "Wow, guys. This is a better surprise than I thought. Talk about elaborate. I'm game. Please, Mister Kidnapper. Please don't take me," I add with a giggle. Not a word from my friends. "Maddie, if you're gonna go this far and take me from my bed in the middle of the night, at least grab my overnight bags. They're right by the door." I point in the general direction of my bags. "P.S., this hood stinks! Please tell me I don't have to wear this the whole time, 'cause that is so not gonna work for me."

Still not a word or a giggle from my friends.

I continue playing along. In a few moments I will be riding in the car with Liam, hopefully the backseat. Not that I'm brave enough to try anything. I feel someone lift one of my feet and I realize that they want me to slide into my slippers. "Thank goodness. I thought you were going to walk me right out the front door barefoot," I say.

I wish I knew if the strong hands holding me belonged to Liam or Stevyn. If I knew for sure they belonged to Liam, I'd trip on purpose just to have him catch me.

The air is cool and windy—April in Las Vegas. If I didn't have the stinky hood on, I could feel the nighttime breeze that I love so much caressing my face. Knowing that triple digits are on their way, I like to appreciate the crisp April winds.

I can hear a car door open and the tug on my arm indicating that I am to enter the vehicle. My right leg is lifted to guide me up the high step. Wow, an SUV—they went all out. "Can I take the stinky hood off now? I'm seriously over this thing already." I get no response.

The door clanks shut and echoes. Huh? I sit in my seat and am quickly belted in. Before I can utter another word, we are on the move.

"Okay, guys, seriously, if you think I'm riding for another minute under this fowl hood..." I start to remove the hood from my head.

"Leave the hood where it is," a deep voice warns me. That voice does not belong to anyone that I know.

In a flood of adrenaline, the hairs raise on my arms. I'm on high alert now. I'm in trouble. My heart starts a steady drumming that is so strong I can feel each beat pounding in my ears.

"What the fuck is going on?" I shout.

No response.

I hear a faint conversation in front of me. The driver...no, the passenger is talking. I strain to hear anything that might help me.

"Yes, boss. We have her," the deep voice says. I don't hear an immediate response, so I can only assume he's on a call. "No, boss, we didn't have to drug her. Get this, apparently her friends were supposed to kidnap her for some surprise." He laughs.

Fuck you, mister. That's the only way you got me so easily.

"She let us put the hood on and walked right out the door." He laughs again. "Her family had no idea," he continues. "It was priceless. I wish they were all so easy. We'll be at the airport in about twenty minutes."

The conversation ends and I realize how many mistakes I've made. I let them take me from my home. From my fucking bed! I have willingly climbed into a kidnapper's vehicle! Now they think I'm getting on a fucking plane! Hell no!

Oh my God, what am I going to do? What the fuck? My mom and dad. My little brother, Shane. Why didn't I realize that my friends like their sleep too much to wake up in the wee hours of the night! Fuck, fuck, fuck. I can't get on that plane! I'm as sure as dead if I do. Better they toss my dead carcass on the side of a Vegas road. At least my parents will find out sooner what happened to me.

I take two or three deep breaths and am almost knocked out by the foul, rotten egg smell. Fuck you, assholes. I remove the hood. I only grab a few mental snapshots. Four men. Two in back with me. Two in the front seat. It's not an SUV, but a certified, kidnapper-issued, blacked-out van. That's all I see before my mouth is covered with a cloth saturated in a chemical. I go into black, dreamless nothingness.

2

LIAM, LOST BOY

This is going to be the most exciting weekend of my entire life. Vivian and I have been in the friend zone since seventh grade, and it's long past time to change that. I have it on good authority that Vivian wants more with me, too. Our mutual friend, Maddie, has told me in no uncertain terms that if I'm ready to take our relationship to the next level, the ball is in my court. In other words, I need to stop being a pussy and tell the girl I have been in love with for years how I feel. When it comes to Vivian, though, I am, indeed, the biggest pussy on earth.

Vivian is no ordinary girl, and everyone knows that I'm in love with her. Well, she hasn't caught on. She's the most beautiful and sexy creature ever created. Her pale, dewy skin, contrasts with her near-ebony hair, which is set off by the most electric steel gray eyes. Her beauty is rare. Her body is toned and fit, with the perfect amount of curves. But the thing that sets Vivian in an entirely different league from other gorgeous girls is that she is even more sensational on the inside.

There is nothing more attractive than a sizzling hot girl who doesn't know she's gorgeous. The drawback is that every yahoo thinks he might have a shot with her because she's approachable. Her kindness should not be confused with stupidity. She is sweet and all, but she has a tough side. She kicked my butt a couple of times growing up, until I got my man muscle and she stopped trying to take me. If she only knew I secretly loved our little fights. Her temper is even hot.

Over the years, I have had to sit back and endure the guys in her life—the ones who she only gave the briefest moment of her time and, worse, the ones who she really liked. Those were the most painful. My stupidity and weakness threw me right into the role of friend. I played the role well because I loved her and really was her friend. I did it with pride, and being on the receiving end of those mesmerizing eyes peering into my soul, or her smile that turned my heart into a puddle on the floor, was a gift. For her, I would play any role I was cast in. Protector is the role I have claimed for myself. If I couldn't be the one she fell for, then I would make damn sure that no one had the chance to hurt her.

Then something in our friendship changed. It's like I received a promotion over the last year or so. Recently, she and I began spending more time together, alone. I still haven't made a move. Big wuss. I did manage to tell her how absolutely beautiful she is.

She became more forthcoming about her boyfriend troubles, and listening only added more nails to the friend coffin, to the point where I've buried any chance at her seeing me as anything else. My wussiness knows no bounds. Then, one night about six months ago, she called me and asked if she could stop by. This wasn't out of the norm. Well, maybe her calling first was. Usually, Vivian and Maddie popped by whenever they wanted. When I opened my door, I could tell she'd been crying. She didn't say a word. She didn't need to. I immediately wrapped my arms around her. I loved her.

That night solidified my feelings for Vivian Marie Travis. I knew that my role forever more would be to love and protect her. She was all I ever wanted. We stayed up until three in the morning talking about everything and nothing, including the jerk who broke her heart. When neither of us could keep our eyes open, I made up the sofa for myself and told her she could take my room. She smiled at me sweetly with silvery-gray twinkly eyes, and I felt my heart stop.

"What?" I asked her. If I was really a man, I would have made my feelings known at that very moment. I would have stormed over to her, grabbed her into an embrace, and stoked the fire behind her eyes. I would have sacrificed everything to have her. That night, I was no man. I was what I have always been, her loyal friend.

"I'm not putting you out of your own bed, Liam. We can share the bed, if you don't mind." She blushed and I momentarily couldn't speak, blink, or think.

"I...I...don't mind if you don't," I stammered.

And that was it. The first night Vivian slept over. It wouldn't be the last. Nothing ever happened, but I could feel an electricity, that I assumed was coming from me, when our skin touched. Every night she slept with me, we moved closer and closer. Until waking up with her in my arms was the norm and some of the most exhilarating mornings of my life.

If Maddie hadn't stuck her nose into our business, I would probably still be the world's lamest. It seemed immature as fuck that she was going back and forth between Viv and I, but I thank her daily for the intrusion. When she told me that Vivian had feelings for me, that was all I needed to hear. The bottom line is, we are in love. So, this weekend, based on all the facts I have tabulated about us, I will not be a pussy anymore. I fully plan to kiss and love every inch of my beautiful Vivian. I know that she has little or no experience with that part of a relationship, so I will be patient with her. I have hopes of her being my wife one day soon, so I have that kind of time. When we get back from her surprise San Francisco birthday getaway, I intend for her to be mine.

I have never in my life wanted anything more than Vivian, and I can't wait. She's what I live for.

3

UNWANTED FLIGHT

*W*here am I?

Oh my God, my head is pounding. I try to sit up, but I can't. All I can do is grab my head and hold on. My brain feels like it's in a vise. I open my eyes one at a time. My most recent memories flood all of my senses at once, making the pain much worse.

They didn't kill me like I'd hoped. I'm on the plane—a fancy, private leather and glass number. Fuck. This shit just can't be happening to me. Why couldn't they have just killed me?

I dare to look around. I see the four kidnapping assholes are all sleeping. How can they sleep and just leave me free and unrestrained? I know exactly how. We're in an airplane...in the air! What can I do? Even if I was some amazing Jackie-Fucking-Jet-Li-Chan badass fighter, I'd only be able to incapacitate one of them. Then I'd have to deal with the other three. Also, I have no idea where the nearest exit is. Even if I found the emergency parachute, I have no clue how to use it. I have been unconscious for who knows how long? We could be in a foreign country by now. A thousand stranded movie scenarios play through my mind. What would I do? Where would I go? What if we're over international waters?

My best chance of escape is on the ground, but I know that the odds are not in my favor. I curl in on myself and cry silent sobs and silent prayers.

Liam.

Maddie.

Mom and Dad.

Shane.

Fuck.

I fall asleep again and awaken to the plane's smooth descent. If I have any chance of escape, it'll be when the plane lands. Four two-hundred-plus-pound men versus all one hundred and twenty pounds of me. Let's do it! The plane sets down easily and I immediately steel my nerves for the fight that is to come.

I don't even get a chance. Before I know it, I'm restrained in cuffs and a hood is going back over my head.

"Hope this one smells better, miss," a deep voice says. This hood is fresh-smelling, like it was recently laundered, but it is still a hood. Does he expect me to thank him?

I am quickly ushered—more like pushed—off of the airplane and down the steps. I'm so upset, I trip. Liam is surely not coming to my rescue. Liam. I'm caught by a pair of strong hands.

"Nice catch, Tyson. Can't bring her to the boss all banged up," another deep voice laughs from behind me.

"Maybe if you'd stop pushing and shoving her and let her fucking walk, she wouldn't trip. She is sightless, dumb fuck. Remember?" I assume the person who caught me was the one who had the kindness to offer me the clean hood.

"My bad, Tyson."

Tyson? At least I know one of their names.

"This way, miss." Tyson says.

Miss?

Next thing I know, I'm being stuffed into another vehicle. My sense of smell is heightened, and I catch whiffs of the ocean. Wherever we are, the ocean is close. I also note that wherever they are taking me it is close to the airport because we do not travel far before we stop. I'm quickly ushered out of the car and into a building. The lack of air and breeze and the slamming of a heavy door clues me in.

I'm guided forward. The sound of our footsteps bounce and collide off of the walls, cluing me in that the space is massive, made of stone or brick, and the floor under my feet is rough like concrete. I'm trying to use every sense I have to gather information to escape. Long plane ride, near the ocean, vacant stone edifice.

More stairs? A hand guides me up what appears to be a winding staircase. Round and round we go, climbing up and up. A sob escapes me. This can't be fucking happening to me. I'm cuffed and blinded, heading up a staircase that can only lead to my doom.

Why didn't I let Liam love me? Why were we so stupid and scared? I'll never see him again. I'll never get to see those dimples or those blue eyes again. According to Maddie, he secretly loved me, too. Maddie. Mom and Dad. I won't get to see Shane graduate from high school. Fuck. And Growl, he's gonna be lost without me. The sobs are coming out of me louder and faster now.

"Quiet," a voice urges me.

"Fuck you. Just kill me now and get it over with."

I don't know what comes over me, but I stop dead in my tracks. I have made this far too easy for them. They are not going to get any further cooperation from me. I'd rather them kill me than the alternative. "Skin suit" comes to mind. Enough is enough. My life, my terms. I'm sure heaven is a beautiful place.

"Miss, if only it were that easy. The boss would be devastated if any harm came to you. Please keep moving." It's the same kidnapper —Tyson. He's still by my side.

I don't take another step.

"Miss, please. Please continue forward." He tries to convince me. "You will not be harmed here."

Even though his voice sounds kind and reassuring, I continue to stay exactly where I am.

The man lifts me from where I stand and carries me the rest of the way. Not without a fight, though. I kick and try to use my head as a weapon. I scream at the top of my lungs and hammer my fists into his back. The beast of a man doesn't budge or lose his balance once.

When he sets me down my leaden arms ache and my body is marathon exhausted from fear, emotion, and my puny attempt at fighting to get away.

The hood is removed.

My hair sticking to my sweaty face would normally drive me nuts, but I endure it and squeeze my eyes shut in an effort to delay my reality. Collective noises echo off the walls of the room—sobs that are not my own. When I can no longer take it, I open my eyes, and what I see drops me to my knees. My legs are no longer capable of holding up my weight. I rest my head on the hard, cold stone floor and break down, chanting a slew of silent prayers: for safety, for this to be a dream, for rescue. A skin suit would be a better end to what lies in wait for me.

My God. Where am I? Please let this be a dream...a nightmare. Please.

There is a heavy presence in front of me; heavy dark work boots come into my view. When a pair of hands grasp my shoulders, I squeeze my eyes shut, blocking out what will happen to me next and the person lifts me to my feet. I take the opportunity to scan my environment, there is no way I can shut out the world with my eyelids; it is hardly enough of a barrier from reality.

I gaze around and take in the six other wide-eyed, frightened faces. Six young women. All have their arms cuffed behind them, and all wear the same mask of fear and anger.

The other thing that becomes alarmingly apparent are the guards surrounding us—more than ten, no doubt carrying guns. I can't see guns, but their military posture and attire suggest it. There is no way out but to make them shoot me. One thing is for sure, they are going to have to shoot me because this situation has "sex slave" written all over it.

I study the room for more facts to catalog for my escape. If I wasn't terrified for my life, I would think this is a very handsome, masculine space. It is circular with stone walls, like I suspected. The floor is very old-world European cobblestone. There are seven large built-in bookshelves that appear so ancient they would crumble if you dared to touch them. Each bookshelf boasts aged, expensive volumes. In the center of the space there is a circular bar, and I suddenly feel thrust back into another century—one with castles and moats, when being a woman wasn't exactly an asset.

Just before I force one of these gun-toting fuckers to shoot me in the head, a strange sound catches my attention. The floor in the center near the bar opens and a bright light blasts through the hole. As the light fades away, a head appears. A dark-haired man, dressed in a smoking jacket, rises out of the floor.

"Ladies. Welcome to this year's Chamber." I can't see the person clearly yet, but his voice is excited and cheery.

He gives us what is supposed to be a warm smile, but I'm not fooled—he is the devil for sure. Maybe he'll shoot me and put me out of my misery.

"Allow me to introduce myself. My name is Mason Wilde. Of course, that is not my real name. You will soon learn that none of us use our real names inside the world of The Chamber." He steps off the circular platform that brought him up and begins walking toward us.

"You will use new names during your time here." Mason stops and takes a pause to glance at each one of us. He casually walks down our line with his hands threaded together behind his back. "You have all been handpicked to make this year's Chamber the most exciting and sensual in its history."

I can't help the bile that rises in my throat at the thought of what he means by sensual. Skin suit, please. At least skin suit implies my death. Sex slave is what he's implying. I've never even had sex before. Liam was supposed to be my first.

This can't be happening to me, but glancing down the row of girls, I realize that it is indeed happening, and not just to me...to all of us. We were all stolen from our lives, our families, and our futures. There has to be a way out of this.

"If any of you are contemplating your escape..."

Is he a mind reader? Mason is standing almost directly in front of me when he plucks the thought right out of my head. I never understand why the bad guys don't think a victim wouldn't want to escape or deserve to escape successfully. I'm supposed to be celebrating my birthday, not my certain death. Every second, minute, and hour I'm here will be spent on surviving and escaping.

"Please use your energy on anything else. The Chamber's success comes from our rather Byzantine approach to planning. In the ten years that The Chamber has been in existence, no one has ever escaped. You will all understand why once the rules are explained to you." His devilish smile explodes across his face.

Before I'm prepared, he's a hairbreadth from my face, and I flinch in response. My brain is telling me to look away, avert my eyes from the devil, but my body doesn't listen.

I smell his strong, musky cologne. The energy between us is thick and heavy. His eyes, almost coal-black, bore into mine and I match his stare. He softens his gaze and steps back, and I am thankful for the distance he has put between the two of us. He moves languidly down the line, continuing to regard each one of us. Tears shower my face and my shoulders rise and fall. This isn't happening.

"Beautiful," he states simply as he takes a step back and admires us. "Whew!" he shouts. "This is what I've always wanted—the perfect mix of beauty, innocence, and seductiveness." He continues to gape at us.

He stares.

And stares.

And stares.

We are all startled by his hands clapping together. "Back to business." He shakes off his thoughts. "Where was I, Gabe?" he asks.

"The rules, sir," Gabe answers from behind us.

Mason snaps and points in Gabe's direction. "Right. The rules." He begins pacing. "I'm so excited, I can hardly stay in my skin." He smiles a comical smile and spins around, as if we are waiting with enthusiasm for him to tell us what prize we've won, instead of news of our shared doom.

"Rule number one. You are all safe from physical harm here." He stares at us for a long breath, as if searing his promise into our very souls. Truly, I wouldn't trust him with my garbage.

He continues. "No one, and I mean no one, is allowed to beat or brutalize you. Any pain you feel will be sexual in nature." He sings the word. "You will learn to appreciate that pleasurable pain during your stay here.

"Rule number two. The Chambers, which I will introduce you to in due time, are for fucking, not sleeping. There are designated areas for sleeping. If any one of you falls asleep in her Chamber, she will be punished sexually. Tyson and Gabe, step forward please."

I remember Tyson, the gentle guard who caught me when I fell down the airplane steps. I knew he was a big man, based on how easily he handled me when I almost fell and how his body felt against mine when he carried me, but I had no idea.

Gabe is tall and well-built with fair skin. His long brown hair is tied in a ponytail. He is attractive in a rugged and outdoorsy way. Tyson is completely the opposite. He is also very attractive, and resembles a professional football player or wrestler. He stands well over six feet tall, with deep, olive tanned skin. His hair is buzzed, so I can't tell what ethnicity he is. He could be a mixed race, African-American, Asian, or Latin. He's nice, but that doesn't mean I want to kill him any less.

"Gentlemen, show these beautiful ladies what's in store for them if they fall asleep in their Chambers," Mason instructs them.

Without any hesitation, they unzip their pants and pull out enormous cocks. Each one of us gasp in unison. They are, no lie, near a foot long and pointing up like snakes about to attack. I never knew anything that large existed on a real person. Gabe's smile is seductive, and to my surprise, he grabs and strokes his organ, eyeing each one of us. Tyson, is not as boisterous. He stands silently as if he isn't exposed in front of us. He actually looks as if this is the last thing he wants to do.

"You see, ladies, my guards are all chosen based on their skills and endowments..." Mason emphasizes the last word. "Also, their good looks. Trust me when I say my guards love it when you ladies fall asleep in your Chambers. Let's just say they'll enjoy punishing you."

I can't help but stare at Tyson's endowment. There is no way all of that could ever fit inside of me without inflicting some serious harm. Mor bile creeps into my mouth .

Never fall asleep in The Chamber. Never fall asleep in The Chamber.

"Thank you, gentlemen," Mason says, making my eyes dart to him.

"Rule number three. Your job assignment will end next April, approximately one year from today. You will be paid handsomely for your work. No one is to ever know about your stay here. If it makes it easier, you can think of this as the highest-paying job you never applied for."

Mason walks over to the bar and pours himself a drink. He takes a long draw of the brown liquid before continuing. With glass still in-hand, he turns back to us.

"Rule number four. You will all be allowed to get to know one another. The middle level of the estate is the only level you will be allowed to roam freely. This area includes your sleeping quarters, dining area, media room, exercise room, spa, and salon. As this is a sex Chamber, it is required of you to maintain your beauty and physique."

There is a commotion in the room, but I can't bear to look around. Suddenly, I am freed from my binding cuffs. My shoulders cry from their unexpected freedom. I'm guided to a soft, comfortable chair. I finally gaze down the line of us. The same thing is happening to each girl.

"Much better," Mason states. "Now, let's get down to the nitty-gritty. What is this place? What does it mean for each of you? These are all good questions that I know are swimming in those gorgeous heads of yours." He pauses and smiles at all of us like a proud father.

"The Chamber started out as a very small business. A couple of women, a few clients... Back then, the women were call girls who wanted the job. Then, my partner and I got an idea to grow the business. We decided to make it more audacious and choose innocent girls who would never dream of this lifestyle. Even though we steal them away from their lives, we treat them like princesses. How sexy is that?"

I squirm in my chair. Is he insane? Does he think we are excited by this information?

"We expanded, and, well, I can't give away too much, but I will tell you some of the richest, most powerful men in the world have been chosen by a lottery to participate in this year's Chamber. They pay millions to be a part of this secret world. Are you wondering what kind of wacko nut creates something so taboo? Was I abused? Am I a sociopath? Well, the answer is no and no. I just happen to love money and fucking. So, I have the best job in the world. The next question you might have is, why you?" He takes a seat in a regal, high-backed chair that a guard sets in the center of our line. "That's easy. You are all fucking amazing!" He shouts with excitement. "I have a team of scouts who work tirelessly to find each group of women. You were all chosen two years ago!"

I'm going to be sick! Two years?

A large projection screen drops from the ceiling. Mason pushes buttons on a controller and multiple screens come to life. There we all are.

There's footage of us living our regular lives. I'm hanging out at Wet'n'Wild with Maddie and Liam. I'm walking on the UNLV campus...sleeping in my fucking bed!

The images start to become more personal, if that is possible. My stomach twists when images of my younger brother, Shane, at his high school, flash across the screen. There are my parents in their daily routine. There's even a picture of us sitting at the dinner table!

Images of children and people who are strangers to me, but must be the loved ones of the other girls, also cross the screen.

We all sob loudly and heavily as we each realize why no one ever escapes this place. We don't come to harm if we don't follow the rules or don't play Mason's sex games.

It will be my family, my best friend, the love of my life, and our loved ones who will be punished. That is how Mason has had such successful Chambers. He holds women hostage by threatening people they won't gamble with.

I was willing to die, to fight my way out of here, but this sick bastard has been surveilling my whole life for two years. I bury my face in my lap and sob uncontrollable tears.

"I can see that we have an understanding. There is no further need to continue this conversation. You all know what is at stake. I always find showing you is much more powerful than telling you. Please take a moment to compose yourselves." He gets up from his seat, walks over to the bar, and pours himself another drink.

Vivian Travis, Sex Slave. Never in a million years would I have thought to string that sentence together.

Some unknown amount of time passes before most of the sobbing subsides. I look into the eyes of a tear-stained face of a girl with sun-kissed blonde hair. Her eyes speak volumes. She is obviously terrified, mirroring the stare that I am giving her. She offers me a tight smile that says, "You are not alone." I return it.

"Back to business." Mason clears his throat. "Now that I have your full cooperation. You will each be assigned a bedchamber, a name, and a personal guard. Like I said before, no one uses their real name in The Chamber. Your job description is as follows. There are thirty-five very eager lottery winners who can't wait to spend the next year with you."

He has mentioned the word "year" more than once. Am I to understand that he expects to keep us here for a whole year? There is no way I can survive a day, let alone an entire year. Kill me now and get it over with. There won't be anything left of me in a year. I turn my attention back to him, fearful of missing anything that might be vital to my survival, even though I know the odds are not in my favor.

"You will be their lovers, their submissives, their whatever they want, five days a week. Sundays and Wednesdays you will rest and recuperate. Some of our lottery winners have cleared their books and intend to spend the entire week with you, while others prefer the notion of dropping in whenever they desire. For this year's group of winners, you ladies represent the sky, and the sky is the limit. Now, enough details. I'm ready for some fun. How about you?"

Mason steps over to the girl on the end and stands directly in front of her. He pulls her to her feet, takes a syringe from his pocket, and injects her in the upper arm with it. She jumps and rubs her arm, her eyes are wide with fear. Mason drops the used needle into an open box one of the guards behind him holds.

"No need to be alarmed, ladies. That is a birth control shot. You will each get one today and every three months. No condoms are used in The Chamber. Each lottery winner has been handpicked, just like you. All of them are healthy and disease-free. We will apply an additional form of birth control until these shots kick in." He returns his attention to the first girl in our line. He grabs her face between his two hands and kisses her like she is his lover. From where I'm standing at the end of the line, she appears to be kissing him back. The exchange is intimate and familiar. He runs his hands down the length of her arms, pulling her shirt up, exposing her full breasts as if they are alone, sharing a tender sensual moment. He takes her nipples into his mouth and sucks them one at a time before stopping abruptly, letting her shirt fall over her exposed body.

"Exquisite," he says.

I can't see her expression, but I can feel her fear, because it's mine. We all share a bond. My mind rushes through scenarios of the fate that awaits the rest of us in the line when we are given our shots.

"Long red hair, porcelain skin, green eyes that sparkle like a jewel. We will call you Ivy."

He kisses her again, takes her by the hand, and gives her to a waiting guard. The guard leads her to stand before one of the grand bookcases.

Mason steps in front of the next girl. She has shoulder-length dark hair and light brown skin.

"Beautiful Caribbean princess." He gives her the injection quickly, then kneels down in front of her, lifts her skirt and buries his face between her legs. Her hands ball into fists as this stranger spends much too long there. When he reappears he comes to his feet and wipes his lips on his sleeve.

"You are my Sunshine." He stands and takes her by the hand. Another guard leads her to a bookcase.

The next girl stands before he can guide her to her feet. "An eager, exotic Pacific island beauty. Dark hair, olive skin..." He gives her the injection in the arm. He reaches into the front of her pants and I can see him moving around, exploring. "...and ready—so moist and ready. I like that." He pulls his hand out of her pants, sticks two of his fingers in his mouth, and sucks them. "You even taste divine, Raven." Like the others before her she is led to a bookcase.

The girl who follows is the blonde who I locked eyes with. I realize, as he reaches her, that my turn is coming soon. I squeeze my legs together. I watch as she receives her shot. "The sky lights up around you, lovely one. I shall see if you taste as good as you look." He stands in front of her and stares. "If only I could tear my eyes away from your stunning baby blues. I find that I cannot. Ivory, please come and do a little taste test for me. Don't take your eyes off mine," he instructs the blonde.

Out of nowhere, a stunning, statuesque blonde woman appears by Mason's side. She seats the girl back in her chair and begins to pull down the girl's pants and panties to her ankles. She spreads her legs apart and buries her face between them. The girl squirms and writhes as Ivory continues her taste test. Ivory stands abruptly. "Heavenly," she says as she wipes her mouth.

"Then, Sky it is," Mason names the girl as he pulls her to her feet, her bottom is on display for everyone before she can scramble to pull up her pants. She is led to a bookcase.

I witness each girl being violated and named like property, one by one, getting closer to me.

One girl gets up from her seat with a pride that doesn't seem natural for what is happening to us. She holds her arm out and receives her birth control shot. Mason stands before her, and I can see her chest rapidly rise and fall. She is so close to me, I can hear her shallow breaths.

"A Latin beauty right off the beaches of Brazil. Please, kiss me." She leans forward to kiss him, and the sound of his pants unzipping echoes in the room. "No, no, beautiful one. Not on my lips."

She looks down as he pulls his cock out of his pants. My eyes widen.

His cock is not as humongous as Tyson's, but it is thick and long. I gag. I watch with frightened fascination as the girl kneels down and takes Mason's full and erect cock into her mouth. At first, she licks him like a popsicle. Then, as Mason's hips move forward, she begins to suck him in earnest. I've seen porn before, and she knows what she's doing. She takes him further down her throat until his dick isn't visible anymore. Mason throws his head back, and the girl rises up on her knees and pulls him in more. Mason stops her, swiftly. He takes his cock out of her mouth. He doesn't put it back into his pants. He guides her to stand and she reaches out and grabs it into her hand.

"Oh, my, my. Sapphire is your name, and I can't wait to get my hands on you. You might just be my next wife."

He grabs her by a fistful of hair and pulls her into a passionate kiss. His cock is still in her hand, and she strokes the shaft. He appears reluctant to let her go, but soon enough, she is standing in front of a bookcase.

The next girl is shaking. She's sitting right next to me. I'm right after her. Oh my goodness, I'm right after her!

"My dear, Violet. So beautiful and innocent, like the flower. Fair hair, rosy cheeks..."

She extends her shaky arm out and receives her shot. Her eyes, like mine, are staring at his hard cock that is sticking straight up out of his pants.

"Don't worry, darling girl. Your first time won't be like this. But I do want you to get used to seeing dicks. Take a good look."

He gives her, and me, full vantage of his erect organ. It moves on its own. It sort of jumps. I jump in response.

"Please have a seat," he instructs.

It's my turn. Oh no. It's my turn.

Mason stands before me with his onyx-black eyes and fully erect cock. I stare down at his cock because it is so close to me, and I'm freaking out. My body shivers and my blood is running colder. Will he show me the same courtesy that he showed Violet?

"Don't worry, I saved my two virgins for last. I will not ask you to display your affection for me. Please stand."

I do as I am told, because my family deserves my strength. I can do this. A year of sacrifice is nothing if they remain safe.

"I heard about your fire, your fight. I can see it in those steel-gray eyes of yours, Flame. That name suits you. Feast your eyes on me, Flame. Because you will become well-acquainted with my dick before the night is over. Please be seated."

He turns away from Violet and me. His cock swings out of view.

"To your Chambers, ladies." His hand sweeps lavishly toward the other girls.

He pushes a button on a remote and the bookcases slide open along the walls, revealing hidden staircases. Only five bookcases open. Five girls disappear into the darkness of the staircases, and the bookcases close behind them, leaving me and Violet behind.

"Now, back to my two innocent virgins. It would be cruel of me to let you begin this Chamber without being fucked thoroughly."

He is interrupted by one of the guards. He whispers in Mason's ear.

"Oh my dear, Flame. Seems I forgot your shot. Virgins always get me all scattered and excited. Look at my dick! It can't wait!" He points to his hard erection and thrusts his hips forward, as if we need help to see its length.

Liam and I were so stupid. Why didn't we tell each other how we felt? How many nights did I sleep over at his house, in his bed, with him right beside me? I always wanted him to touch me. I can remember that pulsating feeling between my legs. I wanted it. I wanted him. The love was there, and so was the trust. I should have devoured him, lost my virginity to him. Now I'm going to lose my sacred virginity to Mason—an evil, kidnapping stranger!

"Ivory," Mason says. "Show these ladies to the Deflowering Chamber."

4

LIAM, GONE TOO SOON

Three police cars are parked in front of Vivian's house. I can't go inside; doing so will make this true, and that is a reality that I am not prepared to face. I wrap my fingers around my steering wheel and tighten my fingers, trying to crush it with my bare hands. My hands burn and ache.

"Vivian! Vivian!" I shout until my voice is raw.

She's gone. Vivian is gone. I rest my head on my hands and I don't fight back the tears.

Anger sears through me, causing my body to shake. My heart. I startle when there's a rapping on my car window. It's Maddie. I roll my window down. She's as broken as I am.

"The cops have questions for us. We need to tell them anything that might help them find her." She can barely get the words out before she is sobbing again.

I'm out of my car at once. I wrap my arms around Maddie and the two of us quietly console one another. We head for the front door. I can barely walk through it because I don't want confirmation that she is gone. My eyes sweep the room and take in the panicked faces of Vivian's parents and her brother. Three police officers take up most of the space in the room.

"Mr. Travis, please continue," one of them says.

Maddie and I sit on the sofa with Shane.

"My wife and I wanted to tell Vivian happy birthday," Mr. Travis says. "She's twenty-one today. We had a gift for her. She loves those little fairies..." He can't continue. He and Vivian's mom cry into each other's arms.

I can't sit any longer. I'm so angry, my skin is crawling. "Why are we sitting here?" I shout. "We need to be out there finding her.

"Sir, I understand you're upset," another cop says. "We already have an APB out with Miss Travis' description. These questions are necessary."

I want to punch something. I have never felt so helpless in my life. Maddie is by my side. She urges me to take a seat, but I just can't. Instead I pace.

"Mr. Travis, sir." The cop urges him to continue.

"Right. So we bought her a watch with little fairies on the band. We went to give it to her at about seven in the morning. She wasn't in her room. At first, we thought her friends must have come early for her. So my wife and I went into the kitchen to make coffee, and that's when my wife noticed the back door was ajar. Not just open, though. Broken. The lock was busted. So, in a panic we ran up to our son's room, and he was sound asleep, with Growl, our dog. We ran back to Viv's room and saw that all of her overnight bags were still there in her room, along with her house keys, purse, and cell phone. That's when we called the police and her friends."

I can't fight the tears. Someone came into her fucking house and took her? She can't be gone. She just can't be.

"Mr. Travis, you mentioned your home alarm?"

"It never went off. Whoever came into my home and stole my baby bypassed it. We never had a warning. If we would have, they would not have taken our daughter from our home. We would be cleaning the bastards from my dammed walls!" He shakes his fists.

"Is there anything else you feel might be important?" the officer asks Mr. Travis.

Then he turns to Maddie and me. "Are you the boyfriend?" he asks me.

"No. I'm not the boyfriend." I say between gritted teeth. For some reason, I don't like his tone. "We—" I gesture to Maddie and I, "—have been friends with Vivian since the seventh grade. Today is her birthday and we were taking her to San Francisco for the weekend. I happen to be in love with her, though, so, I would be honored to be her boyfriend."

"And how did Miss Travis react when she learned about your feelings for her?" he asks me while scribbling some shit down in his little tablet.

What the fuck is he implying?

"Officer," Vivian's mom says. "My daughter is in love with Liam. We spoke yesterday while she packed. She was excited about this weekend with him. He's practically a part of this family."

This revelation from Vivian's mother warms and breaks my heart at the same time. Why was I such a fool? Why didn't I take my chance to be with Vivian while she was with me, in my bed, across the table at the coffee shop, next to me in the movie theater, dancing with me at the club, running next to me on the treadmill? Why did I wait? Now, I may never see her again.

"I'm sorry, I need some air." I rush out of the house with every intention to get as far away from Viv's house, but I only make it as far as the porch, and there, I let go.

5

TAKEN, NOT GIVEN

*W*e are standing in front of double doors with a sign that actually says, "Deflowering Chamber." My heart races and clangs around inside my chest. Whatever awaits us behind that door will destroy me. We follow closely behind Ivory and cross the threshold. The room is white and celestial. Too white, and even under duress, I don't miss the purity joke. Ha.

I also notice the pair of naked guards standing at attention on either side of the entrance. Their expressions are blank as we pass, as if they are not standing there with erections waiting to do who-knows-what to us. There are three oversized beds that form a triangle in the center of the room. The only splashes of color in the room are the satin pillowcases adorning each bed. It doesn't take a rocket scientist to figure out that the crimson pillows are on my bed and the lavender ones are on Violet's bed. My blood runs cold.

Another pair of naked guards stand before us. The one directly in front of me is Tyson. Thunderdick, my brain accidentally names him. He glances down at me and offers a kind smile. He is completely naked and his cock is awake and alert, ready to inflict the only thing an organ of that size is capable of inflicting—pain. Maybe he gets first dibs.

"Flame. I like that name. It really does fit you," he whispers. Does he think I care if he likes my name? The only thing I care about in this moment is what is about to happen to me, what I stand to lose, and the fact that I have no say or choice here. My body does not belong to me here.

I swallow and glance down at his massive organ. My knees turn to jelly, and my head swims.

"Touch it. It doesn't bite."

My eyes shoot back up to his. There is kindness behind them that is out of place here. Under these circumstances, I expect to find aggression, power, or even savagery. Not kindness. When I gaze into Tyson's eyes, that is all I see. He isn't making me touch him. He is giving me a choice, even though I know there really isn't one.

He really is beautiful up close. He should be modeling for some athletic magazine. Everyone would want to exercise if they saw him on the pages of a magazine. His skin is the smoothest deep olive, without so much as a visible pore or blemish. His lips are full and naturally pouty. What has come over me? I am standing in front of a naked, very well-endowed stranger who was directly involved in my kidnapping and plans to have sex with me against my will, and I'm admiring his body? I have lost my mind.

I bite the corner of my lip, as I do sometimes when I must make a difficult decision. Tyson has the sexiest smile. Dimples appear on his face, and the most perfect set of teeth in creation appear. Oh my.

I reach out and touch the massive tip of his erection and it jumps. It just moves of its own accord. I snatch my hand away like it's on fire and my eyes shoot back up to his.

"Sorry. That happens when he gets excited. He really likes you."

He?

Tyson pulls me toward the bed with the red pillows. "Do you want to take your clothes off yourself or do you want me to do it?"

This is happening. How can he be my first? My eyes sting and mist with tears I refuse to shed. What good would it do here? This is happening regardless of how many tears I shed. What I need is strength and courage. It is time to stifle my tears, detach myself from this nightmare and figure out a way out of this shit that won't put my family in jeopardy.

"Umm. I'll do it." My heart is beating into a frenzy, causing my body to shake. My eyes don't leave his massive erection. He's sitting, and I would swear his own mouth could reach it from that position.

My hands shake as I go at the task of removing my top and bottoms. I'm in my pajamas, so once they are off I'm as naked as Tyson. I've never been this naked with a man before. I've had boyfriends, and we've made out and touched this or that, but down to my bra is about as far as I've gone. My virginity has always been too special to give away to just anybody, and I've never liked a guy enough to explore further. Except for Liam. Apparently, we were both too idiotic to act on our feelings. I liked him too much, and I think I couldn't get past the fact that he might not reciprocate. Or worse, that we would be lousy together and ruin our friendship. Now I wish I had just dove in. At least my first time would have been with someone that I'm madly in love with, instead of this stranger.

I stand completely naked in front of Tyson. He is very attractive and is going out of his way to make me think he is sweet and that I have a fucking choice in the way this all goes down, but the bottom line is, he is a stranger—a kidnapper—who is about to break me in half.

He pulls me close to him and wraps me in a tight, and unexpected embrace. His erection is thick and smooth and warm against my breasts—too near my face for my comfort. While he holds me in his strong arms, I see the other guard isn't taking his time with Violet. He has her sprawled across the bed, her legs wide open, and his face buried between them. My heart breaks for her because her moans mean that despite her fear and desire to be anywhere but here, her body won't allow her to ignore her physical feelings. Based on the moans and sighs escaping her, it must feel good. The sounds coming from her bed causes warmth and moisture between my legs. My stomach churns and roils and it's like a horrific traffic accident that I can't look away from even though I should.

Tyson's touch brings my attention back to my own horror show.

He places my hands on his cock. I say silent prayers for a way to survive this. He is bone-hard with warm, smooth skin. My hands shake as he guides my hands up and down the shaft. When I dare a glance at his face, I can see by his hooded eyes and the way his head falls back that he is enjoying what I am doing to him. For some crazy reason, I like that I have the ability to make him feel this way. My stomach flip-flops and flutters, and my body clenches and contracts.

"Mason says that we need to spend some time letting you two get used to these." He gazes down at his erection. "Since I'm your personal guard I get to show you. I won't have sex with you, though. It'll be too much all at once, but I really want to," He breathes as I continue to stroke his shaft.

Electricity shoots through my entire body at the thought of this massive cock inside of me. Just the idea of looking into his gorgeous face while he is inside of me has a cocktail of chemicals mixing inside of me, making me want something that I should never want in a place like this. I hate myself for being reduced to weak flesh when I should fight or run. I don't respond to him. What can I say?

"I'm told we have a few days to turn you two into sex pros before the big coming out party." He guides my hand to stroke faster. "That's it." His hips roll in subtle circles. "You're a natural at this," he compliments me, and for the briefest moment I forget where I am. I imagine I met Tyson while out with Maddie, and I've decided to hook up. People give into their basic animal instincts and do it all the time. I squeeze his shaft tighter and pump my hand faster, urged on by his moans. I can do this, I can fake that I am anywhere other than here. That is, until Violet yells out, her voice wet with ecstasy. I freeze. The room and my circumstances come back into view and a shiver runs through my body.

Tyson stares at me and the expression on his face, just for the briefest second, is the fear that I feel. He quickly covers it. We are locked in a stare before he snaps out of it. He reaches his hand out for me and guides me to the bed on my back. I stare up at him, looking for the glimpse he shared with me. His features rest in a position that tells me that he wants to be here about as much as I do. His mouth forms a grim line and his brows furrow. There is sadness in his eyes. He shakes his head quickly.

"Sorry," he mouths. Then he rubs his cock on my stomach. He is warmer against the tender skin of my stomach than he was in my hands. My body betrays my every wish. My sex warms and clenches with want. Liquid moisture prepares me for what is coming.

Sorry? Did I misread his lips? I've never been a good lip reader. I'm so confused. He's so gentle with me. So kind. He's sorry? Who is this guy?

"How does that feel?" He stares down at me and asks.

I don't know how to answer his question. If this was the scenario I trumped up in my imagination for the sake of survival, I'd have an answer for sure. I nod. He is confusing me with his kindness, making me feel like I could tell him no and he would actually stop. He smiles down at me like a lover and not the stranger that he is. My body betrays my mind and my hormones crave his touch.

"See? Cocks are not as scary as you thought." He leans over and kisses me on the lips.

What?

"I know this is scary," he says as he rubs his cock around the opening of my sex.

A gasp escapes me. The feeling is delicious. No matter what my mind might want, my body wants this, especially down there. I'm slippery with wetness and anticipation. My body moves in a rhythm that I don't understand. The moaning coming from Violet and the other guard makes the feelings even stronger. I am losing the battle between my mental clarity and the sensations that are wracking my body.

"I asked Mason if I could be your personal guard during your stay with us. I admire your fire. I want this journey to be smooth for you, not scary." His voice is low, as if on purpose, but I am sure there can be no secrets between these walls. Mason gives the impression that he is the all-knowing ruler of this world he has created.

The head of his cock slips on the wetness and dips inside and the pressure is all consuming. My voice shakes and vibrates on an exhale.

He is killing me. My conscience is at war with what it knows is right and what it definitely knows is wrong. My body is telling me that it wants more—more pressure at my apex, more of his soft voice that blankets me in comfort, more of him. I need to get back to my hookup scenario quickly.

How can this stranger make me feel like he cares for me? He's fooled me so far. I don't know if he plans to flip the script on me and turn out to be crazy or abusive, but right now in this moment he has a modicum of my trust. As much as I can, I give it to him in this moment, in this space. He has been nothing but gentle with me. I remember his voice—him being protective of me with the other kidnappers. He caught me when I stumbled. He is taking his time with me now.

But this is wrong. It should be Liam. He's the man that I want to be devoted to. He's the one who I have shared a bed with many nights. I imagined him touching me and kissing me a million times. He's the one that my virginity belongs to. Liam isn't here.

When Tyson's mouth claims mine, I return his kisses. Our mouths fit together like intricate puzzle pieces. How is that even possible?

His scent is heady—a hint of musk and him. I decide in this moment that I want him to want to help me. I need him to.

"Thank you," I say around our kiss. "For making me feel safe in this house of horrors."

He pulls his face away from mine and stares down at me with sadness in his eyes. A slow smile tugs at one corner of his mouth, then disappears from my sight. He begins spreading my legs apart. His head lowers and his mouth is on my sex. His tongue slides slowly up my flesh and my body. My legs tremble in his hands, as he slides his tongue back down.

"Fuck. Oh." His tongue dips inside of me and the sound that comes out of me is foreign. I've never felt anything like this. Every nerve in my body has zeroed in on the new and unfamiliar feelings down there and what is happening to me. "Ooh. Ohh," I cry out as Tyson's tongue glides across my over-sensitized opening. His lips and tongue suck my clitoris and my hips can no longer stay on the bed. My heartbeat is erratic and begins to increase. This is different than any time I have brought myself to orgasm. My skin feels like it can't stay. I don't know what to do with myself. My hands itch and tingle.

"If you come for the first time with me, I just might take you out of this place and keep you for myself," he mumbles from between my legs.

I can't keep my thoughts straight. Liam, I'm so sorry. I was saving my first time for you. The next thing I know, Tyson slips two fingers into my opening and I can no longer take it. I explode around his fingers. My body is all nerve endings and fiery sensations. I can't catch my breath as he continues to punish me with the pleasure of his expert mouth devouring my sex, while his skilled fingers drive in and out of me. My orgasm splinters and fragments, going on and on. I scream out.

I let everything out—rage, pain, fear, and shameful pleasure. I scream and scream. A heavy weight envelopes me, and I feel terrible...and good. He pulls me onto his lap and wraps me in his arms.

"That was so fucking beautiful." His mouth is close to my ear and he continues. "I hope you fall asleep in your Chamber so that I can spend a proper evening with you." He kisses my tears. "I know this is scary for you. I promise to help you. I won't let anyone hurt you. Okay?"

I nod my head. I want to trust him, but I can't. For his promise of service to protect me, though, I will say anything. I'd be lying to myself if I said I wasn't clinging on to the hope that there was a sliver of truth in his promises.

There is a commotion at the door.

"More guards are coming. Mason wants them all to get to know you, help you with your innocence." I can't stop that, but I will make sure that they are kind, and I will make sure that they are gentle with you. Okay?"

I nod my head at my new, very valuable ally in understanding. My stomach tightens with anticipation at the nightmare that awaits me on the other side of the door.

Within moments, the room is full. There are now four more guards with us, and all are naked. None are as well-endowed as Tyson or the other guard, Gabe. I'm alone on the bed. Tyson is no longer by my side, and I'm gripped with fear.

Two of the guards stand before me, eager to get their turns with the virgin. I glance at their faces, and my heartbeat is palpable. A lump grows in my throat. I scan the room and find Tyson, who has not taken his eyes off of me. Instantly, my fear dwindles down to something I can handle instead of this large bundle that feels too large to contain. I can do this. It's just sex. It's not my mind or my soul. I can keep my loved ones safe. I smile at Tyson and he returns it with a dashing grin. He can feel my strength. I nod at him and he nods back. I turn my attention to the new guards. I'm less afraid. Nervous, but less afraid.

"Kiss me," says the guard right in front of me. His eyes look down, instructing me to exactly where his hand grips his erection.

I kneel down like Sapphire did earlier in the round room and he puts his erection in my face. I glance over at Tyson and he watches intently. The guard shakes his erection in his hand, urging me to take it. I wrap my hand around him, and, closing my eyes, I run my tongue on the tip of it. It tastes saltier than I expected. I put the whole tip in my mouth and begin to suck. I suck harder and his hips thrust forward and I like the sense of control I feel when he moans.

"Fuck, yeah, bitch! Suck it!" he says.

I guess those were the wrong words because two seconds later he is getting up from the floor, with a very naked and angry Tyson standing over him.

"Respect! These women are employees and no different than us. Respect them, or I guarantee you that you'll be out on your ass! Now get the fuck out of here. I will relay the details of your visit to Mason."

The guard runs out of the room with his erection flopping up and down against him and his hand holding the side of his face where Tyson decked him.

"Are you okay?" Tyson is beside me at once.

"Yes."

He stays close to me while the other guard allows me to use his dick to practice giving blow jobs. I work my tongue around him in circles. Tyson guides me back onto the bed. I comply because right now I would follow him just about anywhere. I pull the guard with me with my hand and he follows. I begin to suck his erection. I'm on my hands and knees on the bed with the red pillows.

Yesterday I was a virgin, going to sleep excited about my birthday trip. Today I'm on all fours with a naked man's dick in my mouth. And as I feel the bed depress, I know I have a naked, well-endowed Tyson behind me. I smile inside, because he's the one who is there. I realize that today is my birthday.

Happy fucking birthday to me.

I feel Tyson's lips on my bottom. His soft breath against my skin makes my body tingle. Next, I feel the heaviness of his large cock, rubbing against the length of my sex—from opening to clitoris. It feels good. I push back against him, but he avoids my advances. What the hell is wrong with me?

I continue to suck the dick that is in my mouth, but my true attention is on one man. He is the safety net I have latched on to. I roll my hips and moan at the pressure of his erection running along my heated flesh. I arch my back and press my bottom back into him.

"Behave. I'm not going to go inside of you. It'll rip you apart." He leans forward and whispers in my ear. "We will have our time together, when you are ready for me." He kisses me on the cheek. I smile with excitement at the thought. I continue to mouth the guard's penis. My jaw is getting tired. The door swings open and a very naked Mason walks through.

"I have to leave now," Tyson says. "I trust Mason with you. He'll be gentle. Happy Chambermaids equal happy customers," he promises.

I nod my agreement. Everyone leaves us alone. It's just the three of us.

"Ladies. Ladies. Little Mason can't wait to get to know you." He grabs his full erection and shakes it in our direction. "I hope that my guards eased your tension about dicks and pussies? It's not as gross and scary as it seems. If done right, it can be the best feeling you'll ever experience in this lifetime. You will learn this year that sex, and some pain," he holds up his thumb and index finger to indicate a small amount, "can be a mind-blowing combination. Just think how exciting your sex lives will be when you return home."

Liam. Will he even want me after this?

"Flame, please climb onto your bed."

Me first? I don't want to be first. My heart slams against my chest. I need Tyson. He calms me. But I can't ask for him.

"Face up and close your eyes," he instructs.

This is it. My innocence is gone. I will be a woman in every way. Liam won't want me because I will have nothing to give him.

"Violet, please climb onto your bed. Same position."

I lay still and wait for what seems like forever. I try to fight the tears that escape my eyes, but I can't. My chest heaves. Tears spring free from my eyes. I don't want to be afraid. I want to show him strength, because I have a feeling that he respects it, but I am shaking.

"Hi, there."

I hear the familiar voice and a calm washes over me. It makes no sense, this connection that I feel to this stranger. A smile grows across my face, and my eyes fly open to see Tyson standing over me. It's like he heard my silent plea.

Mason pops into my view.

"I watched earlier and noticed how at ease you are with my head of security. It's rare that we have two virgins in a Chamber. Not many Chamber candidates remain chaste into their twenties." He offers me a smile that comes off as more creepy than comforting. "Seeing how I can't help two virgins at once, this is my rare gift to you. Consider it a birthday present to you both. That is, if you can handle that much man your first time," he says and winks.

I do my best to contain my excitement. I don't care if I can't walk for a month. I need this. I look at Tyson in surprise. We share the same birthday? Maybe that's the connection I have with him. Maybe this won't be my worst year ever.

I nod my agreement. Both of these men have shown me kindness. My fear ebbs. I stare with intent at Tyson. If my first time can't be with Liam, then I want my first time to be with him. Sure, I may be left disabled, but the feeling that he gives me—that this is somewhat in my control, whether that's imagined or not—makes this entire moment less scary. At least with Tyson I will feel cared for. He has shown me that much in such a short time.

"Are you sure about this?" he asks and he looks down at his massive erection. "I'll try to be gentle with you."

I nod again. In a daring, bold move, I come up onto my knees and take him into my hands. I ease my mouth onto his erection. I have to stretch my lips as far as they will open to get the tip into my mouth, and there's not much room left. So instead of ripping my mouth, I suck the tip and swirl my tongue around and around it. I draw the tip back into my mouth and suck in earnest, showing my appreciation. I gag a couple of times, and hear his soft giggle.

He moans, which makes me try harder. I quickly realize if I drop my jaw I don't feel the urge to gag as much. I take more of him into my mouth, much farther than before. His hips move. He likes it. He moans again when I pull and suck harder. I look up at him and he is gawking at me in shock. I have at least half of his length in my mouth and I taste his saltiness. He has given me the best gift. He has eased my fear and I will be forever grateful to him.

In a swift move, he's no longer in my mouth. I lick my lips. I want to remember how he tastes. I may need to recall this memory when times get rough in The Chamber. He directs me to lie on my back. I do as I'm told. He leans down and puts his mouth on my nipple, and I squirm as heat and tingling sensations rock my body. He sucks on each nipple and gives them a tug. They answer back with how hard and sensitive they become. I really didn't know my body could feel this way. He lets go of my nipples and trails kisses up my body until his lips find mine. My moans are an invitation for more and he gives it to me, as he trails kisses down my throat, my neck, my ear. Fire ignites within me and blazes across my body.

"Did I mention that today is my birthday, too?" he asks.

"Happy birthday," I moan.

"Happy birthday to you."

His skillful fingers find my sex again and my body awakens more. He works his fingers in and out and around inside of me. My hips lift to meet him, telling him I don't want him to stop.

"You are so wet and ready for me. Tell me if it's too much."

"Okay." I'm breathless.

He pulls his fingers out of my sex, leaving me gasping. I watch him move over me. He takes a second and kisses the inside of each of my thighs. He stares down at me with hooded, lustful eyes and he is panting. "Ready?"

I nod yes, but my heart beats double-time. I'm nervous. I'm afraid. And the feelings are wound up in a tight knot sitting in my stomach and throat. There is no going back now. I will be forever changed, starting with the moment I was taken from my home. Tears drain down the sides of my face and I squeeze my eyes tight to dash them away. No one is coming to rescue me. There are no saviors here. I must show strength on the outside, no matter how strong fear is twisting its way through me.

The pressure of him spreads the opening of my sex, causing the outer walls to sting and bite. There is so much pressure. I open my eyes to find his eyes pinned to mine. The pressure turns to pain as he tears away one of things I held dear and precious. The pressure is delightful and foreign and overwhelming and I think about Mason's words about how pain can feel good. He eases deeper inside of my slick flesh and my body is hit with a swirl of sensations. My skin prickles and goosebumps cover me and my heart pounds in my chest.

He pulls back out and emptiness invades me. I want to feel his fullness inside of me again. No, I need it. The sensations take me away from the here and now, allowing me to get lost and wrapped up in them. He slides his length inside of me, deeper this time, and my walls contract around him. My body is more relaxed and allows him to penetrate more, going farther into the back of my sex. I arch my back and thrust my hips forward and Tyson gets a little braver and pushes deeper inside of me.

"Yes. More," I hiss at him.

He pushes his hardness deeper still, filling me. I am replete. His length takes up every inch of me, stealing my breath away. When he pulls out of me the fear creeps back in as the emptiness takes over, leaving me cold.

"I want more of you, please. I'll be okay. I won't break," I plead because the sensations crawling and biting through my body are all-consuming and exactly what I need. In this moment, this is all I can think about and all I want.

When the hood was pulled from my head, and I learned that I would be a sex pawn, I thought I'd rather die. Now sex might be the only thing that keeps me alive.

His eyes widen. "Are you sure?" Tyson asks.

I nod, and in one quick motion, he plunges his entire length deep inside my sex. My body vacillates between pleasure and pain. I fight the tears because in this place, taken away from my family, things could be so much worse than sharing my first time with this gentle stranger.

When I raise my hips he slips in deeper. I move in rhythm with him, rolling my hips as he eases in and out of me. I start to feel an intense new feeling down there as he moves in and never quite out of me, faster and faster. His moans excite me more. My bones soften, and my knees spread as his body slips and slides against mine, consuming me.

He stares down at me, frozen in time. My breaths are an uneven staccato, hell-bent on catching up to my racing heart. He says something with his eyes that I can't read. With my eyes, I plead with him to show me this kindness forever and to be someone I can count on in this castle of unseen horrors, even though I'm a complete stranger to him, and he doesn't owe me anything. What have I go to lose? I allow what I hope is a sweet smile to grow on my face and travel up to my eyes. Tyson returns the smile and nods his head as if he can read my mind, before he pushes inside of me again. This causes me to forget where I am for a moment as his overwhelming cock fills me. Greedily, I roll my hips as close as I can to take in all of him.

"You are so fucking amazing!" he moans into my ear, and that is my undoing.

My body shakes and bucks underneath him. Unintelligible words escape my lips as I lose complete control around his Thunderdick. He joins me, burying himself even farther inside of me as we ride out our orgasms together.

After, we both lie still, trying to catch our breath.

"I might just fall asleep in my Chamber nightly," I whisper in his ear.

He kisses my shoulder and playfully bites and nips at my sensitive skin. "Maybe not every night. Don't want anyone to catch on."

In the wake of what just happened, the room comes back into focus. It's still too white, foreign, and scary.

I forgot I was here. How could I have sex with a stranger and forget everything that has happened to bring me to this moment? Can the hormones be that strong, or is this a defense mechanism?

I'm not done with him yet. I don't want to think about my fucked up life. I need more. With him still inside of me, I roll on top. He's rock hard and I show more appreciation. I'm not sure what I'm doing, but I figure if I like it, he probably does, too. I move my hips in a circular motion, grinding hard on him. In this position, he fills me even more. I throw my head back and move into a forward position. The room disappears again, and I feel butterflies and clenching between my legs.

"I'm sorry to interrupt the party over here, but it seems I've worn my virgin out completely," Mason says.

We all glance over to find Violet passed out.

"I know I said that you can break Flame in for the next few days, but I must have a few minutes to sample this nectar," Mason continues. "I have been checking the two of you out, and, damn...makes me want you both. Sit over there and watch, Ty."

How can I protest? He's the one who has given me this gift. What's the saying? He who giveth, can taketh away. I know now that I need Tyson. Without him, I won't survive the next year. Tyson lifts me off of his length, his vacancy leaves me void.

"On your knees, please," Mason says taking Tyson's place.

I comply.

Mason plants a kiss on my bottom, taking a cheek in each hand. He smacks me hard, causing my ass to sting and warm, but it doesn't hurt. Without the same tenderness Tyson gave, he slams into me. He isn't flowers and candy, that's for sure. He pounds in and out of me. The rhythmic sound of his skin slapping against mine is what I focus on. I allow myself to get lost in the rhythm, smack-thump, smack-thump. The welcomed and already too-familiar sensations begin again. Mason's cock continually pushes on a spot in the back of my sex and I am responding. My breath rips through me, and I pant, unable to think straight. I push my ass back to get more of him. It's not romantic or sweet. It is pure fucking. No wonder Violet passed out.

"Look at Tyson," he commands me.

I glance over at him and he's even harder than he was before. He's rubbing his hand up and down his shaft as his hips move. He's getting off on Mason fucking me. I don't know why this is so hot to me. My cheeks warm, thinking about how his massive cock was inside of me, and I'm undone. I slip off the edge. Waves and waves wrack my body and it gives way, letting the orgasm take me. I tremble and shake, and my walls tighten around him as he plunges deeper inside of me and yells out.

"Fuck! Best Chamber ever!" He falls onto my back and grinds his cock inside of me playfully.

After a few moments, he pulls out of me, curls into a naked ball and passes out on the bed next to me. Fuck hard, sleep hard.

Tyson makes his way over to me. Round two? He motions for me to follow him to the empty bed. I do as he requests, eager for anything he wants to give me.

"Sleep," he says.

He must be able to read the disappointment on my face, because he adds. "Not to brag, but I'm a lot to take for an experienced pussy. Yours is a new, tender little flower that needs to be handled with care. We can explore more tomorrow," he promises.

I scoot in under the covers. When he scoots in after me, I'm shocked. This is insane. Now that the room is again stark-white and uninviting, my world tips and turns. It really is true. Somehow, I allowed myself to believe this was all a dream: part fantasy, part nightmare. Tears spill from my eyes and roll down my face and our arms, as we lie together in silence. I'm aware of every sound and movement he makes. Tyson. My first. No matter what else happens in my life—whether I survive The Chamber, the choices I make, the career I choose, who I marry, where I live—that statement will always and forever be true. Tyson. My first.

My only hope is that for Liam this doesn't define our future. I hope he can get past it. I fall asleep effortlessly. Tyson's slow, even breaths are my soundtrack.

6

A NEW ALLIANCE

*W*hite-hot, blinding light floods the Deflowering Chamber, bouncing around the alabaster walls and white marble floors. The effect pulls me away from my much-needed slumber, and I wake with a start.

Healing sleep is what I require. My body feels broken and ravished. How do they expect me to do this five days per week? Last night with Tyson was a rough ride. His cock should only be allowed to enter a horse. It'll take me weeks to recover. No female vagina is suitable for his girth.

Still, I'm relieved that my first time in a place like this managed to be tender. As raw as my flesh feels, I appreciate the merciful generosity and kindness he showed me. The reality is that his Thunderdick broke me in two. I doubt I have the strength to move or walk. Even turning over is proving to be a challenge, but somehow I manage it. If only I could be in Liam's bed right now, waking up after our first night of lovemaking in his strong arms. I flip over completely so that I'm on my back and Tyson is smiling down at me, snapping me out of my deep thoughts. Now I'm awake.

"Good morning, beautiful," he states as if this were any morning of any day and we were rising as lovers rather than what we really are —strangers, captive and capturer.

I don't hate Tyson for my predicament. He's just doing his job, and I know that if it were not him, it would have been someone else who might have treated me so much worse.

"Hi," I respond.

"How are you feeling?" he asks.

"Exhausted...split in two," I mumble through a yawn and stretch my arms over my head.

The room is empty. It's just the two of us—no Violet, no Mason.

"Sorry about that. I seem to have that effect on women," he says and laughs.

I want to ask him what's going to happen to me next, but I'm afraid of the answer. What if he says more sex with him? There's no way my body can endure another go, even if being in the moment allows me to forget that I am here and not home. I want to ask him if he will help me escape, but I already know the answer to that question.

"What happens to me now?" I go ahead and ask. Please, no more Thunderdick.

Tyson raises himself up and rests on his elbow. He gazes down at me. He really is very attractive. Up close, his eyes take on a hazel hue that can't be appreciated from a distance. Back home, Tyson would be a catch, a guy that any one of my friends could fall for if not for his involvement in The Chamber. I want to ask him how he came to be here.

"Today you meet with your groomer, Zion."

He pops out of bed, and my eyes greedily take in his massive cock. I'm still getting used to seeing them everywhere...even behind my closed eyes. His swings in and out of view as he walks away from me. I just don't get how he carries that thing around in his pants. It must weigh a ton. His backside is quite spectacular in its own right. He's perfectly muscled and toned from the top of his shoulders to his calves, but my eyes linger on his buttocks that I want to touch.

He grabs a robe from a nearby chair and turns to walk back to me, giving me the full-frontal view. He smiles and winks approval of my visual exploration. His cock swells even more with each step he takes. He tosses me the silky crimson robe, and I rise to put it on. I have a strong feeling that I'm going to hate the color red by the end of my year here.

We don't speak as Tyson leads me to my next destination. He nods and acknowledges the other guards we pass in the corridors. He isn't distant and cold. It's almost like he's remaining professional on purpose. For appearances. There's a very subtle current of energy bouncing between us. It shocks me every time our skin accidentally touches. I don't know if he feels these things, but I do. He's all business when he drops me off in front of an area that looks like the lobby of a high-end spa.

A young woman at the counter offers me a kind smile. She introduces herself to me as Zion. She's beautiful. I'm starting to think that beauty is a requirement for employment here. She has long, auburn hair, pale green eyes and a petite figure. Maybe she can take my place. I extend my hand out in introduction. "I'm Viv...I mean, I'm Flame," I say. My voice is tight and small.

"Welcome, Flame," she says. "I'll be the one keeping you Chamber-ready at all times," She motions with her hand. "Follow me."

I turn and wave goodbye to Tyson, who nods and walks away. But he gives me a quick wink and a flash of a smile before doing so. Zion and I walk through a small waiting area to a more secluded room.

"Have a seat," she instructs.

The chair is plush leather and reclines. When I take my seat, the material caresses my skin. I've never given much thought to chairs and how they feel against my body, but I plan to appreciate even the tiniest of pleasures. I don't know how many of them I have left.

The room is small in comparison to the rest of the place, and it has a calming effect on me, like a warm blanket. The color scheme of warm beige, brown, and splashes of blue add to the feel. Recessed lighting creates a dim, faint glow. The clawfoot tub in the center of the room is already filled with water and sweet-smelling petals. I close my eyes, prepared to drift off into a deep sleep. That all changes when I feel the a pluck on my eyebrow. Reflexively, I jump. I have never waxed or plucked anything.

"Sorry," she offers. "You'll be used to having hairs snatched out of your face in no time." She continues to pluck and tweeze and wax every place but the top of my head. My skin is a live wire of pain and sensations.

"My job is to keep you groomed, and your vagina in good shape. This job can take a toll on your nether regions. I'm going to put some healing salve on you right now, then I want you to soak in the tub. Open your legs, please."

I've been to the gynecologist before, and I treat this moment as such. I tell myself that this is a regular check-up. I'm holding onto and creating anything to ground myself to my reality.

After my evening with Tyson, I am eager for anything that will take away the sting between my legs. Her fingers are warm.

"You'll get used to this, too," she says and plasters a weak smile on her face. I know that it's weak because it doesn't reach her eyes and it falls as quickly as it appears.

Tears prickle my eyes as her fingers go to work applying the thick salve. She layers on a heavy coating, covering my entire vaginal area. I close my eyes and concentrate on her deft fingers and nothing else, and soon, my body responds to the friction of her rubbing the cream in. All my nerve endings hone in on my sex. I pretend I'm anywhere but here. I'm in my room with Liam. I squeeze my eyes tight as the image takes shape. His blue eyes are staring into mine, his lips graze and tickle my neck, my cheek, then come close to my lips. A low hum of electricity pulses along the space between my skin and muscle. It's Liam's fingers, not hers, that spread me and massage the folds and opening.

I gasp when fingers slip into my sex, I'm tender and raw. Soothing menthol cools my tenderness, and it starts to feel better right away. When I open my eyes Liam is gone. I am back in the small space, back in The Chamber. Zion is busying herself with washing her hands. What just happened must be an everyday occurrence to her. I am thankful that she treats this bizarre situation clinically.

She turns back to me. "All right, hit the bath. The salve is full of herbs that promote healing. I heard that your first time was with Tyson." She stares at me with big eyes and bared clenched teeth. "Brave girl. It's gonna take a few days to recover from that much man."

"Thank you." I climb off the chair and let my robe fall to the floor. After my grooming experience, there is no reason to be shy. The claw-foot tub, like everything here, is regal and classic.

I drop into the hot water. My girl parts scream out as the heat slaps against my body. Once I settle into the bath, all parts of my body get used to the temperature. All I can do is close my eyes and let the warmth take me over. A soft melody plays in the background.

"I'll leave you to it," Zion says. I hear the door close behind her.

My thoughts drift to Liam. Is he the key to surviving this place? If I can hide myself away in a fantasy of him, could that be enough? Stolen moments in my own world will allow a mental escape until a physical one presents itself.

Everyone has to know I'm missing by now. I don't know where I am or what time it is back home, but I know I have witnessed one sunrise, so it's been one day. They must all be frantic with fear and worry, and in some ways, what they are going through is worse than what I am going through. At least I know that I'm alive. Sure, my body doesn't belong to me, but I'm not chained up to a wall. I'm in a spa, soaking in a tub, while they are home wondering if I am lying in a shallow grave, or worse, being tortured.

My tears drop into the bath and mix with the water. Mason has put all of us in the worse possible situation. He promises release in a year, if we behave. Then what? I suddenly reappear? What will I say, that I wanted to find myself and I ran away? They would never forgive me. I would never forgive me. If I try to escape, then what? Everyone I love will be in danger? Shit. I slam my hands into the water and it thrashes in waves around me. I let go. I bring my legs up, wrap my arms around them, and wail, unconcerned for who might hear me.

This is my last show of weakness. When I get out of this tub, I must embody the survivor I know that I am. I have to be strong. More importantly, I have to learn to separate my mind from my body and become Flame when I'm traveling through the halls of this horrid place. I can only be Vivian when it's safe for me. I believe I might be able to be Vivian around Tyson, and possibly the other women. I'll have to determine what other scenarios are safe for me to be me. I have to survive this year, and I can only hope and pray that Liam still wants me when I find my way back to him.

7

WELL GROOMED

*Z*ion wakes me from my bath and helps dry me off. I slip on another silky red robe. This one falls to the floor dramatically and flows behind me in a train when I walk.

We are on the move, and I follow close behind her. This place is a maze of tunnels, dimly lit halls, and an untold amount of levels. I keep waiting for Lancelot or Lady someone or other to grace my presence. They shouldn't worry much about our escape in here, because I don't think we could even find our way out.

Zion interrupts my thoughts. "While you were busy being deflowered, the other girls got the grand tour. This is level two. This level houses the Beautification Chamber. Also, the spa, indoor pool, exercise room, jacuzzi, and steam and dry sauna."

I nod and gaze around at the lavish appointments that I would imagine only finding on Rodeo Drive or in some upscale spa back home in Vegas. High ceilings meet tall windowless stone and brick walls. Ornate chandeliers bathe our path in sparkling lights. Majestic carpets dot the floors in pops of royal purples, silver and grays.

"You and the rest of The Chambermaids are allowed complete access to this floor. Mason wants you at your best physically at all times. That's why you'll have a trainer to ensure you're exercising properly. Of course, I'll make sure that you are always flawless in the looks department." She smiles at me as if she's proud of her talents. "You'll have daily visits with me to make sure that every pore and hair are operating to perfection. I'll also offer you salves and creams to help ease your sexual discomfort."

I don't respond. What the fuck am I supposed to say? Instead I keep in step with her. There's no need for words. It's not like I have a choice.

We step into an elevator. Inside, the opulence continues. The elevator has gold on the walls, ceiling, and floor. A beautiful jeweled chandelier hangs from the ceiling and adds brilliance that bounces off the walls.

"We are heading to level five, the Sleeping Chambers. As the name implies, this is where you'll sleep," she informs me. "You'll be two or three to a room. There's a conversation lounge and media room on this level. There is also a jacuzzi and smaller lap pool."

We exit the elevator on the fifth floor. I wonder to myself what secrets lie on the third and fourth levels, but I'm quickly distracted. We step out onto the Sleeping Chamber foyer. It's breathtaking and fit for a princess. Directly in front of us is a spacious living room, with a massive fireplace and high-backed sofa. The glass ceiling is open to the sky above and the clouds that float across are astonishing.

I follow Zion across the living room, stepping on what has to be a Persian rug. She takes me to my bedroom and I can identify my space right away by the crimson bedding. I'm clued in to my roommates as well—the light blue bedding belongs to Sky, and the deep blue bedding could only belong to Sapphire. The room is gorgeous. The walls are painted a soft beige. Each bed is king-sized, with a table on one side and bookshelf on the other. What immediately catches my eye are the three staircases opposite each bed. Our Chambers?

"Looks like you're in a triple. Right this way."

I follow Zion up the center staircase. It's an iron structure that winds up at least two or three floors. There are small windows that offer light on the way up. I also notice the sconces that must be the night's light source. When we reach the top of the staircase, we come to a heavy, deep cherry curtain—no door. Zion gestures for me to walk through the opening.

I hesitate and take a couple of deep breaths before I pull the heavy drapery aside and cross the threshold. I have no words. I have to make myself breathe, because my air is caught behind a huge lump blocking my throat. What I see first is the huge canopy bed, draped in the softest silk, satin, and velvet. Of course, all shades of scarlet. The Chamber is round, like the room I started in. The four bedposts are thick and heavy, in a raven black that compliments the red. The floor isn't stone like the rest of this palace. It's covered in pillowy red plush carpet that you could sleep on. My stomach twists and rolls.

Across from the bed is a tall, inky black cabinet with brass handles. I cross into the room and open the cabinet doors. I should have left better enough alone. The cabinet contains all varieties of dildos, feathers, handcuffs, belts, gags, and an assortment of other items that I have never seen before. Scary. I swiftly close the doors. This is real, live sick shit.

"What's the horse for?" I ask, pointing to a pony in the corner of the room, attached to a pole that resembles one you might find on a carousel. My eyes follow the pole up to the ceiling. I hadn't even glanced up since I walked into the red Chamber. This ceiling is glass and the sky is visible. If this wasn't so sick and scary, it would be romantic.

"Sometimes the men enjoy watching you pleasure yourself," she says in answer to my question.

"On a horse?" How am I going to get through this? I'm barely not a virgin anymore and now I'm supposed to parade around here doing things I have never done with strange men? What would my family want me to do? Certainly they would all risk their lives for me. If I cooperate, does that mean I'm sacrificing myself for them? No answers come.

"Here, let me show you." Zion walks over to the cabinet of horror and pulls out a dildo. She walks over to the horse and screws the dildo into the center of the saddle. "Do you get it now?"

My eyebrows shoot to the sky and my face warms with embarrassment. "Yep," I say. "I hope I never have to use that horse."

There's a large fireplace against the wall, and what sex Chamber would be complete without a powder room? I don't walk inside. I don't even care. The horse, the bed, the cabinet of horror, my own private staircase leading to my sex Chamber, the whole idea that I can't go home—it's all hitting me right now. "Can we leave now?" I ask Zion. "I'm exhausted."

"Sure."

We head down the winding staircase toward my room. All I want to do is sleep. When we enter my room, Sky is sitting on her bed. She looks beautiful and sad in a long, flowing sky blue robe, like my red one. We exchange brittle smiles in greeting.

"I will leave you now, Flame," Zion says. "Rest up, because you'll be summoned in a few hours for round two in the Deflowering Chamber."

"Okay," I say, sighing. As much as I know my body isn't ready for another evening with Tyson, I secretly hope that I'll be spending the night with him. Before I can utter another word, Zion's gone. I trudge over to my bed and sit on the edge facing Sky.

"Hi. I'm Vivian. Vivian Travis. Flame is not who I really am." I offer her my hand. She takes it immediately.

"Nice to meet you, Vivian Travis," she says in a strong accent. "I'm Romy Janssen. I guess I'll be Sky here."

"Where are you from, Romy?" I ask.

"Holland."

"They took you all the way from the Netherlands?"

"No, I was in America. I was working as a model in New York. That's where they grabbed me. What about you? Where are you from?"

"Las Vegas," I reply.

"What happened to you last night? Did they hurt you?" she asks.

How do I answer a question like that, when given our current situation, every moment is hurtful? "No. I wasn't harmed," I reply. "They took me and Violet into a special room and they took our virginity. From what my groomer just said, they aren't finished."

I move over toward her bed. "Do you mind if I sit?" I ask her before I actually just plop down on her bed. We don't have many choices here, so I don't want to rob her of making one.

"Go for it." She pats the space next to me and I sit down.

We enjoy the quiet for a long time. There is not much to chitchat about, given all of our recent revelations.

"I'm terrified," she finally says.

"Me, too."

She glances over at me. "You don't seemed scared at all."

"Oh, but I am. I don't know how to explain it. When they first brought me here, I wanted them to kill me, because I would rather die, than...than this." I raise my hand up, gesturing to our surroundings. "It was the pictures of my family that clinched it for me. I have to be brave and have faith that he'll release us in a year." I take her hand into mine. "I'm trying not to dwell on everything that is happening every moment. Otherwise I would go crazy. Maybe if I can take it as it comes, then I can break the horror down into survivable chunks. I don't know if that will work, but believe me when I say I'm just as terrified as you are," I admit to her.

"You're strong, Flame. I wish I was."

"Look at it this way. There are seven of us. We have each other to lean on. We're not going through this alone." I wrap her into a hug. She cries softly on my shoulder. "I'm here anytime you need to talk. Okay?" I feel her nod into my shoulder.

She thinks I'm strong? I don't. I'm every bit as petrified as she is, but I can't wear that on my sleeve every second that I am in this place. I can't dwell on all of the details of my circumstances. I have to compartmentalize. Right now, I'm just sitting with Sky, comforting her. This isn't very scary. Last night started out scary, but then Tyson changed that. I imagine in here I will have moments of calm, followed by moments of fear and anger, and moments of release, and perhaps all at the same time. Unless I'm able to take the events as they come, I won't make it.

"Thanks. I do feel a lot better," she tells me.

"Me, too," I say and tell her to keep her head up.

I stand and head to the kitchen. It's crazy to me how my stomach is grumbling at a time like this. My biology doesn't care that I'm kidnapped and locked away in a fucking tower.

It's amazing how different each one of is. Six beautiful girls—seven with me. I wouldn't call myself beautiful. Cute is a more accurate assessment. All of us have different strengths and weaknesses. Mason is quite the collector.

8

COMING OUT

*T*onight is the night. We are all terrified. I think back to the conversation I had with Sky about how I'm strong and brave. This is one of those moments on the emotional roller coaster that is The Chamber. Fear is the only emotion I have—terror of the unknown. One of the biggest sources of my fear is that I assumed that Tyson being assigned as my personal guard meant that he would be with me all the time. I quickly learned that is not the case. I haven't seen him since my second night here. The strange thing is, I miss him, and I don't even know him. Stockholm much? Maybe it's not him, but his ability to make this place disappear if only for a moment.

They call this a "coming out party." I have been at The Chamber for a week now. My family and friends have to be beside themselves with panic and fear of the unknown. Do they think I'm dead? I've learned this week that Sunshine is from Barbados. Sky, from Holland, and Ivy is from Ireland. Raven, Sapphire, Violet and I are from the United States. Raven is from Hawaii, and Violet is from Los Angeles. Mason has amassed quite a variety of women.

Tonight we will be paraded around to the richest and wealthiest sickos in the world. All prepared to spend a year feasting upon us. Reality has officially set in. Zion and Sky's and Sapphire's groomers showed up to get us from our room. We were then bathed and dolled up. My hair resembles something from the Victorian era, with the ringlets to boot. I have a lavish, blood-red long gown with a plunging neckline and a bodice so snug I can barely breathe. Sky's baby blue dress is equally impressive, as is Sapphire's jewel-toned blue gown. We do look like princesses, if only in this moment. All we are missing is our royal court.

"I am so nervous," Sky says in a low voice. "I don't think I can do this."

I have no words of wisdom for her this time. I'm barely holding it together myself. "I'm right here with you, Sky." I walk over and squeeze her hand.

"You two are being ridiculous!" Sapphire exclaims. "It's just sex, that's all! Mindless fucking. Me, I love sex." I'm reminded of our first night in The Chamber, the circular room, and how eager she was to suck Mason's cock. She's apparently more experienced than I thought.

"I wish I could say that, but seeing how I had never had sex before coming here, I don't have the same feelings about it that you do," I remind her.

"Listen, when we walk out these doors, think of a character to be," she says. "Remove you from your mind. It helps." She smiles at us both, almost in a motherly way, even though she can't be any older than us.

Zion adds a gorgeous ruby necklace to my ensemble. Sapphires adorn Sapphire's neck, and the softest blue aquamarine hangs from Sky's neck. We are quickly ushered into the living area. Each of us is as breathtaking as the next. Sunshine is in a beautiful, fitted sunburst-yellow gown with canary diamonds. Ivy is in an emerald-colored gown with matching jewels. Raven has a black gown and onyx jewels. Violet has an amethyst necklace and a gorgeous, floor-length lavender gown. We all look as though we are on our way to a royal ball and not the fate we are all facing. Silence befalls the room as we begin lining up.

~

"WE WILL BE HEADING to the fourth floor ballroom," one of the groomers announces. "You will be introduced one at a time. You will walk to the end of the stage and return. Do not look down. Heads up at all times." He's a good-looking guy in impeccable shape, but I'm thankful that my groomer is female. We all follow the trainers out into the foyer, and we stop when they stop.

"There will be lottery winners on either side of the runway," another groomer says. "Make sure you give your attention to both sides. This will please Mason."

We all nod in compliance, because we fear the repercussions of not pleasing Mason.

The elevator door opens. The seven of us are ushered inside. Surprisingly, all seven of us in our large, colorful, bustling gowns, along with seven groomers, fit easily into the massive freight. Seven hearts hammer loudly and can be heard over the mechanism that allows us to move from floor to floor. Or perhaps the sound is coming just from my own.

No escape.

No turning back.

The doors slide open, with an eerie whisking sound of hydraulics or some shift in the air. We step out into the foyer of a breathtaking ballroom. From my vantage, I can see five elegant archways. Elaborate chandeliers peek out beneath each curve's opening. I'm unable to see the height of the ceiling from my current position. What I do see turns my stomach. Several tables surround a raised platform, and the tables are filled with men in suits. Strangers. The stamped concrete floors that I have grown accustomed to have been replaced by rich and elegant Macassar ebony wood flooring.

Our groomers line us up in the order we were in when we first arrived. I'm dead last, but that doesn't even comfort me at this moment. I could really use a paper bag to breathe in and out of before I collapse.

"I can't do this!" I announce to Zion who's watching me intently. I wring my hands, then shake them repeatedly in panic, my stomach roils and is rocked with spasming pain. I pace out of line, I can't escape into my mind, I am here and now. I shoot a glance at Sky. My expression says, I told you I wasn't strong.

"I'm not some piece of meat to be used by these guys. I'm not going in there," I insist through shallow, panicked, quick breaths. I start backing up into the elevator.

"I want you to stop for a minute and think of your family. Think of your friends," Zion says, walking me to the side.

I shake my head over and over. "My family wouldn't want this for me. They would rather die than see me raped and used over and over," I stare heatedly into her eyes. But would I want death for them? No.

"You were chosen for this because you're strong," Zion says. "You can and will survive this. He only chooses strong women. You can do this."

Her pep talk is eerie and fucked up. I'm not jumping out of a plane or running an impossible marathon. I'm sick of everybody telling me how fucking strong I am. I am not strong, I am scared shit-less. I want to go home! I want to cry and puke and pass out! That is not strong! What would my mom and dad want me to do?

I've already suffered so much and lost everything. To not have them alive and well when I return home would be a worse fate than anything anyone can do to me in here. In here, I can separate myself from my body, like Sapphire said. I can do that. Well, I can try, but if my family died because of me, I would never be able to separate myself from that pain. Could he do that? Would he really hurt them?

I steel myself, pull my shoulders back, force my head up high, and take my place back in line. My cheeks are moistened by my tears. Then a most surprising thing happens. Violet takes my hand and offers a tight squeeze. I squeeze hers in return. I glance down the line at the newly forming sisterhood. All of our hands are interlocked as if we're silently affirming that none of us are in this alone.

This is my only choice.

With our new dose of bravery and sisterly support, we walk in a single file line toward the center arch. One girl is as lovely as the next. Any observer would easily mistake us for a group of debutantes or pageant queens, and not the terrified Chambermaids that we were.

I startle when I see the staircase leading up to a stage or runway that appears to travel down the center of the ballroom, with tables on either side. Fuck.

Ivy takes the stairs first in her beautiful emerald green gown. Her red hair blazes under the lights of the dazzling chandeliers.

"Introducing Ivy. She will poison your hearts, gentlemen," Mason says, announcing her.

The cheers are deafening. Ivy walks down the stage and out of my sight. She comes back into view on her return. As she makes her way down the stairs her resolve crumbles and she breaks down. My heart breaks for her. I follow her with my eyes as she is swiftly taken away by her groomer. My eyes return to the stage again as Sunshine makes her approach.

"The sun just got brighter, gentlemen," I hear Mason shout. "Meet Sunshine!" The cheers are so loud I suddenly want to retreat.

I watch on with fright-filled eyes as Sunshine takes the stage in her sunburst-yellow gown. She quickly makes her way back to us, her face not unlike Ivy's. She also heaves and sobs before being whisked away by her groomer.

Each girl walks across the runway to the sound of thunderous cheers. Each girl is quickly taken away. This occurs six times. Then, my turn comes. I stand at the base of the stairs for what seems like forever, even though I'm fully aware that only seconds have passed. I resolve myself by thinking about my family. I picture them all—my mother, my father, Shane, Maddie, and Liam. I hold his image the longest. I can see him so clearly, I feel as though his blue eyes are peering into my soul. I can do this because they need me to. I make a decision at that very moment to do whatever I need to do to save them because saving them saves us all.

I bravely take the steps. Whatever words of introduction that Mason speaks as I cross the stage roll right over me. My ears immediately cloud. Thump, thump, thump, from my heart is all I can hear.

The lights of the chandelier are too bright. The men on each side of the stage are faceless. Their cheers are thunderous eruptions. I'm happy that I can't make out any of the faces. It's just suits and clapping hands. I pause at the end of the runway, as instructed by Zion. I turn and resist the urge to run the rest of the way back.

Zion is there when I descend the stairs. She takes me by the hand and leads me to a door that reads Preparation Chamber. The doors open to reveal six naked or near-naked girls, with jewels as their only accessories. I turn to Zion. "What's going on?"

"It is time for the exploration. Please, we must hurry and get you out of your gown." She begins unzipping me.

What? She peels my gown from my shoulders. It falls heavily to the floor. I step out of it and Zion goes to work taking the rest of my garments off of me. By the time she's done pulling and tugging me out of my clothes, I'm completely naked except for the rubies on my neck. I fight off shame as I stand there in the buff with the other girls.

Shame comes unbidden when Zion begins squeezing and pinching my nipples. Please just kill me now. I glance around, and to my horror, others are receiving similar treatment. I become completely horrified when Zion dips her fingers into an oily solution then takes her moistened fingers and places them between my legs. I almost swallow my own tongue in shock as Zion easily finds my clitoris. She begins moving her fingers in slow circles around the part of my body that only knows pleasure and sexual desires.

I don't understand how I can lose all focus and thought the second someone touches me down there, touching Petunia. I've been working on giving my sex her own identity, seeing how that part of my body doesn't listen to me anyway or belong to me exclusively. I'm not sure if the new name is going to stick, but I'm willing to try anything. I spread my legs apart ever so slightly to allow Zion more access to...Petunia. Zion slips one finger, then two inside of me, sliding slowly in and out. I can't deny how heavenly it feels deep inside my core. A moan escapes me, and for a second, I forget that there are six other girls in the room. All I can think about is the pleasure coming from between my legs.

"Flame," she whispers into my ear. "I believe you are ready for further exploration."

She's right. My head is light and spinning. The throbbing between my legs is a new sensation for me. It is thrilling.

I find my place in line behind the six beautiful naked young women. We all prepare ourselves for the thirty-five strangers and Mason. My only hope is that Tyson will be there.

The stimulation offered by Zion has helped ease my nerves. At least some of my energy and focus is on the throbbing nugget between my legs that's longing for more attention. Traitor.

9

CONTRAPTIONS

*W*e are all led back into the ballroom. The first thing I notice is that the stage has been moved, but my view is blocked beyond that point. The girls ahead of me are being led inside one at a time. When I make it to the entrance, I wish my view was still obscured. Nothing I have seen up to this very moment is as horrific as what lies before me. Everything else was a cakewalk compared to this nightmare that I may never awaken from. It's the most appalling scene that has ever been thrust upon me in twenty-one years. Each of my new sisters is being positioned onto one strange apparatus or another.

Raven is placed in a device that places her in a supine position. Her knees are bent, and her legs are spread apart. Her sex is open like she's waiting for the gynecologist to give her an annual checkup, but this is The Chamber. In The Chamber, the only doctors in the house won't require a nurse in the room or sterile examination tools. Raven. My heart breaks for her. This is disgraceful.

My eyes find Sky who is being placed on all fours, fully supported by the apparatus that her torso is resting upon. Her rump is in the air and exposed for all to see. I think hers must be the worst so far. Sunshine is positioned on her side—her apparatus has a pulley system. With her top leg fastened into a strap, it is lifted away from her bottom leg—pulling her into a near split. Her sex is open and accessible. I watch in horror as more girls are secured into these sexual contraptions, mortified for them and all too aware of my turn drawing near.

Ivy is in a similar position as Sky, on all fours at first. Then the device moves and her legs slide under her until her torso is resting on top of her legs, in child's pose—allowing her sex and her anus to be completely exposed. Sapphire is next. Out of all of the girls, she's the only one who seems eager to participate in Mason's sex games. Even tonight as we are being displayed like pieces of art in a gallery, she walks with more confidence than the rest of us like she chose to be here. She lays on her back and into her device, and smiles when the straps attached to her legs, pulling them over her head until her feet dangle by her ears.

Only Violet and I are left. We are always the last at bat. We are ushered in together so I'm unable to observe her fate. Zion leads me by the hand. I hadn't noticed the hush that has come over the room. You can hear a pin drop, so they must be able to hear my heart race dangerously fast in my chest. What would the penalty be if I blacked out? Tiny dots are forming on the edges of my visual field. I'm led on shaky legs to the last open apparatus, then guided to stand in front of it. My feet remain on the floor. Zion nudges me to lean my torso on a board, so that I'm bent over, with my back flat. Straps are secured across my back and my arms are placed near my head. There's a place for my head to rest, with an opening for my face to see beneath me, like a massage table. Gee, thanks for making me so comfortable.

As I'm bent forward, I can feel my back arching and my rump pointing further north. This would be extremely uncomfortable if not for all the supports and straps. There are holes in the board for my breasts, and a cut-out for access underneath the apparatus to my sex. My clitoris throbs. The air hitting my entire sex is a new sensation for me.

Zion depresses a button and slowly my feet leave the ground and my legs spread apart. As my back arches even more, the front of my legs are suddenly supported by pads. My anus and sex are on display. Please let me pass out. No would know that I'm not conscious. There is no way that I can survive this. I watch my tears hit the floor beneath me. I count them as they silently splash, one, two, three...

There is no greater shame than what is happening to me, to us. If Liam could see me now.

I lift my head and gaze around the room. Just before the lights go dim, I find my salvation. Tyson. His eyes never leave mine. Even in the darkness, I feel his gaze heavy upon me.

There's not a peep from the room. The men waiting for their instructions, no doubt. We Chambermaids hold our breath, anticipating what will happen to us. Several spotlights begin popping on, lighting up spaces in the room. I quickly realize that there are seven spotlights to illuminate each of us. The audience responds with awe. How wonderfully artistic of Mason.

"Gentlemen, aren't they exquisite?" I startle at Mason's voice. He's standing next to me.

The men agree in hushed, eager tones. His hand caresses my rump, followed by a small squeeze.

"If you remember, this here is Flame."

It feels like he is spreading his fingers across each cheek, and I suddenly gasp as his fingers slide toward my sex. He sinks multiple fingers inside of me. A groan escapes me. My thoughts, feelings, and sensations result in a frisson of terror and pleasure at where I am and my unusual position. Still, as Mason's nimble fingers dive deeper inside of me, I find myself fighting against the apparatus to arch my back more, to invite him to dive deeper into my throbbing sex. I have no idea why my traitorous body wants this, but the quicker my hormones and chemicals mix into that concoction that will allow me to disappear, the better for me. That is the answer to surviving this. For some unknown reason, the second anyone touches my clit or any other part of my sex, I'm able to lose myself in the pleasure and temporarily forget about the pain. I consider this newfound superpower that allows everything to fade into the background a blessing.

His skilled fingers push into me and I push back, needing more.

Waves of tingling prickle my sensitive flesh as he intoxicates me with every thrust. My body climbs and climbs toward oblivion. When Mason pulls his fingers out of me, I am panting and out of breath, and worse, I'm unnervingly aware of my surroundings. I can hear breathing in the foreground. Someone to my left moves his chair, and him dragging it to a new position is like nails on a chalkboard. The heat of the spotlight bearing down on me is apparent now and feels much too bright. The spell is broken.

Mason's lips caress my backside, one cheek at a time. Terror washes over me, reclaiming my body.

"Oh, is she ready!" he says in his usual overexcited tone. Mason leaves me cold and raw.

"Oh, Sky, you don't disappoint," he says from somewhere else in the ballroom. "She's ready, too!" He is so excited. "Gentlemen, it's time. Now, I must caution you. Exploration is about getting to know this year's Chambermaids. You are permitted to touch your prizes any way you wish, with your hands and mouths only. In other words, keep your snakes in your pants. Each of these young ladies has a personal guard who is taking his place nearby as I speak. It's their job to make sure you don't get too carried away."

"Hi," Tyson says into my ear.

His voice is a tranquilizer, sending a calm throughout my body.

"Hi," I say.

"Without further ado..." Mason exclaims.

No sooner does Mason finish speaking than I hear chairs moving and feet shuffling against the beautiful flooring. They are coming for us, all hands and mouths, for journey and exploration. I just hope my superpower doesn't fail me, and the second I'm stroked or kissed I'll manage to lose my grip on reality. It's time to don my new super identity because without it, I stand no chance of surviving.

The first pair of hands find me just as I muster up the courage to allow my real self to temporarily be tucked away. Of course, I can't see who the hands belong to. I can only see the current lottery winner's suit as he kneads my behind. He's greedy going about the task.

Please touch my pussy. Please touch my pussy. Right now, all I feel are his coarse hands groping me. He's close behind me. I can feel his erection pushing against my backside. He reaches around me, pressing his hardness against me. His rough hand cups my breast, kneading again. This isn't going as planned. I'm aware of everything. I can feel his breath on my skin. His musky scent turns my stomach. If I throw up, Mason will be very unhappy with me. Please. I silently beg for him to get on with it. I push my ass into him as a hint. His hands release my breasts. His breath is heavy. He's excited. His hands trail down from my shoulders, down my back, and rest upon my rump. Without a moment of hesitation, he spreads my cheeks and buries his face between my legs. He licks and sucks on my lips and I can release everything. I feel nothing except my sex, which is on fire. The sensation of his tongue upon me is explosive. I arch my back to give him more access. The world will vanish completely if this stranger touches my...

"Oh, yes," I whisper when he finds my clitoris with his tongue. I writhe under his sucking. My entire clitoris in his mouth. Magical. I don't give a fuck who he is at this moment, as long as he keeps sucking. In a swift motion he is approaching my pussy from the front and drives his fingers inside of me. Moans escape in triplicate. What's this? A new sensation joins the party. While he goes about his business getting to know my sex, I feel another tongue take one of my nipples into a mouth, twirling it around and around.

"I can't wait to bury my hard dick inside of your hot little pussy for hours. You are fucking exquisite, Flame." His voice is breathy.

This stranger sticks his tongue in my ear and sucks on the lobe—another new sensation. It sends tingling down the side of my neck.

"Oh, I have to careful I don't break you. I want you so bad," the stranger whispers against my neck. My focus is broken. I'm aware again. Their voices are my kryptonite. I feel myself beginning to freak out. Stop talking to me. Just be a fucking headless stranger.

"My turn to taste heaven," the stranger who won't stop talking announces.

The other stranger takes his tongue off of my sex, and my skin runs cold. In the seconds that it takes for the next stranger to take hold of me, I'm back in the room with the contraptions and aware of the sounds around me. Pleasure fills the room, the other girls express their titillation outwardly. I don't want to hear their sex noises.

The moist heat from the talkative stranger's mouth on the lips of my sex is the distraction I need. His tongue catches hold of my clitoris and he goes at the task of sucking me like I'm his last meal. He isn't positioned

behind me like the first guy. He has managed to fit into the space between me and the apparatus. He is hungry and sucking deter-minedly. I can't keep any thoughts straight. The only thing I'm thinking about is the explosion brewing

between my legs. When he drives his fingers deep inside of me, I'm overwhelmed by throbbing, quickening, and pulsing—he is licking my clitoris like I'm a melting ice cream cone. At the same time, his nimble fingers move in and out of my pussy in a sweet, circular pattern. To my amazing horror, I shatter into a combustion of sensations and emotions. I lay there shuddering,

shaking, while a healthy flow of tears flood my face—thankfully hidden.

That's how the presentation night goes—hours and hours of having my nipples and sex kissed, licked, and squeezed by thirty-five different tongues and pairs of hands. I experience all variations of skillfulness, roughness, and gentleness. While being sucked raw with fingers repeatedly plunged deep within the walls of my sex, I manage for the most part to get lost in my body.

Only during transitions, or the occasional chatty lottery winner, did I become aware of what was really happening to me. I felt thirty-five erections as evidence of how much they wanted me and what I had to look forward to. With my ass positioned in the air, I came so many times I lost count. I'm dehydrated from crying; not one tear is left in my body. The guilt and fear disappeared when my carnal desires were at their highest and returned tenfold when I was left alone long enough to think. Thankfully, that didn't happen often with the five-to-one ratio we had. I felt Tyson's constant presence throughout the night, which also helped me survive. I was grateful to have him there.

Mason received confirmation that the men were thrilled about all of us and the year to come. The men were escorted out of the ballroom, but for some reason we were left in our positions with our violated flesh exposed.

"Hi, beautiful," Tyson whispers in my ear. "You were so strong tonight." His voice is heavy and sensual. His lips graze my cheek, close to my mouth. He wants me.

"Wow, thanks." I can't help the sarcasm. He sounds as if I just played in a sporting event. "I'm glad you were with me, it made me feel safer, somehow."

"I'm pleased to hear that, Vivian." He lowers his voice when he says my name. "I want you to know that I will keep you safe," he promises.

He personalizes our budding friendship every time he says my name. I do believe that I can trust him. How much I can trust him remains to be seen. He'll have plenty of opportunity to demonstrate just how much in the next year.

"Bravo, bravo, ladies!" Mason claps loudly as he returns to the ballroom. His voice is filled with unmatched enthusiasm. The main lights pop on, the spotlights vanish, and I'm moved into a more comfortable position. Slowly, Zion raises my head and torso up. At first I think that I'm being released from my humiliating position, but I quickly realize that it is only to elevate my head to allow for better view of the scene unfolding. I think I was happier with my head down, blind to the activities around me, with blood rushing and pooling unhealthily into to my head for far too long. I'm happy they don't try to stand me up because I would most likely faint.

In my new position, with my feet on the floor, bent over the apparatus, my rump still exposed, I'm able to see what's about to transpire. Each guard strips out of his clothing eagerly. Their large, full endowments hang in waiting between their legs. I know Tyson, who is near me, but not in my line of sight, is ready and waiting for me with his Thunderdick. I'm surprised to see Mason, also minus clothing, come into my view in the center of the room. His dick is also plump and ready.

"You were all amazing tonight. Now in the tradition of all The Chambers before you, the guards lucky enough to work exploration night get to release all their pent up sexual tension from playing the role of observer. As you can see, they're all very ready, and so am I."

So many cocks.

I can see most of the girls now, and the guards move into position to claim them for the night. How long will we be expected to last? I'm beginning to be thankful for my apparatus. At least I don't have to hold my weight.

"Ladies you worked hard tonight and deserve real, deep, penetrative orgasms."

The room goes silent.

"Are you ready?" Tyson whispers in my ear.

A wonderful chill runs down the side of my neck. Tyson surprises me by trailing kisses from my ear to my lips. His mouth is hot, moist, full, and tender as he tastes mine. I answer him with equally tender kisses. My head swims. I'm intoxicated by the flood of emotions I am feeling.

"You are so beautiful," he whispers against my lips. "If you don't mind, I'm going to lose myself inside of you now."

I smile my assent.

Tyson doesn't take his hands off of my body as he walks behind me. Their touch warms me. Even after hours of being fondled, my body is so ready for him. My sex is already quivering in anticipation. With Tyson, I don't want to forget where I am. I don't need my superwoman cape. He makes me feel like I'm in this with him—his partner.

I know better. I have no choice or options here. At least he seems to respect me enough to make me believe that I do. Tyson sinks his Thunderdick deep inside of me. I can't arch my back enough. Mason was right—our hours of being probed only tickled and scratched the surface. Tyson was what I needed. My breathing hitches in my chest, as the impending climax builds inside of me. The sounds escaping me are desperate and carnal. Tyson plunges in deeper still, and instead of pulling himself out of me, he stays deep and rolls his hips, his cock filling me completely. He stays there as I pulsate and spasm around him. Euphoria rains down on me as I roar out and find my release. The tears that flood my face are not from sadness or fear. They are for the strong feelings I seem to have blooming inside of me. For Tyson? What does it all mean?

Tyson leans forward, and the length of his torso flattens across my back. His cock deliciously fills me and doesn't move.

"You are going to make me fucking fall in love with you, Vivian," he whispers, and kisses my shoulders and back like the lover he just might be.

He continues the task of pleasuring me with his Thunderdick, slamming his length deep inside my pussy, pulling it nearly out, then slamming it back inside. I never thought anything could feel so good. The sounds and words coming out of me are not my own. I am a woman possessed.

I pulsate around him, feeling full and sated. I roll my hips around and around, grinding onto him. All I want is him forever. I scream out loud as I go over the edge repeatedly. I shudder, I spasm, I cry. I assign every single sexual sensation I am having in this moment to Tyson. I will recall them whenever I need them to blanket and comfort me.

Tyson finds his release. Animal and primal noises erupt from within him before he collapses against me again, kissing me in a succession of slow, passionate pecks.

"This is wrong. We just made love. I should be able to sleep beside you now. I have to leave you, but please know that I don't want to go anywhere. I want to stay with you and watch you sleep and dream. Dream of me tonight, Vivian."

I nod. He could be very easy to fall for.

Tyson's smile is megawatt, and he kisses me on the lips. I feel naked, depressed and empty when he pulls out of me. Am I being drugged? Is this what Stockholm syndrome feels like? WTF? I'm losing my mind. What about Liam?

~

OUR EVENING IS FINALLY OVER. I am finally released from my apparatus. We are lead to the Beautification Chamber, a good sign. Zion
goes through the already-comfortable ritual of massaging my broken
body. She rubs the healing salve over my entire sex. She slips her
fingers inside and coats me with more salve. This time, I don't get the
slightest bit excited. I'm numb, like any girl would be after spending
the evening with Tyson buried inside of her. Truthfully, I loved every
minute of that part.

Zion leads me to the bath, filled with the healing petals and
water. When I sink into the tub, the heated water cocoons my body
with its forces, pushing against me gently at every point that I am
submerged. I ignore the aches crawling down my spine and the
sharper pains that rest in my shoulders and do my best to unwind.
This is my life now and I have to figure a way out or a way through;
those are my only options. If the rest of my time here is anything at
all like tonight, I don't know how I will survive.

I close my eyes, expecting and hoping to get lost in silence.
Instead, my brain, unlike my body, is wide awake, and I don't have
any idea how to quiet it. My internal information superhighway is
congested with thoughts.

I know I can trust Liam, but how can I trust Tyson? We just met.
He doesn't know me and I don't know him. He has shown me kindness since the beginning. He's even shown protectiveness toward me,
but that's his job, and it could all be an act. None of this matters
anyway. When and if I get out of here, I'm never going to see Tyson
again. His place and life are here. My life is back home with Liam—
that is, if he'll even want me after this experience. Hell, he might find
someone else while I'm in here. A year without a word is a long time
to wait for someone. He won't know if I'm dead or alive. Even if
Mason is true to his word and releases us, I'm sure my family and
friends will have mourned me and moved on with their lives. It
would be the healthy thing to do.

Tomorrow is Monday. I have only been here a little over a week.

The introductions are over. Our first night in our actual Chambers is fast approaching. If I could spend a year with Tyson, I could do this. I've come to realize how much I need him. But, thirty-five different guys fucking me every week for a year? If I survive that, what will be left of me?

The thought that keeps playing on a loop in my mind is to just give up. I could. I have everything I need right here to end it all. One could drown in two inches of water, and I'm surrounded by it. It wouldn't take much; all I'd have to do is allow myself to sink. I scoot my body down until my chin is resting on the surface of the water. My heart starts thrumming and my breaths shake. I scoot down until my mouth is covered and I stare out at the tiny room. Images of my family flash before me as my heart pounds in my chest. A couple more inches, and all I have to do is breathe water until I don't breathe anything.

I plunge myself deeper until my eyes are submerged. My body trembles as I open my mouth and take in water. My body fights to save itself, and I have no choice but to come up for air. I do so in a wild, frantic rush, splashing and spilling water onto the floor, while I hack and bark and wheeze. Water shoots out of my throat and nose and the only desire I have is to catch the breath I so badly wanted to extinguish.

Coughing gives way to weeping silent tears for everything that I have lost. My body shivers with a violence that stirs the water, which no longer offers me peace and serenity. My mind is empty because I have nothing. I wrap my arms around my legs and stare blindly at nothing. My vision is blurring as I let the errant tears fall unchecked.

In the distance I hear Zion shouting, "Flame!" but I don't answer. I am not Flame. I'm nobody. "Nobody" can survive a place like this. "Nobody" doesn't give a fuck what happens to Flame, and that is who I have to be. Zion's hands reach into the tub and I know that she has unplugged the drain when the water retreats. The sound of sucking and whooshing takes the lukewarm liquid into the pipes, and I don't move.

"Flame, oh my god, I should have checked on you sooner!" Zion says. "You'll catch your death sitting in this cold water. Look at you. You're freezing cold." Her warm hand brushes up and down my arm, offering friction that sends heat to the spot. I don't turn to her, I continue to stare ahead at nothing. She wraps a heavy towel around me and attempts to lift me from the empty tub, but she isn't successful at moving my dead weight.

Cool air hits my body when she opens the door and leaves me. The towel slides down into the tub, I feel it resting against my back. The sound of my teeth slamming against each other breaks through the silence. After a short time, the door swings open, but no light filters through.

"Vivian!" Tyson's voice sails through the small space and awakens something inside of me. I turn my head to see him rushing toward me. He scoops me out of the tub and wraps blankets around me with Zion's help.

"I tried to drown myself, but I couldn't do it," I say around a hiccup. My voice is so void of life, I hardly recognize it. He sits down with me on his lap. He takes my hands in his and blows heat into them.

"Everyone keeps saying how strong I am, but they don't know what they are talking about." Sobs wrack my body, and I stare into his eyes. "I'm weak, and I want to die."

He brings his forehead to mine. "I won't let you," he says and wraps his arms around me.

10

LIAM, WE HAVE TO FIND HER

I don't know how the police expect us to sit around and do nothing. Vivian has been missing for over a week. A week! All they do is tell us how they're working on the case, but they have no real leads. It's like she just vanished into fucking thin air. What am I supposed to do?

Everything in my life reminds me of her. If I go to our favorite coffee shop near campus, all I think of is her. When Maddie and I get together to hang out, all she does is cry, which makes me feel like a helpless piece of shit, but she's the only person I can talk to who truly understands. Vivian's parents are also suffering, but I can't exactly hang out with them.

I pull up in front of Maddie's mom's house to pick her up. She and I are going to the police station again. The officer working Vivian's case was moved to the big, fancy station on MLK and Alta, so that's where we're headed.

Maddie comes running out of the house and hops into my car. She kisses me on the cheek, buckles her seat belt and we take off.

"How are you holding up?" she asks me.

"Same. Shitty. You?" I glance over at her. She's wearing her usual tight shirt with her cleavage pouring out and a barely-there miniskirt.

Maddie is hot as hell, too, but she and Vivian are opposites. Maddie is tall, blonde, blue-eyed, and bodacious with a sexy body. Vivian is more reserved, more refined, and more athletically built with steel-gray eyes and near-black hair. If they were standing side by side, you would never expect them to even be friends. It's like Vivian makes Maddie more of an angel, and Maddie brings out Vivian's inner hellion.

Maddie was never my type growing up. A girl like that can get you in trouble. Her combination of hot and wild means a lot of hassle for whoever her boyfriend is. No matter, though, I love her, too. I have and would protect her just as I would Vivian. We've been best friends forever.

When we pull into the police station lot, we pause for a beat. Both of us are hotheads, so we can't just bust in there demanding answers, or we may land in the tank for a night.

"Okay, Liam, we're going to go inside calmly," she says. "Remember, we want them to want to help us."

"You're right—best behavior." I smile.

We walk back out twenty minutes later with nothing. The fucking detective on the case wasn't there, and his partner informed us that they have no new leads. This can't be happening.

"Well, that was pointless," Maddie says. "Can we grab a bite, at least?"

I nod. We head to PT's for their cheeseburger special. I order us a couple of Sapporos. When they arrive, I take a long draw from my beer. "Can you believe this shit, Maddie? What if we never see her again?" My voice cracks on the words.

Her eyes narrow. "Don't say that, Liam. We have to believe she's coming back to us."

I roll my eyes at her. I wish I could feel so optimistic, but deep down I know she's dead. She's a kidnapper's nightmare. There's no way they'll be able to handle her. She has too much fight in her. She's dead. I hold up my bottle. "To Vivian," I say.

"To Vivian," Maddie says, and we clink bottles.

"Let's get drunk," I say.

"Here?" Maddie looks around at the thin, late lunch crowd.

"Anywhere. Here works. It's close to home in case we get too drunk. You wanna call Stevyn?" I ask her.

She looks down at her hands. "That won't be necessary."

I slide around our booth so I'm right next to her. "What up?"

She leans into my side. "I don't know. Ever since Viv went missing...it's just, he doesn't love her so he can't understand. I feel like you are the only person I can talk to about what I'm going through."

I bump her shoulder with mine in an effort to comfort her. "I feel the same way about you. No one else understands." I slam down my beer bottle. "That's it! Fuck him, and fuck everybody else! We are starting an official 'our girl is missing' support group." I stand and ease my way out of the booth. "I'm gonna get us something stronger."

I return with a bottle of tequila, two shot glasses, salt, and limes.

"They let you bring the whole bottle to the table?" Maddie asks.

"Sure. Shana knows Vivian, too." I wave to the bartender. "She said to take some shots for her, and that she will make sure we leave in a cab."

Maddie doesn't think about it any further. We lick the salt off of the back of our hands, throw the poured shot back, and suck the limes. We repeat the ritual until we are slurring our words. The pain becomes dull. We might just be onto something. I don't know why we didn't think of this earlier. Like two fools, Maddie and I start dancing in the middle of PT's. I'm not even sure there is any music. The place starts getting busier as the night progresses. People we don't know, and some who we do, join us for shots of tequila. By the time the cab rolls up, we've forgotten about the pain, at least temporarily.

Maddie and I hang on to each other for support as we climb into the back of the cab. We slur our addresses to the driver. He pulls up in front of my place first. The pub is only a few blocks away. I lean over to hug Maddie and give her a quick kiss before climbing out. I totally miss her cheek and my kiss lands on her mouth.

For some reason, we don't break the kiss. I pull my face back and stare into her eyes, searching for something, and then I see it—need, loneliness. I press my lips back to hers and in an unexpected response, she winds her fingers through my hair. I toss money at the cab driver, take Maddie's hand, fumble with my keys, and rush her into the house. I don't want to think about what we're about to do. I just want to bury myself inside of her so that for one fucking moment, I can feel something other than pain. I'm sure she feels the same way. We're bonded forever by tragedy.

We're practically naked by the time we make it to my room. We burst through the door and pause in front of my bed. I stand in front of Maddie naked. My is dick hard and aching. I'd hoped that by now I'd be inside of Vivian, tasting the sweet nectar of her innocence and making her mine in every way. I never for one minute thought I would be standing in front of her best friend—my best friend— watching her ample breasts move as she takes sobering, deep breaths. Neither of us is as drunk as we were when we walked through the door.

"Are you sure about this?" I ask Maddie. She's suddenly what I want and what I need because she can take the pain away, but I won't do anything she doesn't want to do.

"Yes." Her voice is velvety.

"What about Vivian?" I ask her.

"I think she would understand," she says. "We're hurting. Just this once, okay? Promise me."

"I promise."

The next instant, our lips crash into each other's. We are hungry and desperate. Images of Vivian flash through my mind. I imagine that I'm kissing her. It's only when Maddie pulls away from me that my eyes open. The hottest, most seductive smile crosses her face, and she drops down to her knees.

Before I have a second to react, she guides my dick into her mouth and begins sucking. In all my fantasies about Vivian, she never did this. "Oh," I moan. Maddie pushes me back toward the bed and crawls after me, sucking and licking expertly. Fuck. I should feel guilty, but right now I'm happy to feel anything other than the blinding pain of losing my girl.

Maddie comes up on her knees and leans over my dick. She is

holding onto it, stroking it. She looks up at me and smiles. The next thing I know my entire dick is down her throat. How the fuck? I'm about to come and I don't want to come in Maddie's mouth. I pull her off of my dick. Damn, that felt epic.

I pick her up and ease her down onto my dick. I sink so deep inside her hot pussy. Unlike my Vivian, Maddie has experience, and she shows it as she rides me like her life depends on it. It's deep and hot, and she rides me until I can't take it anymore. I erupt. Fuck, Maddie! I come harder than I ever have. If I convulsed with any more force I might break a bone. Maddie comes, too. She screams out like a feral animal. I flip her sexy ass over so I'm on top.

She's crying—likely, from guilt, relief and pleasure. I feel pretty shitty for betraying Vivian like this, but more importantly, I feel no fucking pain. My dick isn't showing any signs of going soft. My body must know on a biological level what I need, because this is the only thing I've found that numbs me. I slam inside of her. I keep my eyes on hers. We'll never be able to say that this "just happened," that we were drunk. That shit is for suckers. We know what we're doing. We know what we need, and tonight it is this with each other. I grind deep inside of her, taking away our pain, replacing it, if only for one night, with pure carnal pleasure.

Maddie's hips rise up, telling me she wants more. She meets my thrusts with her own, grinding around my dick like it's her lifeline. We both cry out in pleasure when we reach our climax together. I flood her with adoring kisses. She cries even harder, so I wrap my arms around her and hold on. We fuck each other several more times throughout the night. I can't seem to bury my dick deep enough inside of her, and she can't seem to open her legs wide enough to get more.

For one night, we helped each other to ease our pain. We fall asleep with our arms laced around each other. We're comforted, not guilty, about what we have done. I'm sure tomorrow it will be a different story.

11

EXPLORATION

I rise early in the morning. Sky and Sapphire are still asleep. I decide to take a personal tour of my new home. I cross my room, grab the thin, red, thigh-length robe from its hook. When this is all over, the color red is going to elicit a PTSD reaction from me.

The door doesn't make a sound when I slowly pull it open, and it closes just as quietly. The clock in the family room—social room would be more appropriate—says it is six-thirty. Wow. I'm amazed that I'm up so early.

I make it out of the sleeping Chamber and pad barefoot down the stone hall to the elevator. The doors slide open with a soft ding, and I step in. Tension closes in on me like a vise, as if I'm doing something forbidden by roaming around alone. According to Zion, certain areas are all-access. Perhaps the uneasy feeling is coming from the fact that I'm walking around alone for the first time since being brought here. I'm not usually one who likes to be left alone. Growing up, I always had a steady crop of family and friends to keep me entertained. In here, since I have no friends or family, I prefer my own company. More and more, I look forward to spending time with Tyson.

Tyson. I recall how he was there to comfort me last night. He didn't judge me or ask me why I tried to kill myself, not that he should have to, given my current predicament. He also didn't try to pacify me with bullshit about my inner strength. Maybe the fact that I tried to off myself helps him see me for the weak person that I really am.

I depress the button for the second floor. Key access is needed for floors four and five. My mind drifts back to the time I spent on the fourth floor last night. Shivers run down my spine. When I step off of the elevator, I learn quickly that I'm not the only early riser. There's an attendant at the desk who greets me. She is also stunning. What is it with this place? Only the drop-dead gorgeous need apply? Her long, naturally blonde hair falls down her back to her waist in cascading waves. She's tanner than she should be, with pale-green eyes. Her body is perfect.

"Good morning, Flame. How may I assist you?" The moniker slices through the air and my skin. By now I have a ton of wounds invisible to the naked eye—some deeper than others.

The woman seems sweeter than she looks, which is judgmental on my part. She smiles like a schoolgirl, waiting for my response.

"Um, I thought I'd come check out the spa, or jacuzzi maybe..." I'm not really sure what I want. I was hoping to be alone with my thoughts without having to make any decisions. I wanted to feel free, if only for a moment.

"Certainly, Ms. Flame. Would you like a swimsuit or would you rather go au natural?" she asks without the hint of a blush.

I want to ask her how long she has worked here, but I think better of it. "Um, I think a swimsuit would be great." I guess I hadn't thought about it. The attendant disappears and returns quickly with a deep-red two-piece. Of course, it's fucking blood red. I take it from her, grateful for any form of cover. "Thank you..." I pause for her name and incline my head toward her in question.

"Roxy. My name is Roxy." She smiles.

I know that isn't her real name. No one uses their real names in The Chamber. "Nice to meet you, Roxy. I'm..." Nobody. "Well...I mean, you already know my...what they call me here," I stumble over my words and feel my cheeks warm at my inability to engage in a simple conversation. "But...um, it's nice to meet you." Dork much? "I'd better go change." I smile in embarrassment and start walking away in the wrong direction. Roxy quickly points me in the opposite direction.

The changing room, like everything else I've seen here, is lavish and rich. The room sparkles from the large chandelier that twinkles from the ceiling. Deep-purple chaise lounges are spread out around the sitting area. The floor is stone. Whenever I see the flooring I think of moats and drawbridges. The rest of the room is standard—bathroom, toilet and shower stalls. The shower wall in the back is exceptional. It's a wall-to-wall steam shower with beautiful green plant life climbing along the walls. I step inside, curious. Amazing. You could forget you're even indoors in a shower like this.

I leave the steam shower with intention of trying it out very soon. I pop into a stall and shimmy out of my red robe, boy shorts, and tank top. The red swimsuit is one of those barely-there numbers that I would never, ever wear in real life. I don't know what to do with the clothes I just changed out of, so I leave them on the bench in the stall.

The jacuzzi is easy to find. I just follow the sound of the water jets. Sunshine had the same idea as me, because she is reclined back in the jacuzzi with her eyes closed. I clear my throat when I enter, taking the steps slowly so that I don't scare the crap out of her.

"Hi, Sunshine." I wave when her eyes pop open.

She smiles at me and sits up straighter. I make my way to a seat next to her.

"Hey there, Flame," she says with a thick accent.

I remember Mason calling her his Caribbean beauty. She is gorgeous. Her skin is soft, dewy, and lightly tanned. Light brown eyes with a hint of green regard me. I know why she was chosen. She also has heart-shaped, pouty lips and beautiful eyebrows.

"So, you like red, huh?" she jokes.

"And your favorite color is yellow?" I point to her yellow suit. We both laugh. "I hate red now!" I proclaim.

"I used to love yellow before. Now, I'm developing allergies to it," she confesses.

We both giggle a bit more before we fall into companionable silence. My heart warms at the normalcy of our conversation as if these were everyday circumstances we were meeting under.

The water is glorious against my skin. The warmth is my weakness. We are silent for a long time before either of us dares to break into the precious quiet. With my eyes closed, I slice into the calm. "I love your accent," I say.

"Thanks," her voice sings.

We fall back into our quiet. All I can do is think of home—my family, my friends, Liam. Will I be enough for him when I finally return? Will he want me? Would I want me?

I miss him. I miss his stupid jokes that were only funny to him. It endeared him to all of us. We laughed so hard at the fact that he thought he was so funny. He and I would be a couple by now, if things had gone according to plan. He was the best person I knew. Maddie comes in a close second, but even she was no Liam. He was the perfect combination of sexy and nice. Most guys that hot are usually assholes. Liam was one of a kind in that department, until I met Tyson.

Tyson.

"This is a lotta crazy shit we got ourselves into, huh?" Sunshine interrupts the quiet.

"Never in a million years..." I say.

"My mum and dad and my sisters have got to be going batshit crazy by now. I was shopping when they grabbed me. I was with my girlfriends. Of course, I didn't park with them that day." She sighs in memory of the dreadful day. "I bought the sickest red dress..." She pauses. "Sorry," she says.

A laugh escapes me. "I liked red just fine the day you were taken. I promise." I smile at her.

"This dress was the sexiest thing I'd ever put on, you know? It was tighter and skimpier than anything I'd ever worn before. See, we had a party to go to later that night. I wasn't paying attention. I was only thinking about my dress, and I never made it to my car. All I saw was the white cloth coming to my face, and lights out for me." She says it like she still doesn't believe it happened to her. Tears flow freely down her face, as if she's mourning all over again. "When I woke up, I was on an airplane."

I offer her a tight smile and squeeze her hand in understanding. We don't say anything for a while. We sit and consider our unusual circumstances.

"I practically jumped into the fucking kidnappers' van when they took me!" I attempt to make light of my stupidity. "I couldn't get to the van fast enough!"

"What do you mean? Are you a crackpot or something?" she asks with a startled look on her face.

All I can do is laugh at her expression because I probably am a crackpot. I calm myself so that I can explain. "You see, the night I was taken, I thought it was my friends kidnapping me. It was my birthday the next day, and they had this elaborate surprise set up. When the hood went over my head, I went along with it." I still feel like the hugest idiot.

"Some surprise." She shakes her head and bursts into uncontrolled laughter. I join her, because it really is an insane story. We both laugh until we are crying.

"Never thought I'd lose my virginity in a sex club," I add.

"Do you have a beau back home?" she asks me.

"Sort of. I was hoping that at the end of my birthday weekend he'd be my beau." I try the unfamiliar word. "You?"

"Yes, ma'am. I was hoping to be engaged really soon, too. One of my girlfriends told me they saw my Thomas going into the jewelry store recently." She plays with the suds forming on the top of the water. "I'm sure Thomas won't want me after they use me up here."

I know Liam won't either.

"Sure he will, and Liam will want me, too." Liar! "We didn't choose this, Sunshine. We were taken from our beds, parking garages, and wherever else. We were stolen away from our lives and forced to play nice to save the people we love. The least they can do after our sacrifice is take us back with open arms. If they can't do that, then they didn't deserve us to begin with." If Liam doesn't want me I may just die.

We go back to silence. She probably thinks I'm nuts. If she only knew I'm trying to convince myself as much as I am her. I close my eyes and think of Liam. I can't help but wonder what he's going through and how he is suffering without me. He always felt a strong desire to protect me even though we were just friends. He can't save me here. I'm a prisoner for at least another three-hundred-and-fifty days. I've definitely been counting.

Of course, that's if I'm lucky and Mason stays true to his word. Who knows? All of this could be a ruse to keep us compliant. The promise of freedom, money, the threats to our loved ones, the success stories of past Chambermaids, and the kind treatment could just be to get our maximum cooperation. He may really plan to kill us and dump our bodies in the ocean after he's done with us.

Fuck all of us.

"My name is Whitney, by the way."

"Nice to meet you, Whitney. I'm Vivian."

We don't shake hands. We hug each other. We're in this together. There's strength in the seven of us, even in a place like this. I really believe that. I know this year would be unbearable if I had to endure this alone.

Sunshine and I are prunes by the time we leave the jacuzzi. We wave to Roxy as we pass the reception desk. She waves and smiles generously. When we get to the dressing room, we find new yellow and red clothes waiting us.

12

BLOSSOMING SISTERHOOD

*W*e walk back to our living quarters in amiable silence. When we enter the social area, we find all of the girls camped out and dressed in their signature colors. I can almost envision them as my sorority sisters, sitting around the family room before a meeting about an upcoming fundraiser or a big challenge against a rival sorority. Somehow, my imagination is not up to the task.

Once Sunshine and I step deeper into the family room, we see Ivory sitting at the head of our group. All eyes are trained on her as if she holds the answer to the enigma that is the universe.

"Girls, welcome," Ivory says with Mason-like excitement. "You made it just in time. Please sit!"

Sunshine and I do as we are asked and sit side by side on an oversized chair for two. Ivory is even more beautiful up close. Her blonde hair falls in dramatic curls down her back. Her skin is porcelain and perfect. I would guess that she's almost twenty-five. She's wearing a striking white dress that hugs her curves and stops just above her knees. Her blue-green eyes meet mine as she greets us with a gentle smile. She seems relaxed. She's even kicked off her sky-high white stiletto heels. Her bare feet are French pedicured to perfection. "Ivory" fits her.

"Flame, Sunshine, I know we met your first day here, but just in case you were too overwhelmed, I'm Ivory." She rises and pads across the small distance between us to hug us both. "Welcome to this year's Chamber. I asked Mason if I could come down and speak candidly with you. I'm not sure if you're aware of this, but I started out as a Chambermaid here," she says.

I had no idea. We all exchange glances. The name Ivory should have clued us in.

"Yep. Three years ago, to be exact. I sat in the same place as you all, and I was scared to death. I thought I would die for sure. I didn't believe a word Mason said about setting me free, but as you can already tell from your treatment here, Mason isn't in the business of killing. This is his livelihood. Chambermaids are his bread and butter. You will all be pampered with only the best for a solid year, and when it's over you will all be very wealthy young ladies."

She pauses to give her words a chance to sink in. She is right about the treatment. We have not been physically harmed. We're not locked up in dark, cold cells. We are free to roam about. We are free to make friends with each other. There's no isolation.

"Some of you may have heard that I'm Mason's wife. It's rare in The Chamber for love to blossom. In some cases, lottery winners have been known to fall in love with Chambermaids. In rare cases, it does happen."

I don't miss that she glances at me.

"I, too, was taken from my family and my home. I was promised the moon, and Mason delivered. When my year was up, I was paid and sent home. What I didn't expect was how much I would miss Mason. I went back to my life, friends, and family. It was hard for me. What I mean to say is that I also fell in love with this lifestyle. The problem was that The Chamber moved around and was, and still is, always shrouded in secrecy. I would have never found him again. Lucky for me, Mason felt the same way and found me. We were married immediately and it has been my very own fairy tale."

I want to ask her if it bothers her that he has sex with so many different women, but that isn't my business, so I keep my thoughts to myself.

"Enough about me. I'm here to ease your transition into this life. Do you have any questions for me?" she asks.

"If you say Mason is so kind, why does he threaten to kill our loved ones?" Sky asks in her beautiful tongue.

"The way Mason sees it, he spends time and money handpicking his Chambermaids," Ivory replies. "This is a very lucrative business for him. I'm sure no one has actually ever been killed. Financially destroyed, beaten, or broken, perhaps—just enough to ruin their lives without completely destroying them. Then again, I am just speculating." She has a soft smile that doesn't fit the sentences she just strung together.

"How did you survive so many nights with so many men?" I ask.

"Oh, and what about our safety?" Sapphire interrupts before my question can be answered. "Who makes sure these guys don't knock us around?"

"One at a time, ladies. Sapphire, I will answer your question first. Flame, your question is a little harder to answer. Safety is easy. Each of you have become acquainted with your personal guards, correct?"

Some nod. Confusion clouds the faces of others. I certainly have become well acquainted with my personal guard.

"If you are unsure of who your personal guard is, he is the man that fucked you senseless last night after the introduction party," Ivory says. Realization floods the confused faces. "Each of them is given the task of protecting you. They will sit in front of a monitor the entire evening, five nights a week, watching to make sure you are treated properly. Now you know why they love it when you fall asleep," she adds. "After hours of watching you, they get horny as hell." Her expression is smug. We all understand her.

Knowing that Tyson will be there with me the entire time makes me feel more at ease. I plan to fall asleep frequently. My body, my choice. This makes inviting Tyson into my Chamber even more exciting.

"If there is even a hint of danger, they will be in your Chambers at once. The guards take protecting you very seriously. In even rarer cases, relationships form between Chambermaids and the guards who serve them. This is highly frowned upon because a smitten guard cannot do his job properly." I don't miss that she is looking at me in warning as she says the words. "Proceed in all things with caution," she says and breaks contact with me.

"Now, in regards to surviving The Chamber..." She stands. "Ladies, you must become your colors and your characters—embody them. That is how you survive. Be whoever the fuck you want to be outside of The Chamber. If your name is Brooke or Alyssa or Megan in your real life, be her when you're outside of that Chamber, but the second you hit those steps, be fierce! This is all an act. If your color is demure—then be the most demure lady who ever walked the earth. If your color is the embodiment of sex—be a sex-crazed nympho. If dark and edgy is your role, then sell the mystery. It helps to read up on colors and their meaning. Since you have no access to the internet or television, I can only offer you books. Our libraries are stocked."

She sighs as if her work is done, flops into her seat, and speaks as she slides her feet into her heels. "I promise you all, if you walk up those stairs as yourselves, the guilt and shame will eat away at you. It's not going to happen overnight, but if you practice, you will get it." She stands up. "Any more questions?"

Violet raises her hand. She actually waits for Ivory to call on her. She's toast in here. I thought I was in trouble.

Ivory sits back down. Her work isn't quite done. "Yes, Violet?"

"What actually happens in The Chambers? I mean, I know sex, but how does it work?" Her voice is soft and sweet.

Great question. I lean forward expectantly.

"Whatever the lottery winner wants," Ivory responds. "Usually, the guys on your schedule for the night put in their specifications. They may want you tied up or dressed a certain way. They may want you blindfolded or even gagged. Your handler or groomer prepares you for each man, and freshens you up between them. Some guys may just want to eat your pussy all night. Some may want to get their dicks sucked. Some of the true romantics might want to treat you like a real date. You've all seen those horses in your Chamber?"

"Yes," we all mutter.

"Believe me, you will all get to know that horse very well," she says. "I don't know why, but most of these guys get off on that. The bottom line is, they have paid millions to spend the year doing just about whatever they want to do with you. My advice is to be prepared for anything." She rises again.

"We will have to table any other questions for another time. The lottery winners will be showing up in a few hours, and you ladies need your rest. It's going to be a long night. Remember, embody your characters. Good luck." She flashes us a big smile and walks out without looking back.

Our faces reveal all variations of stunned and dumfounded.

Some of the girls stay in the family room and chat. I bolt to my room. My only desire is to bury myself under the covers—under the bed, if I can. I fling the wine-colored blanket back and something light catches my eye when it dislodges itself from under my pillow. It's a lavender envelope. On the front in beautiful script is my name, Vivian.

I tear it open in haste. Before I can begin reading it, Sky and Sapphire appear in the doorway, chatting about something. I turn my back to them in a flash, not wanting them to see my letter. I hide it under my shirt and excuse myself to the bathroom, a lavishly appointed, three-stalled room. I step into the stall in the center and lock myself in. I put the seat down and sit on it. I carefully pull the letter from the envelope and begin reading it. It's from Tyson.

My Dearest Vivian,

It is in bad form that I write this because I risk so much. I knew that I wouldn't have a chance to see you before your first night. It kills me that I can't be inside of The Chamber with you. Please know that I will be watching you, and if you need me I'm only a staircase away.

I'm so sorry that you have to endure this, but know that if I could take you away from here I would.

Yours since Vegas,
Dominic

P.S. Do not fall asleep in your Chamber tonight. Believe me, if it were up to me, I would have you sleep there every night. I don't want anyone to catch on to anything between us. I will send another letter when the time is right.

P.P.S. Please destroy this letter. Might I suggest shred and flush? XOXO

I hold the letter to my chest. Tears fall like a storm. He really does care for me. Dominic. He told me his real name. No one uses their real names in The Chamber, but we are now Vivian and Dominic. I will take care to not utter it by accident. How does a man as amazing as him find himself working in a place like this? I hate to shred this beautiful post, but I know that it is best that whatever is transpiring between us goes undiscovered.

What is going on between us? Why am I having such strong feelings for a man I barely know? What about Liam? I read Dominic's words three more times before I decimate the letter into tiny, flushable shreds, lavender envelope and all. I will check my pillow with hope every single day. I miss him already.

When my stomach growls, I realize that I haven't had a proper meal since I've been here. I haven't had any appetite, but I am suddenly starving. I rush past my Chamber-mates toward the kitchen. I raid the cabinets, and the best I can come up with is oatmeal. It hits the spot—warm and comforting. I head back to my room and fall into a dreamless sleep.

13

THE PLAYLIST

I wake with a start, disoriented from my afternoon nap. I'm alone in my room. Just as I swing my legs over the edge of my bed and put my feet onto the floor, Zion enters.

"Flame, you're awake! I was just coming to get you."

I wish she could take my place. With her fiery auburn hair she could easily be Flame.

"Are you ready?"

No. "Sure."

"Then follow me," she says, and to my horror she heads toward my Chamber stairs.

Why is everyone so cheery around here? I follow close behind Zion. Fuck. I really do not want to do this. When we reach the top of the staircase I can't breathe. I take in rapid shallow breaths, sucking in air, and it still isn't enough. Alarm sets in as my head gets light and starts spinning. My heart is pounding in my chest, and it becomes tight. I'm going to die. Seriously. I can't do this! Five men! How can I have sex with five men in one night? What are they gonna want me to do?

"I can hear your heart pounding from here. Girl, are you okay?" Zion asks.

"I'm fine." I'm dying!

"No, you are not fine. You're on your way to a full-blown panic attack. Listen, we have time—nearly an hour. Just breathe."

I try to relax, but it's not working very well. We walk past the heavily-veiled curtain, and I continue to breathe long, deep, relaxing breaths. I cringe when I glance at the self-pleasure horse, and, to my dismay, the open cabinet of horror. Zion takes my hand when I pause. She leads me past The Chamber to the adjoining bath. There's a stylist's chair in the center of the bathroom.

I sit in the chair and continue to breathe deeply until my breaths are normal again.

"Better?" Zion asks me.

"I think so." My heart slows down and my vision is clearer.

Zion turns the shower on, then turns to face me. "Listen, Mason is a smart man. Why do you think he had that introduction party? You had thirty-five different men pawing at you. Thirty-five! Tonight, you only have to deal with five. Not to mention, your personal guard has the biggest dick on the planet. If you can handle Tyson, none of these guys will even come close.

"I secretly call him Thunderdick." I giggle.

"Thunderdick and then some," she replies.

We both laugh at the absurdity of his organ. I hop into the shower. The warm water engulfs my body, calming me further. I just stand under the showerhead and drown in the warmth. It's too much. I'm in my Chamber. I need to remember Ivory's words from earlier. I need to manifest Flame. It seems like the only time she comes around is once I've been touched in that certain place. I have to suffer as Vivian only as long as it takes for whoever I'm with to touch me there. It's only then that the fear, everything, vanishes.

There's some truth to Zion's words, though.

Before I was brought here, I would have never imagined doing any of the things I've done. In a short time, I have become much more relaxed about sex. I've had more than twenty cocks in my mouth. I've also had sex with Tyson and Mason. I've done all of these things, and I didn't die. I've enjoyed my experiences with Tyson. He gives me control and makes me feel like the decision to have sex is ours. He makes me feel like we're in it together.

I wash my body and my hair, smiling when I think of him. "You're right, Zion," I shout over the water. "Besides, Tyson will be watching the whole time, right?"

"Correct," she shouts back.

"Hey, can I ask you a question?"

"Anything," she says.

I rinse the suds off my body. "Earlier, Ivory came and talked to all of us, and she basically said it's forbidden for guards and Chambermaids to become involved, but she seemed to be speaking directly to me. Do you know what that's about?" I wait for her answer.

"I do," Zion says.

I lean my head out of the shower, and my eyebrows raise in question. I turn the water off so I don't miss a word, then step out of the shower into Zion's waiting towel. I go at the task of drying while she talks.

She sighs, then stares at me as if deciding. "I don't see how telling you this can hurt anything," she finally says.

My eyes don't leave hers.

"Tyson has never been a personal guard to any girl in The Chamber, ever," she begins.

I hide my face in the towel to hide my smile while I pretend to dry my face. "Was he chosen?" I ask as casually as I can.

She sighs again. "No, he requested to be your guard, which is unusual. He has never expressed any interest in any other task besides leading the guards. He has never guarded an individual girl or had sex with any of the Chambermaids."

"Never?" This knowledge thrills me on a level that I can't begin to explain.

"Now you see why the interest that he has taken in you is being observed," Zion says. "Mason couldn't deny his request, but he is concerned."

I turn to hide another smile as I wrap myself in the towel and take a seat in the chair. "Wow, I feel special." He chose me. I have a sudden urge to giggle and squeal like a schoolgirl. He has wanted you from the very beginning. I'm the only Chambermaid he has ever had sex with. Why me? I knew I could trust him.

"You should feel special, but Ivory's warning is real. Mason will never let his best guard get into a relationship with you. It will cloud his judgment, and he leads all of the guards. He has to have the clearest head. Trust me, Mason will be keeping a close eye on the two of you."

Her warning doesn't sit well with me. I don't want to be anywhere near Mason's radar, and I certainly don't want this to make Tyson back away from me. He's the reason I feel safer here. It's not like we're going to be a couple when I get out of here. I have Liam back home. Liam and I have been friends without benefits, and Tyson and I are the exact opposite. His life is here, and mine isn't. In a year, I'm leaving this, and Tyson, behind.

Zion is quick with my preparation, which includes airbrush foundation and giant curlers. She hands me a piece of paper, which I quickly discover is tonight's playlist.

Stranger One wants me sexy and seductive, attentive to his every instruction and desire.

Stranger Two wants me naked, and he wants me on the horse.

Stranger Three wants me in some strange suspension contraption. He also made it clear that I'm not to speak.

Stranger Four wants me to sample several apparatuses.

Stranger Five wants vanilla sex. What the hell is vanilla sex? Whatever it is, it sounds messy.

I don't know if it's better or worse to know my fate. The paper is shaking in my hand.

Tyson is watching. Tyson is watching. I steel my nerves for what is to come.

The time is near. I glance up to the opening in the ceiling. The sky is sprinkled with the brightest stars. Trance music filters in through the gentlemen's room below. My stomach rolls in dread and anticipation.

Zion did her part to help me get into the role. I'm dressed in a gorgeous scarlet nightgown. It's sheer enough to show my breasts and the triangle between my legs clearly. The gown falls to the floor with a train. I don't recognize myself. My hair falls in big curls down my back. I'm wearing five-inch stilettos with red soles.

Who am I?

My face is the most unrecognizable part. I'm more of a moisturizer and lip gloss kind of girl. This glamazon in the mirror is not me. False eyelashes frame my gray eyes, causing them to appear bigger and grayer somehow. Ruby red lips stand out against my alabaster skin. That's it, I'm no longer Vivian. For the moment, she is gone. I stare at the reflection of this beautiful stranger. She is not me, and she is not Nobody either. Nobody is weak and broken, and the reflection staring back at me is none of those things. She is Flame.

The bookcase slides open, and I brace myself for Stranger One. It's my first Chamber, and I don't know what to do with myself. What would Flame do? I sit on the bed, and attempt to lean in a sexy manner, but fail miserably. I don't have to worry. When I gaze at the entrance to my Chamber, there he is.

A strange man in my Chamber.

My heart stops and my breath catches in my throat. His eyes are pinned to mine. To my surprise, he looks a little nervous. I break eye contact first and notice that he is holding a bottle and two long-stemmed glasses. He's very attractive, with thick dark hair, dark eyes, and fair skin. I guess that he is in his thirties. I can't see his body because of his dress shirt and pants, but I can tell that he is fit.

"Flame, you're breathtaking," he says. His eyes take in all of me. He looks at me with adoration.

I blush, then remember he wants sexy and seductive. Compliant. I'll wing it. I take solace in the fact that Tyson—Dominic—is watching.

I find myself wishing I knew where the cameras were.

The music fades into the background. Only my heartbeat is audible while I await instructions from the handsome stranger.

"Please, sit here." He directs me.

I rise from the bed and make my way to the bistro table I hadn't even noticed. The table is only large enough for a couple of wine glasses and our bottle. The stranger pulls out my chair for me. When I sit, he plants a soft, wet kiss on my temple. He's a flowers and romance guy. He takes a seat across from mine.

"You're exquisite, Flame." My stranger pours champagne into our glasses. "Shall we make a toast to what I expect to be an amazing year?"

He raises his glass.

I raise mine.

"To us," he says.

I mimic him. "To us."

"Call me X, because tonight I'm going to ex-tinguish your flame."

Lame. "That sounds intriguing," I reply. We sit in silence so long that I begin to squirm. X stares at me with lust in his eyes. He's showing me romance and chivalry now, but his eyes tell me that he is no gentleman.

"Please stand," he instructs.

I do as I'm told. My chest is rising and falling, giving away the fear that I'm desperate to cover.

"Walk over to the bed, and please do not sit."

I comply.

He stands and crosses the small Chamber.

I squeeze my eyes shut and take deep gulps of air while my body trembles. You can do this, Vivian.

When I open my eyes he is two inches away from me. With my sky-high stilettos, he and I are face to face. I'm lost. I wait on edge as his breathing picks up. In a sudden move, he fists my hair, pulls my face to his, and kisses me. More accurately, he devours me. I do my best to keep up with him and match the intensity of his tongue with mine. I wish that he would just get on with it, though, and help me get out of my own head and disappear. Once he touches my newfound pleasure spot, I'll no longer be present in this room with him, and that is what I desire. Perhaps if I amp up the seductress factor he will end this charade.

I tangle my hands into his hair, pulling him closer to me. His erection pressing into me indicates how much he likes it. I fake a moan into his mouth.

"Oh, baby. I want you, too," he breathes.

It's working. He practically rips my sheer gown from my body, and it falls to the floor in shreds. I step out of it and realize that I'm standing before him naked.

"You're fucking perfect," he says, standing back to admire me. "I don't know what to do first." He sounds like a kid on Christmas.

He gazes into my eyes and then lowers himself out of my line of sight. I open my legs when I feel him nudge my leg, widening my stance. The feeling of his tongue licking and tasting me is just what I need. He's gentle as his tongue acquaints itself with my sex. I let my mind zero in on him licking my clitoris like it's his favorite brand of candy. I thrust my hips forward and licking turns to sucking. I hear the moans escape my lips. Heaven.

I grab one of the bedposts. My body covered in goose bumps, and my stomach starts to clench. My nipples peak into tight nuggets. I want to touch myself. I want to bite something. Fuck. I moan, and he sucks harder. I feel myself climbing higher and higher. His fingers slide inside of me and I nearly slip off the edge.

"Lie down on the bed." He gazes up at me from under heavy lids. "I want your knees bent and legs spread far apart so I can see this pussy."

I do as he asks, and he quickly takes me into his mouth again. He gives a voracious suck, then slides his tongue along my needy flesh. I nearly lose it and I fist his hair and pull his face into me. I'm shaking from the thrill of how my sex throbs, but manage to keep my orgasm at bay. The throbbing is maddening, sending tingling waves through me. I want him to bury himself inside of me way more than I should. The feelings stirring inside of me are too strong to ignore, like a fire that has to be put out, just like he said.

I watch the stranger remove his shirt, revealing a fine body. He has deep contours in all the right places—chiseled abs and a well-defined chest. Tyson has the body of a professional football player, but X's body is like a world-class soccer player. I watch as he unzips his pants, and his very full erection springs free. No underwear.

"Wow," I say. I know guys like when women seem impressed by their cocks.

"All for you, baby." He smiles.

He is no Tyson, but he's pretty big. I seem to have become an authority in a very short period of time.

"Are you ready for me?" He strokes himself.

I nod enthusiastically because the throbbing from earlier is ebbing and I need it back. X climbs onto the bed and without another word, he slams his erection inside of me. I hiss from the contact. He repeats the action over and over. I raise my hips so that his length can reach the spot deep inside of me that makes me lose my mind.

He pulls out and flips me over onto my stomach. I follow his hands with my body and bring my rump toward him, arching my back. He plunges back inside of me. I like this position because I can't see his face. In this position, he could be anyone I want. He drives his cock inside of me fast and hard. It only takes three thrusts to plunge me to the depths of a mighty orgasm that causes my pussy to squeeze his erection. As my body stiffens and sparks shoot through me, I go rigid, pushing my ass back onto his cock.

"You like this dick don't you?" he says as he slams into me, causing my body to catch another wave before I've come down from the first.

"Yes! I fucking love your dick!" I shout through heavy breaths.

"Tell me to fuck you harder!" he hisses.

"Fuck me harder, X. Break me!" It is enough to bring him to the brink of ecstasy. He slams into me so hard that I swear I'll have bruises. He seems more animal than human. He yells out, pushes into me one last time, and he doesn't pull out. His body shudders and quakes, and he collapses onto me.

But he's not finished with me. By the time he's done, I've counted seven orgasms for him. I didn't know a person could come that many times in a few hours. He must have taken something because his erection never waned. He was hard and ready the entire time.

When he finally walks out of my Chamber, I'm suddenly rocked by the avalanche of emotions that hit me. There is no one, only me. I wrap my arms around myself and break down. I let it all out of my system, knowing that somehow I have to do this four more times. Four more strangers. It's my job to act as if I'm there exclusively for each of them, and all I really want to do is go home.

Warm hands on my shoulder startle me. "Flame?"

I look up to see Zion. She sits on the edge of the bed, and I collapse into her arms. "There, there." She consoles me, rubbing my back.

That only makes me cry harder. "I don't think I can do this. Why can't they just kill me?"

"What happened? You were doing so well. What's wrong, Flame? You knew it would be this way, didn't you?"

"Yes, but knowing what is gonna happen..." I can't finish. She won't understand. Once I'm alone with my brain, it's just too much fucking reality. I continue to weep.

I want to be back at home with my family.

When I make the decision to sleep with someone, I want it to be my choice. I can't do this—strangers breathing on me, touching me, violating me.

The low-pitched rumble of a man clearing his throat alerts us that we're not alone. We both look up and see Tyson standing in my Chamber, worry etched on his face. I feel at ease the second I look into his eyes. I want to run to him, to wrap my arms around him, and let him comfort me as only he can, but I don't. I only stare at him and take solace in the concern he shows me with his eyes.

"Is everything okay in here?" he asks.

His eyes never leave mine. Mine never leave his. To do more would reveal too much. I can see his panic in the way his gorgeously muscled chest rises and falls in haste.

"Are you harmed?" he asks, purposely keeping his tone profes-sional. He's a personal guard to a Chambermaid, not Dominic talking to Vivian.

Yes. I nod. "This is harder than I expected," I say. "I'm better now."

Now that I see you. "Thank you for checking on me," I say, but I hope he can see in my eyes that I mean so much more.

"I'm right downstairs," he says with his eyes trained on mine.

I nod and smile at him. There's no way that Zion can't feel the tension between us. It's palpable.

"I think she's good, Tyson," Zion says. "Thanks for checking on her."

"Never a problem. I'm always right downstairs," he states again.

I wipe my eyes with the back of my hand and continue to resist running into his arms. "Thanks, Tyson. I'm okay now." I hope he understands I mean that he's responsible for that.

Tyson nods a final time and leaves. The room feels colder without him in it. I follow Zion into the bathroom. I take a fast bath, careful not to wet my hair. Zion makes quick work of reapplying my eye makeup and dresses me for my next stranger.

Red peep-toed stilettos—that's it.

When I return to my Chamber, the stranger is already waiting for me.

"Your chariot awaits you, Flame," he says, pointing to the pleasure pony. There's a large dildo screwed into it. The room is dimmer than I remember it being earlier. The moon shines through the glass ceiling. I can make out the salt-and-pepper hair of the stranger. The only source of true light in the room is the spotlight. It's a beacon, trained on the pleasure pony.

I comply without a word. It's obvious that he wants to watch. I cross The Chamber as seductively as I can in five-inch heels toward my chariot. I step onto the foot rest and swing my leg over the pony. I notice a button that reads, Heat and Lubricate. I also notice that the phallus is glistening.

Mason thinks of everything.

"You don't know how hot you are right now," my observer's voice says from the darkness.

I catch sight of his silhouette. I can tell that he is stroking himself. I bend my legs with caution and ease. I am not afraid as much as I am ashamed, my body is heated with blush. Being watched this way is freaking me out. I think of Tyson just a few short steps below me, and with a bit of extra courage, I lower myself down onto the phallus. It is warm and firm; its size fills me nearly entirely. At first I just sit as my sex becomes accustomed to the feel of it. I have never pleasured myself with a dildo before.

"That's a girl, ride that pony," the stranger instructs me.

I do as I am told. I begin to roll my hips in a circular motion. The dick is warm and malleable—close to the real thing. It fills me. When I find that special spot, my heartbeat speeds up, and electricity soars through me. I feel throbbing between my legs as my clitoris swells in want and need. Feeling the heady sensations is just what I need. I start grinding on the dick. The feeling is fucking amazing. I lose myself in my own world of self-pleasure.

I'm alone in my Chamber. I can't get the length of the warm cock deep enough inside me. I gasp loudly and hiss and moan. I grind harder. My hips rock forward and backward. I could die right here and now, blissfully riding this pony. My head swims. My body is bombarded by heat, cold, and electricity. I can't describe it. I must find Tyson's camera because right now, this is for him. I hold onto the single pole, rise off of the dick, and quickly sink back onto it. I squeal with delight. I repeat the motion up and down on the warm dick, pushing it as deep into my pussy as I can.

When I'm nearly blind with the sensations my body is producing, I succumb to it and erupt over the edge. I'm loud and feral. My clitoris pulses and throbs between my legs. My body shudders and shakes. I stop myself from screaming out Tyson's name. All I can do is gasp for air. In the next moment, I feel myself being lifted off of the magical pony. The stranger carries me to the bed and slams his erection inside of me before we are even lying down completely. My insides are still a mass of fiery sensations. Coupled with his repeated pounding, I spiral into another orgasm almost immediately. I cry out in pleasure. My stranger comes inside of me with a series of quakes and shudders, followed by a string of obscenities.

The time with Stranger Two passes by quickly. Self-pleasure should be the status quo in The Chamber. Zion enters the minute he leaves. I'm in much better shape. She cleans me up for my third stranger. "Exhaustion" is my new middle name.

When I walk back into my Chamber, Zion is with me. I'm naked, again, and she assists me into a contraption. It is a swing of sorts. "I'm going to be suspended?" I ask.

She shrugs her shoulders. "Look at it this way. You're tired, and you'll be supported by this thing." She grabs hold of the swing. "He'll have to do all the work."

I nod. She has a point. I would love to rest right now and do nothing.

Zion lowers the swing onto the bed. She assists me to lie on top of it. She stretches my arms out to my sides and straps them in. She spreads my legs apart into a near split and straps them in place. Another strap goes over my torso. My head is supported by a sling that my forehead rests on, but my face is free to see below me. This shit is crazy.

"Are you okay?" Zion asks.

No. "I think so."

"Okay. I'm gonna push the remote and you're gonna move up and backward off the bed first, then higher off the ground. Tell me how you feel…if anything hurts."

"Okay," I reply. I begin moving like she says until I'm hovering over the ground of my Chamber a good three or four feet in the air. What I immediately notice is that my breasts are poking out of two holes. Also, my naughty bits are accessible from underneath and behind. It's an all-access swing.

"How's this?" she asks.

"Besides crazy?" I scoff.

"Yeah, besides that."

"Surprisingly comfortable." I think I could go to sleep.

"Now I don't know how kinky your next customer is gonna be. Based on this, he's out there. I want to warn you, this thing moves a lot and it can hold up to five hundred pounds."

Not good. The implication sends my brain spinning and my fatigued heart speeds up. I try to take deep breaths. Not helping.

Even with as much as I've experienced already tonight, the idea of swinging around on this with a man on me and his cock buried in me is freaking me out.

"Can I ask you a favor? This is probably the strangest request anyone has ever made, but I'm really nervous."

She walks around so that she can see my face. "Don't ever be afraid to ask me anything, Flame. I'm here for you."

My face heats, and I know it bares the color of my Chamber. "It's embarrassing."

"Anything," she insists.

I squeeze my eyes shut. "So, for some reason when I go in cold, I'm more...you know...scared. But if I'm aroused, like on the horse, it's easier somehow...and..." I can't believe what I'm asking of my groomer.

She giggles. "Girl, I gotcha," she says.

In yet another embarrassing moment—they are mounting rapidly—she raises me up into the air so that she can easily stand under me. She presses another button and my angle changes, my feet lower to where I'm on a slant. Zion takes my nipple into her mouth and sucks it. I instantly feel my nipple harden in her mouth. The hairs on my arms raise. It seems more forbidden because she's a girl, but it's no less exciting.

She goes to work with her tongue on my other nipple and begins working my clitoris with her fingers. It also hardens, and I feel myself slip into my safe place. My superhero alter ego resurfaces. I love her. She is strong and fierce. She is Flame. Zion slips an unknown number of fingers inside of me and skillfully moves them just the way I like. When I'm moist and ready enough, she pulls her fingers out of me.

"That ought to do." Zion says.

"Thank you," I stare into her eyes and give her the warmest smile I can muster.

"Anytime."

The stranger enters almost the second Zion disappears. He says nothing to me, and I immediately take that as a cue. He takes the remote and lowers me until my face is level with his very erect and very long cock. I never really see his face, but I guess it doesn't really matter. They're all strangers to me.

He keeps his clothes on. The only thing exposed is his erection. He holds it in his hand and takes me by the chin so that my mouth is touching the tip. I open wide and he sinks himself inside. He tastes flavored, like coconut. I'm getting better at using my imagination, and I feast upon his cock like it's a tasty coconut lollipop that I can't get enough of.

He thrusts his hips forward and rolls them. I hope I can hurry him along before the tingling between my own legs starts to fade. I suck his erection with all my might, willing him to succumb to my efforts. I think about what I ate for dinner last night and what snack I might try as I suck—anything to take my mind off of the here and now. He finally comes in a rash of trembling and quakes but doesn't make a sound, not even a moan. His hips thrust forward and I feel the warm, salty fluid flood my mouth. I'm mortified for a second, but with my hands restrained my only choice is to swallow the liquid. Don't throw up. Tears prickle my eyes and I want to die as the warm goo slides down my throat. He pulls himself out of my mouth. His dick is still rock-hard. The stranger walks out of my sight and I'm being lowered. I feel him take position behind me. Finally.

He doesn't say a word when he plunges his entire length inside me. His erection is full, even after coming in my mouth only moments ago. He fucks me first with desperation, his massive organ never quite leaving my depth before he slams back inside of me. I know he's coming again when he thrusts his entire erection inside of me one final time and stays there, quivering and pressing against me as if he can't get deep enough. In complete and utterly creepy silence.

After a time passes, he pulls out of me. To my great horror, he starts swinging me. Forward and backward. Each time I return, I'm impaled onto his erection. He never misses. It's like a game to him. I swing back and he's inside of me. I swing away and he's gone. I don't know how long this goes on, but if he wasn't so silent and creepy this could be pleasurable.

When I come to a halt it's only so that he can hop onto the swing with me and fuck the shit out of me while we swing together. He is relentless with his pounding. His cock is a beast inside of me. I want to come so bad, but sex with this stranger is too weird and erratic for me to get into the right rhythm. I'm also exhausted.

I lie still and endure the incessant pounding of my sex until he shudders and stiffens behind me.

14

SELF-PLEASURE

$\mathcal{H}$e is gone as silently as he came. Early, by my assessment. Well, that was just weird. If I never see him again, it will be too soon. Zion comes in and unstraps, unharnesses, and lowers me onto the bed. I climb out of the contraption and bend and stretch my abused body. With the right person, that swing could really be fun.

"Since the creepy man left so early, do you think I could have some alone time with Dominic?" I ask Zion.

"Who the hell is Dominic?" she asks me.

"My magic pony." I smile and walk over to the pony.

"No problem. You two lovebirds take all the time you need." She snickers and walks out.

"Hey!" I call after her. She pops her head back in around the curtain. "Do you know where the cameras are that the guards watch us from?"

"Why?" Her head tilts in question.

I shrug, feigning casualness. "Just curious."

She thinks nothing of it and shows me the cameras. Two on the bedposts, one on the horse, one in the bathroom, and one by each entrance. Nowhere to hide.

I lean over Dominic, depress the button, and watch with fascination as the warmed liquid spills out of the opening and oozes down the shaft. I look in the direction of the camera and wink. I have never done anything remotely this bold, but I'm inspired to do something spontaneous and unforced as Vivian. Flame has been dismissed for the moment.

In the sexiest eye smolder I can conjure, I mouth, "I want you." I slide down onto the large rubber dick. The camera moves down and I know he is watching me work it. I grind onto the dick with all the torque I can put into my hips. I bounce on and off the entire length. I push forward and backward. It feels even better knowing that he is watching me.

The camera lens makes a buzzing sound and turns up. I'm looking directly into the lens now. It makes another buzzing noise and I can tell he is zooming in on my face. This knowledge is making me insane with emotions and sensations. I drag my tongue along my lips and I stare deep into his eyes. Even though I can't see them I know they are there—I can feel them on me. I bite my lips and knead my tits. My mouth falls open and I explode in the fucking best orgasm I have ever had. I hang onto the pole, completely spent and breathless, staring into the camera.

THE COOLING WATER WAKES ME. It takes me a moment to realize where I am. My eyes scan the bathroom, and I begin to clamber out of the tub after a couple of heavy sighs. I'm guessing Zion headed to bed after putting me in the bath. I wrap myself into a towel and start the process of removing the remnants of the evening from my face. False eyelashes—gone. Heavy eye makeup—a memory. Cleaning the foundation from my skin is a difficult task, but I finally scrub it off and I'm left with my own clean face.

"Much better," I say. A white piece of paper on the vanity catches my eye. My stomach drops for a second, but I soon learn that it is from Zion.

You did well tonight. Keep your head up. See you tomorrow, and get some rest.

Zion

This letter I don't feel the need to shred. I wrap myself in my giant crimson bath towel and head down the winding stairs to my Sleeping Chamber. I barely make it to my bed, thankful that Mason had the common sense to locate our rooms so close to our Chambers.

Strangers Four and Five went by in a flash. One wanted vanilla sex—which I learned is normal sex, without all of the theatrics—and the other stranger put me into three different contraptions, much like the ones from the introduction night. So I spent my time with him with my ass way in the air, and then, even further in the air.

If falling asleep in The Chamber bathroom counted, I definitely would have gotten a visit from Tyson, because I passed out in the healing waters of my heated floral bath. My brain enjoyed the silence, and I was too exhausted to dwell on my very special circumstances or to go over the evening's events. My vacant mind was a blessing.

I open my bedside dresser and place Zion's letter neatly inside, wishing I could save Tyson's in the same manner. I know that is not the best idea. When I pull the covers back, the familiar lavender paper peeks out. My heart stutters and then finds its rhythm. I can barely contain myself. I run to the bathroom stall in an overly excited, childlike manner and plop onto a toilet seat. I rip open the envelope and greedily snatch the letter from its envelope.

My Vivian,

His Vivian. That's becoming truer and truer in my heart as each day passes. I'm such a dork that I can't seem to get past the greeting.

My Vivian,

I nearly scooped you up and carried you away from here when I came into your Chamber tonight. The thought of you being in any pain is unbearable to me. Even though I haven't known you very long, that is not how it feels to me. I risk so much getting these letters to you, but I want you to go to sleep with thoughts of me. I want you to know what is going on in my head. You really enjoyed the pony tonight. That was so fucking sexy. I have never wanted to be a horse more in my life. When you climbed onto it the second time, just for me...I nearly combusted! I have never had an orgasm watching before. I will thank you properly very soon.

I have a final request. I want you to pleasure yourself tonight before you fall asleep, please, and if possible, see me behind your closed eyes. Envision me holding you, kissing you, adoring you, and making love to you. Most of all, envision me falling in love with you, because, Vivian, that is exactly what is happening. I will be doing the same...

Yours,
Dominic

P.S. I love your pony's name...and please destroy.

I wipe the tears that begin to push their way out of my eyes. Against my desires, I destroy the letter. I do it before I can change my mind. All I really want is to curl up with it and keep it forever.

Can this really be happening in a place like this, in a situation like mine? Dominic is falling in love with me? I hope it is true. The tears keep falling. I realize that all of the signs are there. When I first arrived, Tyson was my lifeline—a big, gorgeous stranger who I let protect me out of desperation. The only emotion that I felt was fear and relief that I'd found someone who could fulfill that role—especially in a place like this.

Now, that has changed. I have changed. I am looking forward to the letters like they come from a lover, and sex with him has become more like lovemaking. I need him, I crave him, I want him. Am I falling in love with Dominic? How can that be, when I love Liam?

Surely, Liam won't give up on me. What happens when I get out of here? That is the thought in the back of my mind, the same thought I share with Whitney...Sunshine. Will they even want us after we are all used up?

What about Liam? I push the thought of him back. I won't survive a year with the things I want but cannot have clouding my mind. I will have to work on faith that when I return back to my normal life, Liam will love me no matter what I have endured, and I pray that I will be able to leave this place behind me. The bizarre thing is, before it was thinking about Liam that kept me grounded. Hmm.

I blush deep red at the idea of pleasuring myself for Tyson again. I know now that there is not much that I wouldn't do for him. I go back to into my bed. My crimson bath towel hits the floor, leaving me completely nude. I have never slept naked before. Neither Sky nor Sapphire have made it back from their Chambers, which makes sense. Creepy Stranger pulled a hit and run on me that I was most grateful for, shaving a little more than an hour off of my Chamber time.

Once the covers are up to my shoulders, I bend my knees. A nervous giggle escapes me. I don't know why this is so embarrassing. I wet my fingers with my mouth and find my little pleasure nugget. Images of Tyson flood my mind. I can see his Thunderdick that I have come to adore. Electricity flows throughout my body and deposits itself between my legs. I begin massaging it in earnest. Now Tyson is stroking the shaft of his massive erection and I take him into my mouth. I moan at the image and slip two of my fingers inside of myself. I feel very hot inside, and silky. I move my hips in a slow motion. The next image is of Tyson plunging himself inside of me. My hips lift automatically at the vision, welcoming him. I come apart. My clitoris goes rigid under my fingers. My sex squeezes around my fingers. I whisper his name aloud.

"Dominic."

15

LIAM, GUILTY CONSCIENCE

I roll over and see Maddie's naked body wrapped in my sheets. Okay, it's worse than I thought. I'm overcome with nausea. What the fuck did we do? Now I have to add guilt to my pain.

Good fucking job, Liam. How will I face her when she comes back? Was it worth it, to be pain-free for a night? Last night I thought it was. Last night, I was free. The bottom line is, this can never happen again.

"Hey, Maddie, wake up." I nudge her. Time to face the music.

"What the hell? I'm sleeping here." She turns over to look at me. Her expression goes from realization to shock. She jumps up, keeping the sheet around her naked body. "Liam? What did we do? I thought I dreamt last night." One hand goes up to her mouth. Her eyes show everything. Fear. Shame.

Welcome to the party.

"I know, Maddie. I feel like a complete jackass, too..."

She sits on the edge of my bed and bends forward, burying her face into her hands. "What are we gonna do, Liam? This is the most fucked up thing I've ever done. She's missing, and God only knows if she is dead or alive, or worse, being tortured, and I fuck her boyfriend."

I put my arm around her shoulder and she jumps like my touch burns her.

"Don't, Liam. Just don't." She stares heatedly at me and hops off of my bed. She races around the room picking up her scattered clothes from my floor, and goes out into my hall. I flinch when my front door slams shut. Just like that, Maddie is gone. Fuck, I hope I didn't lose her, too.

What if she never speaks to me again? How do I fix this?

Last night we were two people in severe pain, comforting each other in the most basic way. It was comforting. I didn't forget about Vivian, but for a short time, I forgot about the pain of her being gone. I'll have to give Maddie some time to digest her own feelings, find a way to make it right in her heart and mind. No matter what, this has to get resolved. For starters, we're best friends. This can't come between us, because no matter what, we still need each other.

One day, when my girl comes home, we're gonna have to tell her what we did...what our pain drove us to. I know that Maddie and I will both agree that we shouldn't tell her right away. She'll need time to adjust to being home. That's if she even comes back. Fuck! I really fucked up. Do I even deserve her? I miss her so much. Vivian is the single best thing to ever happen to me. She makes me want to wake up every morning and start my day. When I go to bed each night, it's her face that I see. That thought makes me want to fall asleep so I can start a new day with her.

This can't be the end of my time with her. There has to be more. I need to keep believing that whatever she's doing, wherever she is, she's strong enough to fight her way back to me. When she comes back, I hope she can forgive us for the worst transgression any best friends could ever be capable of.

16

FUN AND GAMES

I wake in the morning to the smell of bacon. It's unexpectedly normal in this strange, new world.

Bacon.

I think back to sleeping in late on the weekends and Mom using our favorite food to rouse us from our deep slumber. My brother and I raced down the hall toward the kitchen and stopped to take in the spread: bacon, biscuits, fresh-squeezed orange juice, toast, and eggs. Smelling it here makes my heart ache and my stomach burn.

I wasn't ready for normal here, but I really love bacon.

I jump out of bed, forgetting for the moment that I went to sleep in my birthday suit.

"Nice," Sapphire calls out from her bed. I glance over at her and she's grinning in my direction, her eyebrows are raised. "Somebody's acclimating to her environment." Her eyes drag up and down my body.

I scramble to cover up with the crimson towel I deposited on the floor. By now, my skin must match.

"Sorry, I forgot where I was."

She pops out of bed, completely naked, but does not attempt to cover up. She has a body to be proud of. She's perfectly curvy with full breasts, a small waist, and an ample behind. She could be a swimsuit model, for sure.

"That shit can be hazardous to your health around here," she calls back as she struts to the bathroom.

"Bacon! I smelled the bacon!" I yell after her.

Never mind. She doesn't care why I was naked. I grab a short dress from my dresser next to my bed and slide it over my head. Of course, it's red. I pull on a pair of fresh panties and set out in search of bacon.

When I make it to the kitchen, I find Ivy, Sunshine, and Violet working.

"What smells so good? I mean, besides the bacon." I'm practically licking my lips.

"Morning, Flame," Violet says. The other girls smile in my direction.

"Morning, ladies." I start helping by grabbing a bowl from under the sink to crack eggs.

"We decided we should eat healthy breakfasts together as often as possible. We can take turns," Sunshine says.

Hope blossoms inside of my chest and warms my center. The possibility of a real sisterhood in the midst of all of this crazy is something I didn't even know I needed.

"I'm down for that," I smile and start beating the eggs.

"Hey, anybody else wanna search for the nearest exit and risk breaking out of this bitch?" Sunshine asks.

Three heads whip around in sync to stare at her. By the expressions on their faces, I have no doubt they are thinking the same thing as me. Is she serious? If she is, could we succeed, and what would the cost be if we did? We all raise our hands.

"Fuck a year," I say. "I don't think I can make it another night. I don't know if we could pull it off, but I'm not against it. We might not have a choice." We just got here. Who knows how dark this place is going to get for us?"

The girls all nonverbally agree with me. Ivy nods, Sunshine sighs and shrugs, and Violet gives me a noncommittal head bob.

We start placing platters of breakfast fare on the dining table. By the time we're finished cooking, we have eggs, bacon, sausage, biscuits, sourdough toast and orange juice on the table. The other sleepyheads drag their broken bodies into the kitchen.

Bacon gets you every time.

We say grace before we eat. Ivy leads this morning with a beautiful prayer and plea that this year goes by with the speed of sound, that each of us grows in strength, and that we keep our sanity.

I notice that she doesn't pray for our release, and I guess I can understand that. While we're all silently hoping and praying for that, what we need even more is strength. Each day, we die a little on the inside. We want to actually make it to the end. We need to find the strength to escape our mental and physical cages.

Like zoo animals we get a little patch of land to graze upon on the floors we're allowed access to. We get to swim, eat, and hang out with the other animals in our habitat. If we're good at pretending, we can even make ourselves believe that we're free. We're not delusional, though... We are not free. We are in captivity.

The Chamber is our zoo.

When people come to see us in captivity, they don't have to worry about appreciating us from afar. The visitors who come to this zoo aren't merely spectators. This is a petting zoo. Visitors here are welcome to enter our pens and touch, feel, and admire us up close.

Still, this is nice. I gaze around the table at the six beautiful, different women. We are all strong in our own right. If not, we wouldn't be here. We all had lives before we were brought here.

None of us speak about what happened to us last night. I don't know why they're keeping quiet, but I feel like saying it aloud makes it true. Even though part of me wants to warn them about the creepy stranger, I'm not ready to admit that I'm really here and this is really happening.

Instead, we talk about ourselves. I soak up what I can about my new sisters.

For example, now I understand why Sapphire sounds like she's from New Jersey, even though Mason calls her a Brazilian beauty. She tells us how she and her family moved from Brazil to New Jersey when she was only six. I learn that Ivy is a model back home in Ireland. Violet, like me, is a college student. Raven was once Miss Teen Hawaii. Sky is a model from Holland who lives in New York. Sunshine is one of those really smart people who finished college before most people finish high school. She was actually beginning a PhD. program in the fall, and she's barely twenty.

Now we can all add Chambermaid to our resumes.

I tell them about living in Vegas, and how we don't all live in hotels on the strip. That there are actual suburbs, schools, community centers and churches. It gets just as cold as it does hot, and people have real jobs. I probably eat five pieces of bacon before breakfast is over. The girls who didn't cook volunteer to clean up. This is how a wonderful bonding ritual starts. Half of us cook, we bond over daily breakfast, and the other half clean. We share these mundane tasks in a bizarre place.

We'll slowly make this zoo into our home.

~

AS THE WEEKS GO BY, I find myself falling into a routine.

Breakfast with my sisters, time in the gym, then grooming. While I'll never get used to what happens to me five days a week when the sun goes down, I continually remind myself that I am surviving this.

I don't get to see Tyson very much at all, and I really miss him. That scares the crap out of me.

He has found a place in my heart. Small as it is, it's there.

I never stop looking for letters from him. When I see him in passing, a palpable spark travels between us. A butterfly war almost always starts inside of me, and he knows it. I flush pink and he gives me a lopsided smile that stops my heart.

He's the type of guy who makes innocent girls actually believe he's in love with them, just to get in their pants, then drops them the next day. I can tell he cares. He never says much to me when he greets me in a professional tone that I mimic. It's more about what he doesn't say. He gives me a buttery smile, and his eyes burn through me intensely, caressing me.

Our secret.

He tells me without uttering a single word that I mean something to him. The way my body, mind, and heart react freaks me out.

We both have a much harder time a couple of months into my stay, when Mason invites us all to a mandatory social indoor barbecue.

THE DAY OF THE BARBECUE, I dress in my swimsuit, grab a towel, then set out for the designated barbecue area. The event will be in part of the castle that we've never seen. I find the party in an indoor "backyard" paradise. There's a huge lagoon pool, complete with a built-in slide, and a hidden jacuzzi, set deep into a cave-like structure. It could be a perfect hiding place for newly budding relationships, if that were allowed here.

There's a gourmet kitchen and a massive grill. The skylights are retracted and open, allowing heavenly sun to pour in and beat down upon us. It's June, and the heat is delicious on my skin.

Every type of food imaginable is laid out. A man tends bar at one end of the buffet, and a line of swim-trunk-clad guards is already forming.

An onlooker would think this is a normal pool party at a mega-millionaire's palace. Everyone is wearing clothes. Image that. The guys are in board shorts, and of course we all have our signature-colored bikinis.

All are in attendance: our groomers, Roxy from the spa, all of the guards, and Ivory. I decide to enjoy the moment in the sun, allowing myself to forget where I am, and focus on the people here that I like —my new sisters, and Tyson.

Suddenly, the music quiets, and we all turn to see Mason in front of the pool.

"Welcome," he says. "I hope you're all hungry and ready for some fun in the sun." He looks up to the skylight.

"We decided to throw this little soirée so that you all can spend some time together in a social, nonsexual setting. The guards need to get to know who they are protecting, and you ladies need to know who is protecting you. I find that when you care for one another, trust follows. Now, don't get too into each other. That is forbidden." His eyes meet mine and linger there before moving on.

"However, you ladies will feel much safer when you know who's downstairs waiting to come to your rescue should you need it." He pauses so what he's said has a chance to sink in.

"Enough with the lecture. Eat up, drink up, have fun!" He drops the mic.

This could be either good or bad. How do Tyson and I interact and make it look innocent or casual?

"What's up, sexy?" I hear his voice behind me and I bite my lip to fight the smile.

When I turn to see him, he looks equal parts casual and seductive. I would never be able to ignore him, even if I'd met him somewhere else. Something about him speaks to me. I take the glass he offers me tentatively, worried about who's watching us. Around here, I'm sure someone is always watching.

"Are you sure?" I glance around.

"You heard the man. We're supposed to get to know each other." He gazes down at me, and the intensity makes my bones feel soft and squishy. He and I take a seat on the pool edge. We sit close, but do not touch, but I still feel him against me. My body aches with want.

What the hell is he doing to me? I could spend a lifetime under that gaze.

"Besides, if we avoid each other that'll make it worse."

True.

I stare down at my legs in the cool refreshing water and focus on slowly kicking them back and forth. If I stare at him as much as I want to, I have no doubt Mason will switch him with another guard, and then I would be truly fucked.

With so much to look at, I gaze around, pretending to watch the other partygoers, anything to decrease this intense urge I have to hold his hand...or to jump into his arms and crush my lips to his .

Any contact could send me over the edge.

The energy between us sizzles, It's wonderful, but makes it hard for me to breathe. It's crazy, beautiful and scary as hell.

As if he can read my mind, he scoots closer to me, so that our arms are touching. Mmm. My eyes close instinctively. There are no sounds, no people, only his skin on mine searing and molding us. For me, it is everything. I take a gulp of air, but my eyes remain closed. Heat and vibrations start in the center of my chest and move toward my fingertips and toes. If I spoke, my words would come out shaky.

"I feel it," he says at a volume that I hope only I can hear.

I open my eyes and everyone reappears. The sounds of the party compete with the thrumming of my heartbeat in my ears.

Not looking at him, I take a long draw of my beer, act dumb and say, "What?"

Sitting here so naturally with Tyson, even my beer tastes good, and I don't even like beer that much.

"The buzz of energy between us. The tingly feeling in the pit of my stomach, like I'm going down a steep drop on a roller coaster." He inclines his hand and moves it up, before cresting over the imaginary edge. My stomach goes along for the ride.

"I've never felt like this before. It's...it's..." He pauses.

"Indescribable, mystifying, overwhelming." I breathe out all of the things I've been feeling.

His pinky finger moves on top of mine, and I stare down at our hands.

He doesn't have to say a word at first, he answers with his eyes—they say it all. Then he says, "All of that."

So he feels it, too.

What are we doing? Is this just a strong infatuation? Or, is he a temporary solution to my current situation—a lifeline that I grabbed hold of to survive? Worse, what if Mason doesn't approve and takes him away from me? Will I drown? Yes.

"You don't know how much I want to kiss you right now," Tyson whispers, looking down at me. His eyes rest on my lips, before finding my eyes again. His filled with desire and hope, mine answer back in kind, as shivers run down my spine and I part my lips on a sharp inhale before I break contact.

I look back down and kick my feet in a slow rhythm, enjoying the resistance.

"Believe me, I do," I say, but I don't look at him. I can't. Instead I stare everywhere else.

Suddenly, we both go into the pool with a splash. I squeal in surprise, and turn to find the culprits—Sapphire and her guard.

Good thing I can swim, because the water is deeper than I expected.

Tyson turns and bathes them in retaliatory waves of water, and we burst into fits of laughter. It's what we needed. Our trance is broken.

"Fuck, you look even better wet," Tyson says.

"Whatever!" I splash him. Big mistake. Tyson takes this opportunity to pick me up and toss me into the air, and I crash into the water. When I come to the surface, sputtering and gasping for air, his eyes are full of mirth. I jump onto his back and try to no avail to sink him.

Not a good idea. The close proximity is killing me. In a brave move, while I'm on his back, I whisper into his ear, "I want you."

Tyson flips me suddenly, and I go under again. As I come to the surface, I feel his lips kiss an exposed spot on my bottom. Oh. I sigh.

This is bad. Anyone watching has to know that there is something already between us. I make a fast decision, swim to the edge, and start pulling people into the pool. Zion, Roxy, Mason.

What I start is the mother of all water fights. One of the guards tosses in a bunch of water guns—the huge, super-soaker kind—and that's it. It's a full-blown battle royale, with every man and woman for themselves.

I must swallow a gallon of water from screaming and being splashed and dunked. Even in the madness, I never lose sight of Tyson. When my eyes find his, he's always watching me.

Damn, I want him.

By the time the fight dies down, I'm famished. Before I can get a towel around my body, Tyson is standing before me with two plates heavy with food.

"Thanks," I say.

We find a table off to the side, away from the water in case another fight breaks loose.

"I'm starving," I say and drive my fork into a heap of macaroni and cheese.

"I figured as much," he says, watching me.

"Aren't you going to eat?" I ask around a mouthful.

He blushes, caught. "Sure. I guess I can't help it," he says, taking a bite of his steak. I massacre the macaroni and move on to the next item, grilled salmon.

So good.

"I never get to see you like this." He looks around. "We could be anywhere right now. I can imagine that you're mine and we're at a buddy's barbecue. Not here. That's how I want it to be. I'm taking little snapshots," he admits.

I blush into my hand, stunned that he just said these things to me. I'm sure my skin is tinted an embarrassed shade of pink, but inside I'm thrilled by his admission. "That sounds...wonderful." My heart aches with how much I wish his words were true.

He starts eating his food, never letting his eyes leave mine.

If I was his.

Could I spend a lifetime under that gaze? When he looks at me he makes me feel like I alone am the reason for his existence, as if I'm the only person in the room, on this earth, in the universe. That's what his hazel-eyed gaze does to me.

When I leave this place, I know that I'll never forget him. Ever.

"So..." I move food around my plate with my fork. "Do you expect that I'm going to be too sleepy to descend The Chamber stairs anytime soon?" I ask, hopeful. I make sure no one is in earshot of us.

"Very soon."

As night falls, I realize that with the exception of the water fight, a couple of potty breaks, and a brief conversation I had with Mason and Zion, Tyson and I are together. We're tethered together by whatever it is that connects us. I never want to leave his side, even for the brief times that I have to. Even when I was caught up in a conversation with someone else, my eyes sought him out, and he was always watching me.

Maybe he's right. Maybe I am his. If only for now.

17

BACK TO WORK

The pool party was a perfect idea, and Mason is kind of an evil genius.

He manages to create a social environment under the worst possible conditions, so much that I feel guilty for surviving here. We're safe, just like he said we'd be. No one has harmed us. We do have our brains fucked out five days per week, but somehow, even that isn't as bad as it could be.

Because everything else is...nice.

The pampering, the food, the clean and safe housing, the friendships, and even the parties. I guess they try to make it as bearable as possible. Mason gives us many opportunities to forget why we're here. We're not locked up in some dank, dark concrete cell. We aren't shackled and fed rations of rice and bread. We aren't beaten, either. I'm not saying I like it, but Mason has found a way to make it...habitable.

Yesterday, I actually had fun. The best part was spending time with Tyson in the open getting to know him. He's such a serious person, but I can tell he has a funny side, and I can't wait to peel back the next layer to find more.

It was like any other day with a group of twenty-somethings hanging out. It reminded me of tailgating at UNLV football games.

It made me miss school. My friends and I didn't just attend classes, we made ourselves a big part of campus life. Will my life ever return to normal? Will I care about getting my degree in interior architectural design? How can I? Will I ever get the chance?

Tonight it is back to business in The Chamber.

After I clean up the breakfast dishes, I rush back to my room to do what is now my routine envelope check—every day after breakfast and again after dinner. When I see the lavender envelope poking out, I nearly jump right out of my skin. I snatch it and run to my spot in the bathroom stall.

My Vivian,

Yesterday was like a dream. I don't know if you noticed that no matter where you were, my eyes were on you. I can't get enough of you. I want you to fall asleep in your Chamber tonight. I crave more time with you. I'll be watching closely tonight. If you need me, I'll be right downstairs.

Please remember that.

Yours,
Dom

His words and knowing that I get to spend time with him two days in a row fuels me.

"Somebody woke up on the happy side of the bed," Zion says as she gets me ready.

I smile at her. "I slept like a baby."

When Zion hands me my lineup for the night, I cringe at one name that stands out. I would know him by his list of expectations: do not speak, do not make eye contact. Mr. Creepy.

I've been through the entire lottery. Most of the guys aren't too deviant in their desires. Only a few stand out to me. A handful of them, including this one, show up periodically, not every week. I was hoping he got bored and crawled back underneath whatever rock he came out from. I guess I was wrong.

Do not speak, do not make eye contact. Fuck.

Tonight is my lucky night.

"I know, he's a creep. Tyson won't let him hurt you," she promises. "At least he's first."

I turn and scowl at her. "He is fucking creepy in any place in the lineup," I say.

Dominic, Dominic, Dom. I repeat his name like a mantra as I descend The Chamber stairs.

Mr. Creepy is already on my bed when I walk into my Chamber, flat on his back and naked with his erection pointing into the air. Zion follows close behind me.

Why? She never comes into the room if one of them is inside.

I learn all too soon when she covers my eyes with a satin scarf and guides me toward him. I climb onto the mattress with blind faith and my hands are pulled above my head and secured into cuffs above me. How the fuck am I supposed to see what I'm doing?

"He wants you to ride him," she whispers into my ear.

Why can't he tell me what he wants? Zion helps me find the location of his erection. I sink down onto him, using only my legs for balance. His erection is long and hard, and I can feel it throbbing inside of me.

The room is quiet, no music. The worst.

I tune into my racing heart and match its rhythm with my thrusts—quickening them until my body takes over and I forget where I am, who I am with, and I'm able to ignore the eerie mattress bouncing sounds in the room. I use the muscles deep inside of me to squeeze myself around his cock, thereby increasing my pleasure.

A moan crawls up my throat, but I stifle it. Do not speak.

I breathe heavy and loud as I grind myself onto his long cock. I rise off of his cock, using my legs to push up, and slam myself back down. The pleasure builds, but I will not come for Mr. Creepy. I attempt my very first fake orgasm.

I shake and shudder, and breathe erratically.

He must buy it because he comes right after me. I'm hoping he does me a solid and vanishes.

He doesn't.

Instead he pushes me to my feet on the bed with my hands still tied above my head. He pushes my legs apart with his hands. His mouth attaches to my nipple, and he begins to suck each one hard.

He is so rough that I hiss at the contact. He drives his fingers inside of my sex, and begins thrusting them in and out while he tries to remove my nipples with his mouth. Just when I cannot take the agony another second, just before I'm about to scream for Tyson, he stops the brutal sucking. His fingers leave my sex, and before I can prepare for it, he slams his cock inside of me. Standing.

His face is so close to mine. I can't see him, but I can feel his hot breath against my skin, meaning his mouth is so close to mine.

Please don't kiss me. I will vomit all over you if you do.

He breathes hot, heavy, and pounds his cock inside of my sex with almost angry desperation. Over and over. His hands squeeze my body too hard.

I can't breathe. I can't think. I can't disappear. I am here.

My body aches...raw.

I am thankful that I'm blindfolded. My tears soak the cloth through.

I hate Mr. Creepy. I fucking hate him.

I don't know how long I stand with my arms over my head while Mr. Creepy reminds me of where I am. With every thrust he brings me back to reality. His eerie silence as he does whatever he wants to me makes me feel that I am a sex slave, nothing more than a captive plaything, a prisoner of The Chamber.

He punishes my tender walls with the violence of his pounding while I silently cry. Mr. Creepy reaches multiple climaxes inside of me, while I endure them all in silence.

When he leaves as silently as he came, I break down. Heavy, desperate sobs escape me.

My hands are released from their bindings. The blindfold is pulled from my face. When I see that it's Tyson who frees me, I let go. He takes me into his arms, and I fold into him, trying to bury myself inside of his embrace. My body is shaking beyond my control.

"I can't do this anymore."

He peppers my cheeks and forehead with feathery kisses, like a parent would when soothing an ailing child. He takes me into the bathroom. The sobs that break free don't sound like any sound that I've ever produced in my lifetime.

He doesn't say a word. He is pissed, I can feel fury pouring out of him.

"What happened?" Zion asks walking into the bathroom. Her voice laced with alarm.

"I'm gonna fucking kill that motherfucker! That's what's about to happen," he says, setting me down gently into a chair. He starts pacing immediately. "Look at her!" he shouts.

"Oh, my goodness!" she gasps.

I turn to the mirror and see what the fuss is about. The bruising is already sprinkling my fair skin. My breasts are covered with bright blue and red, that twists into brighter purple and every place he grabbed me is turning before my eyes. I gasp and cry harder.

"That's it! I told Mason to leave her the fuck alone!" Tyson shouts as he starts to leave.

"No!" I reach for him. "Don't leave me," I plead between sobs. "He didn't really hurt me." I lie, anything to keep him from leaving my side. I have no doubt the money that Mr. Creepy brings in is more important than keeping Tyson here, and I can't lose him.

I have already lost so much.

His eyes cut to slits and his shoulders rise and fall as he stares down at me.

"He scared me more than anything. He scares all of us." My voice is small, almost a whisper.

"He will never hurt you again." Tyson caresses my face and I lean into his cupped hand.

"Mason," Tyson speaks into a handheld device. "I need you in Flame's Chamber immediately." His voice clipped and sharp.

"On my way," Mason says through the speaker.

We only wait a few minutes before Mason comes through the bathroom archway. He stops in front of me. I look worse for wear. Tears streak my face, and I have bruises everywhere.

"What the hell happened here?" Mason breaks character. His eyes are wide and his jaw slack.

Zion begins covering me with salve.

"That fucking asshole Serge did this, boss!" Tyson spits. "I told you not to bring her here. This is your fault." This part he says low, but not so low that I don't hear him. That's the second time he's said something about me not coming here.

He grabs his head and paces. "I'm gonna fucking kill him!"

Mason turns to Tyson. He takes a healthy breath, then another.

"No, you're going to let me deal with the asshole. We are not going to kill him. We are going to give him our version of a stern warning. After, we'll have to decide whether he remains a part of our Chamber."

Tyson stops pacing and looks at Mason. "Understood."

Mason comes to stand in front of me again. "I am so sorry about this, Flame. If—and it is a big if—he remains with us, this will never happen again." He kisses me on the cheek. "You have a couple of hours before your next...guest. Are you up to it?"

"I will be," I say. I don't want to miss the opportunity to spend the night with Tyson.

My next guests are much kinder.

Mason claps his hands together. "Then it's settled. I'd better go have a chat with Mr. Serge."

"I'm coming with you," Tyson states.

My heart picks up. No. Tyson may kill him.

"I don't think that's a good idea, given your present state. You stay here with Flame, make sure she's okay," Mason orders.

Thank heavens.

He is gone without another word.

"Time for you to soak." Zion says after I'm gooped up with salve. Before I attempt to stand Tyson already has me in his arms. I wrap my arms around him and while my face is so close to his, I plant tiny kisses along his jaw and cheek. His warm smile makes me feel better, even though his anger is still palpable.

"I will leave you two to talk," Zion says.

The hot water stings my tender spots. I really try to hide my pain and discomfort. I grimace only when I think Tyson isn't looking.

"Why didn't you call out for me?" He gazes into my eyes, his laced with sadness.

I look down, my stomach twisting with guilt for the pain behind his eyes.

"I almost did. It took everything I had not to. I'm still new to sex and all of this kinky shit. I wasn't sure if this was supposed to happen." Tears explode from my eyes again, as sobs break through my chest.

"I'm sorry."

Tyson stands and begins disrobing. He strips down to his boxer briefs, and climbs into the tub with me. Thank goodness it's big enough for us both. Some of the water displaces and spills out onto the floor. He wraps me into his arms, my head resting on his chest. We spend an unknown amount of time like that in silence. His slow, steady breaths comfort me.

"Baby, you never have to be sorry about anything. You are the bravest, strongest person I know. Your strength gives me courage."

I snuggle closer into him and he increases his embrace, but not too tight. "Courage to do what?" I ask.

"Make a different choice." He sighs heavily. "Listen, Vivian."

At the sound of my name on his lips, my heart lights from within, warming the walls of my chest.

"Let me tell you this. If you're in pain, if you're scared, you call me. If some jackass is scaring the shit out of you or hurting you, I will remedy the situation. I will protect you."

I nod against him.

"Next time, call out to me. I'm just downstairs."

"Okay."

He kisses the top of my head. I don't know how long we're in the tub. But I fall asleep listening to his breathing. When I wake, he is there, his arms wrapped around me, protecting me.

"How do you feel?" he asks me.

"Like a sore prune," I say, moving my limbs around. "But, better. How long were we asleep?" I ask, gazing at his beautiful face that I'll never get enough of.

"You were asleep for about an hour." He smiles at me.

"You didn't sleep? What did you do for an hour?"

"Watched you," he says, his eyes never leaving mine. "And listened to you snore." His finger gently touches my nose.

"I do not snore." I punch him in the arm, but I smile. Why couldn't we be anywhere else? It makes me nauseous to experience any form of normal within these walls.

His arms go up into the air in surrender. "Whatever you say."

I don't know what comes over me. The fact that I'm naked in the bathtub with Tyson. Relief that I wasn't harmed more, or how incredibly wonderful it feels to be with him. My lips meet his without further thought. Tyson answers back with his own and they tangle passionately with mine.

"I don't know if I can go back out there," I say when our lips part.

"I don't know if I can let you...I want to take you away from here, Vivian."

I sit up in the tub in a slight panic. I know he means every word he says.

"You can't," I whisper. "I want to go...to leave this place, but I don't want to look over my shoulder for the rest of my life. I can survive this. As long as I have you," I confess. "I need you."

He pulls me back into his chiseled chest. "I'm not going anywhere. But you say the word and I won't hesitate to take you away."

I shoot up in the tub again in panic, a sudden thought popping into my head.

"This doesn't count as our time together, does it? I can still..." I lower my voice to a whisper. "I can still fall asleep?" Please say yes.

"Absolutely. I never get enough of you."

I shiver inside at the thought.

Zion walks in stating that it's time to get me prepared, interrupting our bath time.

"Right downstairs," Tyson says, and I nod in understanding.

He disappears from the room without another word, and I feel empty without him. If he wasn't here, there would be no surviving The Chamber. I have no idea how the other girls are able to do it without a guardian in their corner.

The other four guests are tame in comparison to Mr. Creepy. They actually show concern when they take in my bruised body. Two refrain from touching me at all, making for an even shorter night. I go at the task of pleasuring with the joy of knowing my evening will conclude in Tyson's arms.

18

FAKING SLEEP IN MY CHAMBER

*W*hen the last stranger leaves, I have to restrain myself so that I don't haul ass to my en suite bathroom and wash him away. Just in case there are cameras other than Tyson's— and I'd bet my life there are—I'd better make this appear to be any normal night. The smart thing would be for me to pass out, like this night in The Chamber just got the best of me, and I didn't have the strength to make it down the stairs.

I can't.

There is no way I can spend the night with Tyson with another man's sweat dried up on my body. I jump into the shower and wash up with the speed of a cheetah. Once I'm clean, dry, and very naked, I would normally head to my bedroom, tonight I stop short at my Chamber bed.

How do I fake this? I move slower, exaggerating exhaustion. I sit on my Chamber bed and stare out into space for a while. Then I collapse backward onto the bed. I lie still for a few minutes.

I feel like an idiot. Next time I'll just pass out, because the shower has made everything awkward. I'm acting now, and I'm a terrible actor. I roll over and move deeper into the bed. That is the best I can do. All I'm missing is the back of my hand to my forehead.

I hope my year in drama club paid off. I'm doubtful.

When the light filters into my Chamber, I tuck my face to hide my smile.

Twice in one night. How did I get so lucky?

I don't move. I don't react. I wait. If I were really asleep, I'd be scared shitless because he is stealthy. He has a part to play, too. The part of sex-starved guard, surprising the unsuspecting Chambermaid who mistakenly fell asleep in her Chamber. This is no mistake. I have waited for what seems like an eternity for this moment.

"Hello there, stranger," Tyson whispers into my ear. He plants a soft, tender kiss just under my lobe.

My heart flutters and joy fills me like sunshine. Hmm.

"Hi." I stretch, pretending to be awoken. I turn completely over to face him. "I missed you."

Tyson brings his lips to mine slowly, sensuously. His breath teases me, sending tiny tingles across my skin. I inhale his natural scent, mixed with the crisp sage and jasmine of his cologne, and I want to climb inside of him. His tongue slides into my open mouth, and I lose myself in his kiss, pulling him as close to me as I can. This is the first night I have fallen asleep in my Chamber and I plan to make it memorable—plenty of mental screenshots of us enraptured to recall later when I need them.

He is responding favorably to my advances, his breathing is quicker, his movements more frantic, but he doesn't allow me to pull him on top of me like I want. Instead he stays put, his fingers playing in my hair, leaning over me, enticing me with each kiss.

"I know what you are trying to do," he says. "We aren't making love tonight."

"What? Why?" I attempt pouting.

He pulls his face back. His eyes peer into mine. I blink at the intense blaze behind his eyes.

"You have been through enough tonight."

My stomach drops and I don't even try to hide my disappointment.

"Hey." He pulls my chin up when I look down. "I want you that way, always, but that's not the only way I want you...even if that means spending the night with you in my arms."

Well, damn. A girl can't argue with that.

"Are you okay?" He rolls me to my side and spoons me.

I shrug. "What happened to Mr. Creepy?"

"Not enough, if you ask me. Mason had the guards rough him up. He got the rich asshole version of a slap on the wrist. Next time, he's out."

"Oh." Shit. I was hoping that he would just get kicked out now.

"Are you sure you're okay?"

No. I'm scared to death of him. "I'm fine."

"He won't hurt you again. I won't let him," he promises me.

I nod.

Tonight is the first time since my arrival that I have felt real fear. Mr. Creepy brought me back to that first night with my head hooded and my arms restrained. I should have screamed out. I should have yelled for Tyson. Now, Mr. Creepy will definitely make another appearance in my Chamber, and the thought chills me to the bone. I just want to forget all about tonight. I want Tyson to bury himself deep inside of me, to help me not remember.

I feel dizzy when he nuzzles his face into the crook of my neck. His intoxicating scent overwhelms me.

"All I want to do is keep you safe. When I saw what that animal did to you I wanted tear him apart."

I wrap my arms around his arms that are holding me, and squeeze. He really does care for me. "That would be a bad idea. I can't have you getting yourself kicked out of this place. I wouldn't survive here without you. Without this." I scoot back even closer to him, as if there were any space left between us.

"Well, we can't have that, can we?" He nuzzles my cheek with his. "What's the first thing you're gonna do when you get out of here?" he asks me.

"Go home," I whisper. My heart instantly aches. I miss my family, my friends. I wonder what they're doing right now. Are they still searching for me?

"I'm sorry. I didn't want to make you sad. I know how much you must miss them."

He tugs a little more on me, pulling me so close that his end and my beginning are undetectable. How does he know how his question affects me? Is he that in tune with me, enough to sense the very subtle shift?

A single tear falls down my cheek and settles where his arm meets my skin. "It's okay. You can ask me anything."

"Do you miss him? Liam?" His voice is quiet, uneasy.

"I do."

"I know he's going crazy without you. If you were mine, the world would lose all of its color. There would be no sound, no taste, no light without you—only darkness. I'm so sorry I took you from the people you love."

If he only knew how much he is becoming one of them. "Thank you."

I fall asleep easily in his arms. I feel safe, free, at home there. When I awake in the morning, he's gone.

19

ADAPTATION

I never thought I would survive this long. The first couple of nights nearly killed me, but it's becoming less and less scary.

I can never escape my fear completely, but I'm becoming skilled at compartmentalizing to shorten its duration.

When Zion comes and gets me, my heartbeat speeds up. I break out in a cold sweat. By the time I make it up the stairs to my Chamber and past the cabinet of horror, I calm myself down. I know at some point my body and mind will get used to what is becoming a daily routine. It has to. The human body is designed to adapt to its environment. I'm glad that my body seems slower to conform to the demands of my life here, because this is unnatural.

Conversely, when I'm spending the day doing something normal like hanging out making breakfast with the girls, I treat it like the best most normal moment in my life.

If I ever need a reminder of just how unnatural this crap is, Mr. Creepy definitely reminds me.

It's been a week since I saw him and I'm not looking forward to meeting him again. When I spoke with a couple of my sisters about him they said that he has been on his best behavior, much less creepy.

I hope that sticks.

Still, I have to thank him for the reminder, because I never want my Chamber experience to be second nature to me—just a part of my life now. I never want to go about it like a regular nine-to-five job, just because I chose to stay to save my family. This is not my home and this is not my life. This is a temporary hell, and I hope I get a free pass to heaven when I do die, just for enduring this.

The only source of light and happiness is spending time with my sisters and Tyson.

The more time I'm with him, the more I realize just how special he is, and just how much he cares about me. He has shown me that he doesn't just lust for me, that I'm important to him. Our time together in my Chamber last week was tender and sweet. When I recall it, we aren't even in my Chamber. It was so innocent that I can fantasize that we were at my house, in my room, or anywhere else.

It scares me that my feelings for Tyson continue to grow. When I leave this place and leave him behind, what will I do with these feelings?

I'm heading to meet a couple of the girls in the gym. We have an early morning workout, followed by spa treatments, in preparation for tonight. It's the start of a new week. Get me some normal.

"Hey, Roxy," I say when I pass the reception desk. As always, she has a friendly greeting for me.

"Hey, Flame. The other girls just walked back. Have a good workout."

"Thanks."

I make my way to the workout room. Our trainer, Stephan, is already in the front of the room. There are five yoga mats on the floor. I hate yoga. I'm more of a sports enthusiast—tennis, basketball, boxing...anything other than yoga. I make my way down the line to the red mat. They're in Downward Facing Something by the time I step on my mat.

"Flame, nice of you to join us for some relaxation and cleansing," Stephan says.

Am I that late?

I fall onto my stomach and arch my back into the new position. I follow Stephan's instruction into every contortion and pose. I perform the deep breathing, and I even manage not to fart. That is the other thing I don't like about yoga—all that contorting and bending makes my stomach go crazy. When you are in a group with your rump pointed into the sky, farting is the last thing you want to do.

"THAT WAS SURPRISINGLY RELAXING," I say when I sink down into the jacuzzi with Ivy, Sunshine, Sky, and Raven.

"Everybody thinks yoga is for prissy girls," Raven declares. "It's tough. Put any football player in a yoga class and his real weaknesses will show."

"Back home, the football players take ballet," Sunshine adds. "It's supposed to give them more agility and flexibility. I wonder if your American soccer players do the same."

I lie back and let the heated water cover my body up to my chin. "I'm not saying it's not hard work. It's just too slow for me, I guess," I clarify. I don't wanna get jumped by any yoga girls.

"Sure. Flame saves her athletics for her Chamber," Raven jokes.

I sink under in feigned shock for a second. I know she's joking. Someone needs a sense of humor in this place. I splash her with hot water.

"That's not what I heard," I say. "I heard Ivy was working on making Chambermaid of the year!" I tease.

Ivy gasps in shock and splashes me. In the next moment, the five of us are in an all-out water fight, splashing each other and dunking each other's heads. We're laughing so hard that we are near tears, and it's just what I need.

"Stop. Stop. I can't breathe," I shout out, desperate to take a real breath.

Can you die from laughing?

We settle down and a quiet settles over us. We scoot as close to one another as we can, our heavy hearts lightened by our ever-growing bond.

BY THE TIME we make it back to our rooms, we've been plucked, tweezed, waxed, massaged, conditioned, and even fed. We have The Chamber tonight, so, in what is becoming a routine for us, it is time for our pre-Chamber naps. It's just what my gooey bones need. I nearly scream when I pull back the covers and find a lavender envelope.

I don't even remember running to the bathroom stall, but when I do, I tear it open in. Please say fall asleep in The Chamber, please say fall asleep in The Chamber. I pray silently, before I can read a single word.

My Dearest Vivian,

Tonight, please fall asleep in your Chamber. We really need to talk. I am finding it increasingly difficult to watch you each night with these men. The second one of them touches you, I want to rush upstairs and rip his arms from his body. Especially after your most recent encounter with Serge. You can see how this is becoming a problem for me. I guess this is what Mason means about not becoming attached to the Chambermaids. Too late now. I couldn't stay away from you for all the money in the world.

I can't wait to see you tonight.

XOXO,
Dom

P.S. As much as I loved watching the theatrics last week, don't bother with the shower. I plan on us getting very dirty tonight.

I nearly yelp with excitement. Thank you. Now I'm not going to be able to sleep. I thrill at the thought of getting dirty with him. Lately, it's thoughts of Dominic that keep me up at night. I'm starting to want him, any way that I can get him.

WHEN ZION WAKES ME, I hop out of bed, perhaps too eagerly. Zion's eyebrow raises in question. I ignore her. I'm gonna see Dominic tonight. Yes, finally. I approach tonight with a new zeal. There is no fear, there is only excitement. Five strangers. Bring 'em.

In the time I have been here, I have been visited by all thirty-five lottery winners, and I'm still standing. I didn't die like I thought I would. Tonight's fab five go by in a breeze. I spend some time on my pleasure pony. I'm tied to the bedpost and even gagged. It didn't matter. I approach tonight like it's the last day of school—no matter what goes on, your attention is on the end of the day, not the moment at hand. I'm assuming they enjoy themselves. I suck their cocks, I arch my back so they can slam their erections further inside of me. Tonight's guests even have multiple orgasms.

I do as I'm told, and I do not shower tonight after the last guest leaves. Tonight I pretend to drift off into sleep. My heart is racing and my breathing is wild.

My stomach drops when the bed depresses. I pant when he climbs in. He moves my hair from my neck, and I feel his lips upon me, depositing tender kisses from the bottom of my earlobe down to my shoulder. I moan at the feel of it.

"Vivian," he whispers in my ear.

I turn to him, overcome with the reality of just how much I missed him. I wrap my arms around him and mash my lips into his, my need for him evident in the abandon I display. My fingers grapple and fist his hair, pulling him closer to me. I moan around our entangled lips, my tongue weaving around his with want. "Dominic," I breathe his name.

When I can't take another second of the sensational agony throbbing between my legs, I roll on top of him, climbing to my place of honor. I stare down into his eyes. He tells me without words what I want to know. He is falling for me. In this place, he is mine, and I am his.

I sink down on his Thunderdick. My sex squeezes and throbs around him. Dominic's hands palm my ass and he pulls me down onto him deeper. It is a-fucking-mazing.

We don't move. Both of us are in a perfect spot. He holds me down onto his length and I can't think of a place I would want to be more. I stay still, pulsating around him. I could die right here and be at peace. We are in a deadlock, my steel gray eyes never leaving his.

In this moment, with his eyes adoring me, and his cock buried deep inside of me, I can be still no longer. My heart is swelling with a new feeling for him, one I can't describe or understand. I start a slow grind, around and around on his cock. There's not one spot in my sex that is not filled by him.

He swells more inside of me, and I know he is building toward an explosion. My eyes are trained on him, peering through my heavy lids—drunk on him. His breaths increase, his moans and pleasure sounds are killing me. Fuck.

I grind forward and backward on him, as he creeps deeper inside of me...his home. I shatter into a million pieces around him, my screams loud and desperate, and I lose control of my body as it clenches, jolts, and quakes. I throb and contract aggressively around him, sending him over the edge as he fills me with his essence. The whole time, our eyes locked.

When I come down from the orgasm I lose it, sobs break through, and tears rain down my cheeks. He wipes them tenderly with his thumbs. He brings my face toward his and kisses me.

"I love you," he says. His voice is so low, that if I wasn't looking at him, I might have missed it.

It's a declaration that makes the tears flow harder because I believe him. More than that, I'm beginning to feel the same way.

Somehow we manage to roll to our sides, with him behind me and still inside of me. He pulls me as close to him as physically possible. I can't speak. I can't think. His words blow me away, and I can't deny the way my heart is singing.

"I didn't tell you I loved you to hear those words back," he says. "I said them because I mean them, Vivian. I am in love with you. I want you to know how I feel, always."

I nudge my body closer to him. My sex tingles at the sensation of him shifting deeper inside of me.

"I missed you, too," I bring his arm up and kiss it. "I'm kind of an addict, looking for your letters every single day. I'm so happy when I see the lavender envelope. I don't know what to say. Something is happening between us."

"You are destroying them after you read them, right?" He sounds almost fatherly when he asks me.

"Yes, but I don't want to. I want to read them over and over until the paper falls apart."

"You understand that it would be too risky. If anyone knew. If it got back to Mason, he could remove me from the guard."

"No. I'd die." My heartbeat picks up at the thought and I squeeze him closer to me. If Dominic wasn't here, I would not survive.

"Yes. I want to take you away from here," he whispers into my ear.

My head turns in a snap. "You can't! I have to finish! I can't risk my family!" I whisper. "Besides, as long as you're with me, I know I'll be safe. Right?"

He sighs. "Right...you are so fucking strong." I can tell that he is not happy about my desire to stay. I probably seem like an insane person.

I shake my head. "No, I'm not. I have you, and you give me strength."

He pulls himself out of me. For a moment the emptiness is almost depressing. He rolls me over to face him. "That is not true." He takes my hands into his and kisses them. "Your strength is one of the things

I fell in love with, Vivian. I know it sounds crazy after a few months to say that I love you. You must think I'm nuts."

I don't understand. "Fell," past tense? He sees my expression and begins to explain.

"I've known you for two years," he reveals.

I stare at him with wide eyes. "That's impossible, Dominic. How? I would have remembered you." I think about all the people who have come in and out of my life. I don't remember running into anyone like him, ever. I study his face. His deep, olive skin, straight nose, pouty full lips, hazel eyes, perfectly sinewed body... I would definitely remember meeting him.

"Not in person. I've been Mason's head guard for the past four years, but I never get involved in the selection process or the surveillance. I'm not here for that, I was hired to keep this place safe, off the radar, and to supervise the guards and lottery winners. I have never slept with a Chambermaid or a staffer." He is quiet for a beat and the words he spoke sink in. I remember Zion telling me that I am the first woman he asked to guard.

I continue to listen as if what he is telling me is the secret to the universe.

"I was in the surveillance room checking on things when you came onto the screen. Your face appeared, and I couldn't move. My heart lit from within. You must wonder how someone like me finds his way into a place like this."

Yes. "The thought has crossed my mind."

"My world was so dark, Vivian, when I left Hawaii."

Oh, he's Hawaiian.

"I was in the dark, and heading down an even darker road," he continues. "Mason offered me a lifeline. He brought me into his family and gave me a purpose. My previous training was the perfect skill set for this protection detail. It was never about the girls for me. Some of the guys treat this place like a candy store. Not me. This is my job. I'm good at it, and I thought I would never leave Mason's side. Everything changed when your picture came up on that screen two years ago."

He turns me around so I am looking at him. His eyes are pinned to mine. "I stared at your image, your steel-gray eyes, your innocence and beauty, and something ignited within me. I became interested in all things Vivian Travis. I watched the surveillance video with Mason and his trackers. I watched them in my room in the middle of the night. Over those two years, I watched you, and I fell in love with you."

"Wow. I don't know what to say."

"That I'm a complete stalker psycho?"

"I was thinking more along the lines of that is the sweetest thing I have ever heard."

Dominic leans over and kisses me.

"I begged Mason not to pick you. This was the last place I wanted you to be, but he was fascinated with you. For days, I walked around brooding about it. When I realized you were coming, I made sure I was there when you were taken. If I couldn't keep you from coming, at least I could make sure you were treated well. I also told Mason to assign me as your guard. He didn't want to at first, but he said he had never seen me so full of life. He also cautioned me, though. I know I'm babbling on and on, but when a man you barely know professes his love for you, you deserve to know the depths of that love."

"Are you babbling? I hadn't noticed. I'm too captivated by this amazing love story."

He kisses me again. My heart swells.

"I'm just saying, from the first moment I saw you, I wanted things. I wanted to live life, not just exist. For the first time in years, I want to leave The Chamber. There is nothing I wouldn't do for you."

"I have a revelation of sorts, too," I say, in an attempt to lighten the conversation.

"Oh, do you?" he says in a teasing voice.

I nod. "I named your..." I gesture toward his private parts, suppressing an embarrassed giggle.

"And what might his name be?"

"Well, at first it was just Thunderdick. But now I call him Captain Thunderdick, and sometimes I refer to him as The Captain."

He smothers me with kisses, causing giggles to escape me. "Well, The Captain adores you."

"I'm pretty fond of him myself."

"We have to find a name for yours," he teases.

"I was toying with Petunia, but somehow it isn't sticking." I say.

"That will never do. It's not special enough. I'm sure if we put our heads together, we can come up with something more fitting."

We burst out laughing. When we stop, we lie together, enjoying the quiet.

I come up onto my elbow. "Dominic, why was your life so full of darkness?"

"I will tell you that story the next time you fall asleep in your Chamber," he promises.

"Promises, promises," I tease. "I can't wait to hear how your love story ends."

"Well, Vivian. I was kind of hoping we could write the rest of the story together."

In a swift movement, he pulls me close. Conversation over.

I spend the rest of the night with Dominic buried deep inside of me, showing me how much he loves me with every thrust, every adoring kiss, and every passionate caress as he loves me into sweet surrender.

20

GIRL TALK

*L*ast night was the best night of my life. I never thought something like that would come out of my mouth in a place like this. Dominic—I mean, Tyson—loves me. I have got to call him Tyson. Calling him by his real name could change the game for me, and I'm just getting used to playing. Without him, I will forfeit for sure.

He loves me so much, he even tried to prevent me from coming here. Then there was his revelation about the dark road. What kind of darkness could he find when I only see light behind his eyes?

I hope no one was watching us because what transpired was not a Chambermaid who fell asleep in her Chamber, only to be awoken by a horny guard. Last night we were lovers. We adored one another. I realized that I might not have gotten the head start on love that Tyson got, but if things continue to progress the way they are, I just might start gaining on him.

When I first latched on to him, it was out of fear. He presented himself to me like a lifeline in the pit of hell—in a lion's den—and no one would blame me for holding on. To say that is how I feel about him now would be lying. The truth of the matter is, I'm falling in love with him, too.

I really don't know why all of these emotions are at war inside of me. I love Liam, Liam loves me. I'm falling in love with Tyson. Tyson loves me.

This could be just the distraction that I need. A bunch of mental chatter might help me cope with the events unfolding in my life.

I head to the spa for my daily massage. When I arrive, Sapphire and Sky are getting massages from their groomers. I slide my broken and weary body onto the massage table while Zion prepares.

"Damn, girl," Sapphire says. "Tyson must have worked the shit out of you 'cause you were screaming like a banshee last night."

I snap my head to the right and glare at her, embarrassed. "You could hear me?"

"I think the whole castle could hear you," she teases.

"That's an uncomfortable thought," I reply.

"Don't be embarrassed," Sapphire says. "We've all seen his cock. It's massive. I'd be screaming, too."

Zion begins the task of rubbing my shoulders. I sigh at how heavenly the contact feels.

"Did you fall asleep on purpose?" Sky asks the magic question.

To my surprise, everyone seems to be eager for her answer. Their groomers stop massaging, and Sky and Sapphire perk up in wait.

"Of course not," I say. "Why would you ask me that, Sky?"

"I don't know. You guys are different. I mean, I see the way you react when he's around. The way he watches you. When we were at the pool party, you guys were in your own little world—like a real couple. We have a saying back home for the two of you. Ware liefde."

"What does that mean?" Sapphire asks.

I don't want to ask, because it sounds romantic and beautiful in her tongue and I just don't know how long I can maintain my poker face.

"It means 'true love,'" Sky says.

Crap. If she noticed, then others did as well. She's more accurate than she knows. "You're very observant, but the answer is no," I say, trying to cover. "I gawk at him because he's fucking hot, and he probably watches me because he's good at his job."

I can never admit what Sky seems to already know. I don't know about the "true love" part. I'm barely able to wrap my head around any feelings that I have for him at all because they are new and shocking to me. It's not like I can be in a relationship with him beyond this place, and the clock is ticking.

"Whatever, girl," Sapphire says. "If my guard looked like him and was into me the way he is into you, I'd move into my fucking Chamber."

We roar with laughter. Even though, secretly, I wish I could do just that.

We fall into silence and I enjoy my massage. I wish I didn't have to go back into my Chamber tonight. After last night, I don't want to spend any time with anyone else. I really need to think about what is happening to me and my future, not that Tyson made any mention of leaving this place to be with me. His place, I'm sure, is here in The Chamber, not pining after me while I decide whether I want him or Liam. Either way, Liam may not want to have much to do with me when he learns what my job has been for the last year.

What happens if Tyson realizes that his feelings for me are actually just an infatuation or a crush, when the novelty wears off, and he realizes I'm not all that he's built me up to be?

21

LIAM, ANGRY BOY

This is absolute bullshit.

Vivian has been missing for over three months. There is no way she's alive. If she is, then that's even worse. Because she's probably being tortured in some sick fucker's basement.

How did this happen? No one knows shit. The police are tired of seeing my ass, but I refuse to let my girl become some cold case, some never-solved stack of evidence stuffed into a vault. Not gonna happen. I will never stop. As long as she isn't confirmed dead, then she is alive to me.

This means she needs me more than ever to fight to bring her back. My love and vigilance will bring my girl home to me. When we find her—and we will—I will do everything in my power to keep her safe, and I'll make up for lost time.

All I can see is her—gray eyes, skin that's too soft to be real, a full-lipped smile. She's mine, and I want her back. My ringing phone interrupts my reverie. I never answer it anymore. My heart needs to screen the calls in case it is the police or Vivian's parents.

Frankly, the phone ringing scares the shit out of me these days.

"Hey, Liam, it's me, Maddie. Open your fucking door, dude. I know you're screening my calls, 'cause I do the same shit. Liam. Open. Your. Front. Door." She lets each word drag.

When I open the door, Maddie and Stevyn are standing on my front steps.

"Move your ass, I gotta pee." She pushes past me. "And we are not leaving without you!" she calls behind her. "So put some clothes on, assnuts!"

I move out of the way so Stevyn can come inside. We sit on the couch and wait for Maddie to return. Neither of us say a word. The fact that he is still civil and hasn't tried to kick the shit out of me means that Maddie hasn't said anything to him. Thank goodness. Not that I'm worried. Stevyn is more of a preppy boy—small framed, barely five-nine—and I think he gets manicures. Not that I care. He's a cool dude, but I think he's more of a lover than a fighter. Since he and Maddie hooked up, he and I have become boys, and I'm not ready to lose that right now.

Even with the guilt I'm carrying, I'm so glad that Stevyn is here so that Maddie and I can avoid the ever- present elephant in the room—the fact that we fucked each other senseless only a week after Vivian's disappearance. It never happened again, and it never will. When Vivian returns to me, I will be worthy of her. When the time is right, I will tell her what happened. I won't say that it didn't mean anything, either. I will man up and tell her that we were both in so much pain that we thought we could help each other erase it temporarily. Surely, she will understand.

"What the fuck? I said get dressed!" Maddie yells as she returns to the room.

"Madeline, I'm not going anywhere. So just go." I point toward the front door.

"Like it's that easy. You have to get out of the house—somewhere besides the police station or Viv's. You're not gonna fall apart on my watch. Viv needs you strong and healthy when we get her back, and we will. Now put some clean clothes on, or so help me I will dress you myself!" She crosses her arms in front of her body and digs her heels in. She's not leaving.

Fifteen minutes later I'm in the backseat of Stevyn's F150. When we pull up to a local pub I hop out of the truck before it has time to stop. I'm pissed at Maddie for making me leave the house.

This is bullshit. I should not be out kicking it, having drinks, when my girl is suffering somewhere.

"Stop sulking, Liam," Maddie growls at me. "You need this numbing of the brain. Trust me, my brain has been numb since some fucking psycho stole my best friend. If this doesn't help, you can hate me for it. Please, at least try."

"Fine, Maddie. Bring on the liquor!" I shout as we walk through the door. I instantly recognize a couple of my buddies from my MMA gym, Xavier and Blake, waiting for us in a corner booth.

"What's up?" I walk over and greet them. They both stand.

"Sorry about your girl, bro," Xavier grabs me in a tight hug. "Anytime you need to talk, I'm here." He pats my shoulder hard.

"Thanks, man."

Blake hugs me next. "You know I got your back, man. Anything you need."

"I know, Blake, thanks."

Before I'm in my seat, a round of tequila shots appear. The good stuff. I can tell as it slides smoothly down my throat. The music is not too loud for conversation, but the songs are upbeat. It's just what I need. There's no sound from the televisions, just images.

By the third shot, my mind is numb. My heart is still broken, only I can't feel it now. The only thing I feel is heat in my chest and belly.

By the fifth shot, I can barely stand. We're all stumbling drunks. Hopefully, I will remember how cool it was for Maddie to arrange for my boys to meet us, and thank her for it.

"Hey, sexy. Can I buy you a drink?" a very pretty blonde in a tight, short dress approaches me.

"Ish your na...name Vivian?" I slur.

"No." She frowns. "My name is Lindsey. So how 'bout that drink?" she asks again.

Before I can slur another word, Maddie pounces. "Look, honey. This is a private party. I'm sure you can find another hot guy to buy a drink for you, being half-naked and all. Liam is suffering right now, so back the fuck off!" She shoos the girl away with both hands.

The girl is persistent. "I'm just..."

"No, no, no...not another word," Maddie cuts her off with a 'talk to the hand' gesture.

The girl gets the hint and disappears into the growing sea of customers.

"To Vivian!" Maddie holds up a shot glass and we all drink.

My heart aches hearing her name. I want her back more than I want air. I pray every night for her to come back to me. The glasses make loud sounds when they slam on the table. I glance over at the bartenders to see if they are paying attention to our beating up their glasses, and the room tips and spins. Vivian's picture flashes on several of the television screens.

It all happens so fast, I don't remember how I got over to the bar. The bartender points the remote to change the channel. "Leave it!" I shout over the music and voices. "Turn it up, please." He does.

Suddenly, all is quiet—no music or sounds.

The television reporter discusses her case, details about her, when she was taken, and a number to call if anyone spots her. The camera never leaves her beautiful face. She is happy in the picture. It's a recent photo of her and her family on a vacation to Hawaii over spring break. It sat on their mantel. The camera crops everyone else out and zooms in on her. My girl...just like I remember her. She's happy, carefree, full of life, and is a heart-stopping beauty.

"I'd snatch her, too. That bitch is fucking hot!" a heavy voice yells out from down the bar.

"Who the fuck said that?" My eyes frantically scan for the asshole.

"I did, boss." A man stands up to own his words.

All I can hear is Maddie yell. "Liam, no!" It's too late. I pounce.

My fists connect with his face so many times that I can only see blood, no features. My boys pull me away from the bastard before I have a chance to kill him.

"She's mine, and someone took her, you fucking insensitive

asshole!" I can't hold the rage in any longer. I cry heavy sobs. I attempt to go after him again. Xavier and Blake refuse to let me go.

"Man, I'm sorry. I had no idea. I'm sorry," he says holding his face.

I don't know who called the cops, but I'm swiftly put in cuffs.

"Officers, I had it coming. I'm not pressing charges," the man says around the towel he's wiping his face with.

"That will be for a judge to decide," the officer says. They read me my rights and start walking me out.

"Liam. Shit. Don't be pissed at me. We were having a good time, right?" Maddie walks behind me.

"I'm not mad at you, Maddie. I'll be fine," I call out behind me.

"I'm calling your dad."

"Don't call my dad!" I yell behind me. "I'm serious, Maddie, don't fucking call him," I say before they stuff me into the back of the police car.

Fuck. She's gonna call my dad.

The cops throw my ass in a drunk tank. This isn't my first time being arrested. It's almost a rite of passage for a young man.

When I wake up from my drunken siesta, my dad is standing outside of my cell.

Fucking Maddie.

Being the son of a millionaire comes with some perks. Namely, the proverbial get-out-of-jail-free card that I try to never use.

My father and I are not what anyone would call close. Estranged is a better word. He sealed the fate of our relationship when he walked out on my mom for some bimbo only a few years older than me. At the time, I was seventeen. In his defense, he tried to keep in touch, and share custody of me and my brother. After a year, he gave up. It was clear that my younger brother Lincoln and I had chosen our mother's side.

It's been three years since I have laid eyes on my father. He hasn't changed. Lincoln and I definitely took after him with our dark hair and clear blue eyes. I have grown to match his six-foot figure. He doesn't look angry. He looks sad.

"Hi, son. They're doing the paperwork. You'll be out of here in a few minutes."

He's wearing his signature sharp black suit—the kind a man wears on a fancy date or his wedding day. It's exactly what I want to wear the day I marry Vivian. "You look good, Dad. Were you in the middle of something?"

"Nothing more important than you."

I smirk as the cell door slides open and a guard ushers me out.

The summer air sobers me up the second it hits my face. I'm not surprised to see a driver standing outside of my father's Maybach. We both climb into the backseat.

I'm not a stranger to this type of service, but since my father walked out on my mother, our lifestyle has scaled back considerably. My mother and brother still live in the seven-thousand-square-foot house I grew up in. My father's alimony and child support payments have made sure that we've maintained a certain lifestyle over the years, but we have nothing as elaborate as chauffeurs and private jets.

"Nice ride, Dad," I can't hide my sarcasm.

"Thanks. Liam, why didn't you call me when Vivian was first taken? I could have hired someone to help find her," he says.

Maddie told my dad about Vivian.

I look down, angry at myself because I would take anyone's help, including his.

"I wish I would have thought to call you, Dad."

"I'm here now, son. Vivian was always a wonderful young lady, and the cutest little thing when you guys were growing up."

"Is Dad. She is wonderful," I correct him.

"Right, son. Is." He clears his throat.

My father and I sit in silence until we arrive at the Wynn hotel. He's staying in the penthouse. Of course.

As we enter the suite, my father takes off his suit coat and rolls up his shirtsleeves. "Are you hungry?" he asks.

"I am." I rub my stomach and it rumbles in response.

He hands me the phone. "Press six and order anything you want."

I order enough food to feed a family.

My dad has his tablet in his hands. "So, details, Liam. What happened to Vivian?"

"Well, her birthday was on April tenth. Maddie, and her boyfriend, and I planned to take Vivian to San Francisco for her birthday as a surprise. I was going to officially ask her to become exclusive. The next morning, her parents go in to say happy birthday and she's gone. All her stuff—her phone, overnight bags, purse— were still in her room. The crazy thing is, that their back door was broken into, but the house alarm never went off."

I bury my face in my hands. I'm overcome again. My father is by my side, rubbing my back.

"I think the cops thought I had something to do with it."

"Well, that's preposterous."

"I miss her so much, Dad. It hurts." For the first time in years I let my father comfort me.

"Son, let me see what I can find out. I'll make some phone calls. I know some people, Liam. I will use all of my resources. Make yourself at home. There's an extra bedroom at the end of the hall."

"Thanks, Dad."

"I love you, son," he says and disappears behind his bedroom doors.

I devour everything on the table that room service brings, including two pieces of chocolate cake. I pass out, fully clothed, in the other bedroom, with renewed hope that my father can somehow find the answers that I could not, and bring Vivian back to me.

22

OUT OF THE DARKNESS

*W*hen I get my next letter from Tyson, I'm thrilled. I can't get enough of him. I run to the bathroom and flop onto the commode seat. I'm greedy at the task of pulling the letter out.

My dearest Vivian,

The past few days with you have been nothing short of amazing. The time we spent at the get-together was so normal, I forgot where we were for a minute. Our nights together are always something I dream about and look forward to. The more I get to know you, the harder I fall. My fear is not knowing how you feel for me. I don't want to pressure you, because I know how strong your feelings are for him, but I am honest with you, and I always want you to know how I feel. No matter what happens, I will respect your decision, but I want you to please consider me.

I love you.
Dom

P.S. Please fall asleep in your Chamber tonight.

Wow. Does that mean he would leave The Chamber for me? Could I ask that of him? Would I? I never would have thought something like this could happen.

How is it possible that Tyson crowds my thoughts when we have only known each other for a short time? I have dated other guys over the years, and not one of them ever had this effect on me. Is a sexual relationship strong enough to change the tides? Is that all Tyson and I are to each other, sex partners, or are we more?

I REALLY DO FALL asleep in my Chamber after the guests leave. My body was ravished, and I'm mentally exhausted from all of the chatter in my head. I wake to Tyson pulling me into his arms.

"Hi, sleepy girl," he says, kissing me quickly on the lips.

"I really fell asleep." I state the obvious.

"It certainly seems so. Do you want to keep sleeping? I don't mind, if you are tired."

I shoot up in bed when I realize what he is saying. "No way! I don't get to spend enough time with you as it is." I scoot so I'm sitting completely straight up. Tyson smiles when he hears my words.

"How about we just talk, then? Since you're tired," he says.

"I'm not that tired," I say. I would love a visit from The Captain.

He shakes his head. No Captain Thunderdick for me tonight. Even in my disappointment, I smile because this is an important statement on his part. It's about more than sex for him. Yes.

"So, tell me about Liam."

I scoot in close to him and he wraps his arm around me. "What do want to know?"

"Anything you want to tell me."

"Let me see. We met in middle school...seventh grade. He and Maddie and I have been inseparable ever since. He's gorgeous and sweet, but he has a bit of a temper. He's very protective of me, too, just like you are. I didn't start out crushing on him. That's something that changed over time. I love him, but I'm not sure what kind of love it is yet, because I was brought here before we had a chance to figure that out."

"Life can really throw some curve balls," he sighs.

"You said it. I never expected to find someone like you in a place like this. I truly thought my life was over when I was taken. I definitely didn't see you coming." I take a breath, and reality hits me—this place, being in Dominic's arms. Life can change on a dime. "My turn to ask a question. How old are you?

"Twenty-seven."

"Ooh, an older man," I say, and we both laugh lightly.

"Dominic?"

"Yes."

"Why were you in 'the dark?'"

He tenses an almost unnoticeable amount, but I can feel it. He stares into my eyes.

"I mentioned to you that I'm from Hawaii?" He crosses his arms across his chest. "When I was sixteen, my mother was gunned down by some thugs who wanted our car. They shot me, too." He pulls his sleeve to show me the scar on his left shoulder. I reach up and touch it gently, I've seen it before. "I was never quite right after that. When I turned eighteen, I joined the marines. While in the service, I was recruited by a special group based on a certain aptitude I had."

"What aptitude was that?" I ask, even though I see where this is going.

"Let's just say that not giving a fuck about what happens to you, or anyone around you, makes you a pretty lethal government assassin," he replies. "I fell into my new life easily. Every target was just the fucker that killed my mother and left us for dead. I picked them off without thought."

I squeeze him tightly against me. He can't see my face, but tears prick my eyes. I can hear the pain in his voice.

"I performed my job that way for four years. I stopped when it wasn't fun anymore."

"Killing people was fun for you?"

"Like I said, I was in the dark. I came home to Hawaii, to my dad and my sisters. I have two of them. But I wasn't happy. The world was darkness around me. I rarely came out of my room. I was plagued with terrible nightmares almost every night. I ate, worked out in my room and slept. I couldn't get out of my sister's high school graduation, though. That's where I met Mason. He struck up a conversation with me in the bathroom of all places. I thought I was gonna have to kick his ass. He didn't give me much information other than he had a job for me as head of security. I took his card, and after about a week, I called him. I became his head of Chamber security. The nightmares continued, but at least I had a purpose, and I didn't have to kill anybody."

"Do you still have the nightmares?"

"Nope, not one."

"When did they stop?"

"They stopped the first night I saw you on the surveillance camera two years ago. I told you, Vivian. You are my light in every way. You brought me to life. I owe you everything. I will start with my undying devotion. I love you." He kisses my shoulder.

A sudden flood of tears escapes my eyes. I weep for his sadness and his awakening.

"Don't cry, Vivian. I'm a new man because of you."

"I'm a new woman because of you, too, you know."

"I guess you are. Now close your eyes and get some sleep before I change my mind and bury The Captain inside of you. He's really mad at me for denying him tonight," he says.

So am I. "Why are you denying him and me?"

"Oh, believe me, I want to give in, but falling in love isn't about sex. It's about this. Just being together." He kisses me on my nose. "I love you...you horny little creature. Now go to sleep."

My smile is a mile wide. I close my eyes, snuggle into him, and fall asleep in Dominic's arms.

23

MR. CREEPY

*T*he regularity of my nights with Tyson are my saving grace. I crave getting to know everything I can about him. Feelings that I'd only felt for Liam are now there for Tyson. I never thought in a billion years that I would feel love for anyone but Liam. How is it possible to feel such strong feelings for two men?

My only solace is that once I get out of here, I will only have to worry about one of them. The other will remain here in The Chamber. I'll miss him, and I'll mourn the loss of him in my life, but I'll have no choice but to move forward. Knowing him and loving him will allow an extra ray of light to be cast whenever I recall this crazy year of mine.

What if he doesn't stay behind?

What if he keeps his recent promise to leave The Chamber and find me in my real life? Would I let him go so easily then? Would I turn my back on my feelings for him?

I don't find a letter from him under my pillow tonight.

That saddens me. I want him any way I can get him, and especially in my Chamber. Maybe I'm being cruel for allowing this to happen between us. He has told me that I'm his light and he loves me. How much will he suffer when I'm gone? It pains me to think of him finding the darkness again. I do love him and I don't want that for him. If he does decide to leave The Chamber, I could see possibility then. But the possibility of what? A friendship? Him instead of Liam?

Zion prepares me for my night in The Chamber.

I scan my playlist and see that Mr. Not So Creepy is up at bat tonight. His name got an upgrade, because he really has gotten better. He still doesn't say anything, and I find that disturbing, but he is gentler with me. I'm sure he's not happy about getting roughed up, but if it improves his behavior, then it was worth it.

He's first on my playlist.

I never know if that's better or worse. On one hand it's better, because the night ends on a more positive note. Worse, though, because he sets my mood for the rest of the evening.

In a surprise move, he wants me clothed. I don a floor-length sexy sheer nightgown. My hair cascades down my back in ebony waves, and my lips are the deepest red. I resemble a black-and-white movie starlet. When I cross the threshold to my Chamber, he's sitting at the round bistro table.

Before tonight, I'd never gotten a good look at his face. He's older than I thought he would be, and attractive, in an Eastern European way. His eyes are tiny, beady. His lips are thick and full. He's stout and strong. His hair is dark blond.

"Good evening, Flame," he speaks for the first time.

I liked the silence better. "Hi," I say, my nerves getting the best of me.

He even has a European accent. "Please sit." He gestures to the chair. I do as I am told. "You look lovely," he says.

His words crawl over my skin like bugs. I don't know what this is, but I don't like it. I don't like him.

"I've been doing some soul searching," he continues.

What the fuck?

He looks at the table. "After my ass was handed to me by the guards, I mean." His eyes dart to mine and stay there, I want to break his gaze, but I don't.

What? "I'm sorry that happened to you. I had no idea. I thought we were past that. I thought we were...friends." I have no idea where that came from.

"You don't know me, but if you did, you would know that Vladimir is my real name." He leans forward with a smile that makes my stomach turn and my skin prickle.

"I know we're never to speak our given names in The Chamber, but somehow, under the circumstances, I think we're far beyond pseudonyms."

I never called you Serge, either.

"Dear Flame, Vladimir doesn't get "past" anything. I am a rich and powerful man. I have been waiting for the right time...the right moment."

The words pour out of him and affect me like a poison. Dread fills me. "I see." I start looking around. Do I call for Tyson now? No, I wait. Let him lay his cards on the table. I don't want Tyson to walk into a setup. I know that he's watching. The second this creep walked into my Chamber, I know Tyson was on alert. "And what time is that?" I dare ask.

"It's time that you, your personal guard, Mason, and the guards who attacked me pay," he threatens.

I try to buy myself some time. "That sounds expensive."

He's immediately annoyed with me. His dead, beady eyes pierce through me. "Not with money, you stupid bitch! With your lives! No one disrespects Vladimir, especially for some insolent whore! I want you to call for your guard so that I can kill him!" He leans forward. His breath smells of hard liquor.

"I can't do that." I'm not lying, either. If he's going to kill me, then so be it. But I refuse to be the cause of Tyson's death, too. I love him and I will not willingly kill someone I love.

His hand flies up, and before I have a chance to react a hard object connects violently with my face. I fly out of my chair and land on the floor in a heap. Pain blazes across my face where he struck me and my eye immediately swells shut.

He stalks over to me, a gun brushing the side of his leg. I didn't even know that he had a gun. "He will come, and like you he will suffer."

Mr. Creepy kicks me in the ribs with brute force. The pain is so severe that I see stars. The next thing I feel is the cold metal of the gun pressing against my head.

"Call him!" he yells at close range.

My head splits with pain. There are two of him now. I don't know which one to focus on. "No!" I try to match his bravado, but I'm too weak and my face is broken. He cocks the trigger.

I am going to die here on my Chamber floor at the hands of Mr. Creepy. This is not fair. No one should have to meet their end at his hand. I close my eye, the other is already sealed shut.

I hear a commotion coming from the stairs leading from the gentlemen's area.

"I blocked the bookcase. I wanted more time with you. Besides, I can't have your fucking guard sneaking up on us. I was hoping I had more time. I wanted to shove my dick into you one last time before I killed you," he sneers, "but it seems my attention is needed at the entrance." His lips smash into mine, roughly. Bile rises in my throat competing with the lump that is sitting there.

I watch Vladimir stand. There are still two of him, but they are blurred together, touching. "Please don't hurt him!" I call out.

He is not listening. He points his gun down the entrance stairs. I hear more commotion and then light floods the stairs.

"No! Tyson, he has a gun! Don't come up here! I love you." I know that he can't hear me, my voice is weakened to barely a whisper. I can hardly keep my eyes open. Darkness wants to find me.

"Quiet! You stupid whore!" Vladimir shouts at me.

The scene unfolds in a blur. Tyson appears at the other entrance, the one that leads to my bedroom downstairs. Vladimir unknowingly stands vigilant at the wrong entrance. Tyson's gun fires a single, accurate shot to the back of Vladimir's head, and he tumbles down the stairs of my Chamber. My ears ring from the gunshot.

"Vivian!" Tyson yells and scoops me up.

He's alive. I can let go now. Welcomed darkness overcomes me.

I AWAKE TO PAIN EVERYWHERE.

My head, my face, my stomach, and my side are all in excruciating, mind-numbing pain. My right eye won't open. I gaze around the too-bright room and find Tyson sleeping in a chair next to my bed.

"Hey there," I croak. My voice is dry.

Tyson is at my side at once. He looks worse for wear, like he hasn't moved from that spot in days.

"You're awake. How are you feeling?" His relief is palpable.

"Like a truck ran over me, to be honest." My head is foggy, but images flash through my head—Mr. Creepy smashing my face with his gun, kicking me, Tyson shooting him.

Oh my goodness, is he dead?

"Where am I?"

I squint to take in surroundings that resemble a hospital room. Tyson takes my hand in his. His eyes are laced with worry and pain. There's a crease in his forehead.

"You're in the infirmary. Mason brought a doctor in to treat your injuries." He spits the last word out. "I am so sorry I didn't get to you sooner." He inhales a deep breath before continuing, rubbing his thumb back and forth across my hand tenderly.

"At first, when that bastard was sitting across the table from you I thought he came to play nice, like he had been," Tyson says. "The next thing I know, he starts yelling and then he attacks you. I almost left my skin in my haste to get to you, but that fucker rigged the bookshelf so that I couldn't get it open. Those bookshelves may look old and worn, but they're made with reinforced steel on purpose, in case we need to lock this place down and hide you guys. I had no choice but to run as fast as I could to your Chamber entrance. I called

Mason and more guards to rally to get the other door open. I was banking on the fact that he didn't know I couldn't break down the door, and that he didn't know about the other entrance. I have never been so scared in my whole life, Vivian." His eyes, filled with tears, lock with mine, and it hurts me to see the torment etched in his creased brow, the tightness of his mouth, and the muscle in his jaw flexing. "I didn't think I was going to make it to you in time." The tears spill over onto his cheeks.

"But you did. You saved me."

"You should never have been harmed. That fucker should've been banished the first time. Now he's dead and won't be around to hurt anyone else."

Dead. I have never been this close to death before.

"Can I get you anything? How's your pain?" he asks.

"Um. My side hurts and my head and my face. Um, my throat is dry. I would like some water, please."

Tyson jumps up and crosses the room. He grabs a pitcher of water and pours a glass for me. He rushes back to my side. I take it in my hand and drink small sips. "Ahh." The cool liquid feels heavenly as it washes the dryness away. "Thank you." I hand him the cup. "How long have I been out?"

"Almost twenty-four hours. The doctor says you have three broken ribs." He takes my hand into his. "Your cheek isn't fractured, thankfully, but bruised pretty bad. The drugs they gave you knocked you out. All of the girls have come to visit—Mason and Zion, too. Everybody is worried about you."

I attempt to sit up. My ribs scream at me the second I try. Tyson immediately assists me by using the bed controls to raise my head. The movement still hurts, but significantly less. "I've been out that long? How long will my injuries take to heal?" I don't want to ask the real question. Will Mason try to extend my time here?

"Baby, please don't worry about that. It'll be weeks before you're Chamber-ready. Mason is as angry as I am. This has never happened before."

Baby? The endearment soothes me to great depths. "I thought he was going to kill us. That's what he said, that he was going to kill us. He wanted me to call you up to my Chamber, but I refused."

I can tell immediately that he's not happy with my decision. "Vivian, why?" His pained expression grows graver.

"Because...because I love you. I didn't want anything to happen to you. That thought scared me more than anything he could do to me," I confess. "I'm sorry."

For the first time since I wake, I see light in his face and in his eyes. Any signs of anger are replaced with joy. He inches closer to me and kisses me tenderly on the uninjured side of my face.

"My brave, beautiful girl. I love you, too, but if you ever do anything as foolish as that again, I may not forgive you so easily. I'm here to protect you in all ways. That's not just my job. It's my mission to protect the one person I love above all others." He kisses me again.

When I look at myself in the mirror, I'm unrecognizable. I look exactly like what you would expect me to look like in a place like this. My right eye is swollen shut. The right side of my face is a rainbow of black and blue. My lips are swollen and painful-looking. In other words, I'm a hot mess.

The way Tyson gazes at me when he visits, you would think not a thing is wrong with me. I guess that is what you do when you love someone. You see around the ugly, because you have glimpsed the beauty inside. I know beyond a shadow of a doubt that Tyson loves me. More than that, I know that I love him. Leaving him in a few months, when my sentence here ends, will be one of the hardest things that I will ever do.

It takes six weeks for me to heal enough to return to my regular duties. I only spend the first week of it in the actual infirmary. Tyson visits with me every day the entire week that I'm there, spending most of the days and nights with me.

On my last night in the infirmary, he asks me to fall asleep in my Chamber my first night back. I tell him I will count the days.

∿

I FIND my time very restful. My days are spent with my sisters, and my nights spent where any normal girl who isn't kidnapped would spend her nights...in bed. No Chamber.

I haven't seen Tyson since I was released from medical care. No letters, either. I don't check for a letter today. In my heart, I know there will not be one. I'm sure he's watching me. That thought makes me smile.

Finally, it's my first night back in The Chamber. I'm fully healed and recovered.

Physically, anyway.

I never expected to find love in a place like this, but I did. I'm not thrilled about going back to the task of satisfying the sexual desires of so many men, but I'll go at my job with a light heart knowing that my love will be there when my work is done. I don't wait for Zion. I head up to my Chamber and run a bath.

Zion comes in about thirty minutes later to find me soaking in the tub. "Are you okay, Flame?"

"Yep," I say in a flat tone. "I'm just getting a jump on the evening. Six weeks is a long time. I'm sure I will be rusty." My eyes never open. The water feels splendid. I wish I could stay in this bliss forever.

I climb out of the tub when I'm a prune. Zion works on fixing me up for the night. My list is remarkably easy. No one who wants it too rough and no one who wants a fake relationship. Right now, I don't think I could handle either.

Really, I just want to take Tyson up on getting me out of here. I'm exhausted.

I do the math and know that I have been here for close to nine months. I can't believe that almost a year ago I was brought here against my will. What have I missed in my life? In the world? I've been so cut off from everything, the whole world could be gone and I would have no clue.

The theme tonight is one of compassion, proving that although the lottery winners are sexually perverted, they are still gentlemen.

My first guest asks me how I am feeling. He apologizes for what happened to me. Wow, that was nice. He's gentle even, during our sexual encounter. He actually treats me as if I was recently beaten. His touch is caressing. When he comes inside of me, it isn't with the usual explosiveness. Unexpected.

I coast through my evening. I thank each man for his kindness and gentle nature. When the last one leaves for the night, I can't wait to pretend fall asleep.

I don't even get off of my bed when I'm finally alone. I simply roll over and close my eyes. Within a few minutes, I feel the room lighten when the now-repaired bookshelf slides open. I smile inside knowing that my love is here. The bed depresses under his weight. I wait patiently for his lips to touch me, for him to whisper my name. I wait for butterflies to burst forth in my stomach. It has been five weeks.

Still, I wait.

I realize that something is wrong. The energy is off. My scalp prickles. My skin crawls. This is not my love. Fear shoots through me like a firework. I turn in haste to face my visitor. I recognize him from the guard. I believe his name is Carson. He's blond and good-looking. None of that matters, though. He could be the hottest guy on earth, but who cares? He isn't Tyson.

Fuck me.

"Where is Tyson?"

"He's not here."

I want to smack the stupid grin off of his face. "I can see that. Where is he, exactly?"

"He's gone. Mason kicked him out. He said if he wasn't in love with you then they wouldn't have to cover up what happened to that dickhead who attacked you. Mason thinks he can't see clearly because of you, so he's gone. He left about an hour ago. I hear it took several guards to put him out. I'm your new guard." His smile is overly happy. "Seems to me like we need to stop talking and get to fucking. You fell asleep in your Chamber."

Panic rips through me. I've lost all the strength I had gained in my time here. For the third time, the hood is back over my head. I'm back to my first night here.

Fuck. Fuck. Fuck. There's no way I can do this without Tyson. How can he be gone? He left me. He left without me.

"Get out of your head. Your boy is gone, but I'm here. Put that ass in the air."

My own personal hell. I do as I am told. I position myself on all fours. I arch my back and stick my rump in the air, thankful that he can't see my face. Heavy tears fall from my eyes. Everything slows around me, and I fall and fall. I have nothing.

When he sinks his cock inside of me I don't care. I don't escape into my special place. What's the point? There's no place that I can hide from this pain. He is gone. I am alone. Carson continues to pound his cock into me with force and enthusiasm. His moans only sicken me.

He smacks my rump, pulling me toward him, causing me to arch my back more. I wince at the pain that settles into my rib cage from the extreme position. He slams into me in a flurry of convulsions and shivers.

Carson isn't done with me by a long shot. He came to play.

"Go on and hop on that there pleasure horse I've heard the other guards talking about." He sits on the edge of the bed, his erection as hard and stiff as it was when he was inside of me.

I have no feelings in this moment. I am numb. I walk over to the cabinet of horror and grab a dildo. I grab a Dominic-sized one, thinking perhaps it can fill the emptiness that is growing inside of me. I cross the room, feeling too naked in front of this guard. He slaps my ass when I pass him. This causes tears to fall harder. He doesn't know that I'm crying. That, or he just doesn't fucking care. Why should he? Who am I to him but a piece of ass to play with tonight?

I screw the dildo onto Dominic the Pleasure Horse and climb on. I depress the button and watch as the lubricant spills around the shaft. I close my eyes and see Dominic's face. Tears continue to fall from my eyes.

I sink down onto the long cock. It fills me completely, just like Dominic would. I feel heat stir between my legs at the fullness, never letting go of Dominic's image. I grind my sex around the shaft, pulsating myself around it. I lift off of the shaft, but before it is completely out of me, I fall back onto it, forcing it deep inside me. I whimper at the feel of it, as something builds inside of me.

"Yeah, girl, get it!" Carson yells, reminding me that he is in the room.

I open my eyes to see him stroking his own cock and rolling his hips. He has a smile of pure excitement on his face. I close my eyes and search for Dominic's image again. It takes a minute, but when I see him he's hovering over me, telling me he loves me, before he slides his scrumptious Thunderdick inside of me.

I really start working it. I grind around and around. I grind forward and back until I come unhinged. I shudder so hard that it hurts. I cry heavy, broken, ugly tears. I'm fractured and empty.

"That was the sexiest shit I've ever seen. Now, come over here and suck this dick so I can get out of here. Next time you fall asleep, there won't be none of that crying bullshit. You're a big girl. Get over it."

Fuck you. You say that to me and I'm about to put your dick in my mouth? My mouth that is full of teeth? I should bite it off.

I climb off of Dominic. I walk over to Carson and I don't make any eye contact with him. I just take his erection into my mouth and suck it, hard. I want him to come so he can get the fuck out of my Chamber and leave me the hell alone. And I will never fall asleep in my Chamber again.

His hips flex forward. "Ahh. Hmm. Slow down, girl," he says.

I don't listen. Instead I suck harder. He is endowed, but nothing like Dominic. I take his entire length into my mouth, until it is hitting the back of my throat. That does it.

I feel him tense and shake. He calls out random bullshit and my mouth is full of him. I can't swallow it. If I do, I will throw up. Instead, in a sneaky move that one of my sisters shared with me, I bend down as if getting up from the floor takes great effort and I let it run out of my mouth.

"You are the real deal, girl! Amazing! No wonder Tyson wanted to keep you all to himself. But now, you're mine."

The look I shoot him is completely involuntary, but I know that he can feel my fury. His hands fly up in front of himself as if he is surrendering.

"Whoa, girl. Goodnight."

I take my cue and run faster than the wind down the stairs that lead to my bedchamber. I crash through the bathroom door, head into my personal stall, and empty my stomach into the toilet. When I have nothing left inside of me but organs, I climb onto the toilet and wail, until my head pounds and my throat is raw.

I gather myself together because I need to wash Carson off of my body. I need to erase my evening. I will never survive without Dominic.

With sluggish, deflated steps I make it to the walk-in shower. The water is so hot when I step in that it scalds my skin. I don't care. I don't even flinch. More tears come. I can't stop them. I slide down the shower wall in a heap. The hot water continues to pound my raw flesh as I weep.

I don't see the person. I don't hear anyone enter the shower. I only feel the hands around me scooping me up and wrapping me in a fluffy towel. I don't even bother opening my eyes.

Why? What's the point? Only one person can fix what ails me, and he's gone. It is only when the unknown person presses my head to his chest that recognition floods me. I would know the grooves and sinews of this muscled chest above all.

"It's gonna be okay, baby. I'm here now," Dominic says.

My eyes fly open. I throw my arms around him. "How?" I shout in delighted confusion.

He tries to set me down so that he can explain his surprising but wonderful appearance. I don't let him. He might just be a hallucination that my mind is making up out of desperation and sadness.

He attempts a couple more times to put me on my feet, but I refuse to touch the floor. Dominic smiles and floods my face with kisses. He backs us up to an oversized chair in the corner of the bathroom.

"I thought you left me." I begin to cry again, sobs ripping through me. "I thought you left me here alone."

"Never," he says and kisses my tears.

"Where were you?" I stare into his eyes.

He returns my stare, never faltering. "Mason relieved me of my duties because I shot a lottery winner. He says that if you had been any other girl, I wouldn't have reacted in such an extreme manner. I tried to explain, but he says when it comes to you I'm blind. So, I'm not back."

I begin to panic. My eyes lose focus. "You're not back? What does that mean?"

If he is here to say a proper goodbye, I can't do this.

"Are you saying that you are here to say goodbye to me?" My voice shakes with fear. My eyes zero in on his again.

"I will never say goodbye to you, Vivian, but we don't have much time. I'm here to take you away from this place. I won't be able to live a day knowing that you're in here and I'm not with you. You're coming with me."

I'm overcome with joy. I squeeze him tighter, the smile on my face is so wide it might just split in two. "I knew you wouldn't leave me!" I kiss his lips as if they are the sweetest gift on earth. "Wait!" I pull back. "If this place is so impenetrable and you're still on the outs, how did you get inside?"

"I have friends," he says cryptically.

"Oh." I'm so overcome with joy that I can see my life, my first dose of fresh air in almost a year. I don't even know who I am anymore. I don't know what I want anymore, but out of this place is at the top of that list. "I'd better put on some clothes," I nearly squeal.

I can't wait to see my family. I can't wait to see Liam and Maddie. Liam. What will become of me and my first love? Dominic says he wants me any way that he can get me. What if it isn't the one way he truly wants?

I climb off of Dominic's lap reluctantly. I feel safe in his arms. I can remember when I felt safe with Liam. It wasn't the same intimate way as Dominic, but safe just the same. They both love me, but which me will return home?

I creep into my room, careful not to wake my sleeping roommates.

I pull out underclothes, a pair of red leggings, and red t-shirt. I dress in a nanosecond. My mother's face flashes in front of my eyes. I can see my dad and Shane and Growl. I miss them so much. Maddie's face pops into view, then Liam's. The final image to freeze in my mind is Mason's, and fear grips me, just as Dominic wraps his arms around me from behind. He nuzzles into my neck and kisses the spot just under my ear that makes me crazy. I don't react. I am paralyzed. I can't go with him.

"What's wrong, baby?"

"Dominic. I love you."

"I love you, too."

I turn around to face him. My finger shoots to my lips and I glance over at Sky and Sapphire. I pull him out of my room. When we are in the family room, out of earshot, I finally speak. "I can't go with you. I have to stay here." I can't believe the words myself as they pour out of my mouth.

"What?" he whispers. He walks us hastily into the kitchen area, farther away from my sleeping sisters.

"Aren't there cameras?" I look around, feeling open and vulnerable.

"Not at the moment. They will be restored once I leave."

I can tell he's not happy with my revelation. He surely thinks I'm nuts.

"Vivian, listen to me. You can't stay here. Not after what happened to you. Not without me. It was bad enough, you being here at all, even under my protection. You cannot stay here without me." With his hands on the side of my arms, he's pleading with his eyes for me to come to my senses.

"So you're saying that it's safe for my sisters to be here, but not me?" I meet his stare. My mind is made up, crazy or not.

"Fair point. But I'm not in love with them, I'm in love with you. They're not my responsibility, you are. I'm not going to stand here and discuss this any further with you. You cannot stay here."

Wow. Stern, bossy Dominic is somehow sexier. How's that even possible? I understand his need to protect me, but I have to make him understand.

"Listen." I grab his muscular arms. My hands seem so small attempting to encircle his girth. "I want to leave this place more than you want me to. I was ready to run off into the darkness with you, until I remembered Mason's threat. I have to stay. I have stayed this long! I barely have two months left! I won't spend the rest of my life worrying about what might happen to us."

There, he has to understand that. I drop my hands and pace the room. Dominic paces, too. We look like animals about to battle, and we're in the stage where we sum up our adversaries.

He stops cold and slams his hands onto the granite island that now separates us.

"Then we run. Personally, I don't think Mason will punish you, but if you are worried that he will, we run. I'll do anything to protect you and keep you safe. That includes the people you love. New names, new identities, new lives."

I can't help the smile that creeps across my face, knowing what he's willing to go through and give up for me. What he doesn't realize is that I can't let him. There's no way that I will be the cause of him going into exile, and I can't remand my loved ones to a virtual witness protection program. What would we call Growl, Fido? That would never do.

If I thought I would be subjected to this prison for the rest of my life, then drastic measures such as he's describing would be the only way out. That is not the case here. I'm about to get my life back. All of it. "I'm sorry, but that is no life, Dominic. I want true freedom, like I had before The Chamber. If less than two months is the cost for my freedom, your freedom, and my family's freedom, then it's a price I'm willing to pay. I'm not leaving."

Dominic rushes to my side. He wraps his arms around me, and I melt into his embrace. My arms fall in place around him. We stand so close, so tight, that we are nearly one.

"What if something happens to you and I'm not here to protect you?" His voice catches. "I don't know if I can leave you."

I can't believe the words that form in my brain and travel to my mouth. "You have to. I'll be fine."

"But I won't, Vivian." He pulls me tighter. "I'm not strong enough to trust you in anyone else's hands."

"Don't talk like that, Dominic. You are plenty strong, and knowing that you'll be there waiting for me will give me the strength to push through."

I lose myself in the scent of his skin.

"You know, when you found me in the shower it was the lowest point in my life. Lower than being brought here," I say. "The worst part was thinking that you had left me behind."

"Then—" he tries to interrupt me but I don't let him.

I pull away from him and gaze into his eyes. I put my fingers to his lips. He kisses them and my heart stutters. I have never felt this way for any man. Dominic makes me require a crash cart to jumpstart my heart.

"Before you came tonight, I didn't think I had the strength. So that light thing goes both ways. You are my light, too. I was in utter darkness until you scooped me up in the shower."

His eyes never leave mine as I continue. "Dominic, you give me the strength to believe that I can survive. I know that you'll be there on the outside waiting for me."

"And Liam," he whispers.

I sigh and break free from his embrace. I walk to the other side of the kitchen. I really can't believe that we are standing in the kitchen having this conversation.

I feel the same way he does about the choices I face when I leave here. Am I changed so severely that the man I loved, and wanted to be with before I was brought here, will not be enough for me? Or will I discover that the love I feel for Dominic is a love of circumstance for us both? Only time will tell.

"Yes, I love Liam, but I love you, too. My strength is born out of that love. I can do this because of your love, Dominic. You love me enough to break in here and bust me out, and I'm just crazy enough not to go with you, because I love you and everyone else in my life too much to sentence us to living on the run. Isn't love fucking spectacular?" I can't resist the sarcasm, my chin wobbles and shakes, as I fight back the tears. If I break down now, I have no doubt that he'll carry me out of here. Life would be so much easier if we could all be more selfish and less selfless.

"Please come and kiss me before I change my mind," I say.

I see in that moment that my words give way to something for him, in the rise of his thick, perfectly arched eyebrows.

"Don't even get any ideas, buddy. I'm firm on my decision."

Dominic stalks me like I'm prey. He's analyzing. He probably thinks I'm a freaking psycho for this choice that I'm making. In the next moment, the most amazing smile crosses his face. His tongue glides across his most kissable lips. Watching him is orgasmic.

His rippled chest rises and falls. His eyes never leave mine. He is deciding. I can see it in his eyes. Does he follow his heart and give me what I want? Or does he follow his brain, throw my stubborn ass over his shoulder, and drag me out of here, just like he did on the staircase when I refused to take another step? Whatever he decides, he'd better choose in a hurry because I can't stand here squirming and panting. I'm about to pounce.

Butterflies take off deep inside of me when he launches toward me. I leap into his waiting arms and we exchange desperate lips, tongues, gasps, and moans. I want him to bury himself inside of me right now and nothing else. I need him inside of me, liquid moisture builds between my legs. "Oh my fuck, I want you to make love to me, Dominic." It's a whispered prayer, a plea. "Please, I need you to fill me up inside," I cry.

I'm nearly about to combust with the thought of him granting my ultimate desire. We moan in desperation around our kisses. His erection grows in answer as he walks us toward my room, our lips never separating. Yes. He's going to give me what I want. Captain Thunderdick to the rescue! Hell, yes.

Dominic tosses me onto my bed. I glance over at my roommates and resist the squeal that is begging to escape my lips. I swear that I'm so amped up, the second he touches my sex, I will come undone.

He stands over me, his erection full and threatening to tear through his pants. His chest heaves rapidly. His eyes are carnal and animal with his desire for me. I stare at him through hooded eyes. I only know how to be sexy with him. With him, it comes naturally. I'm panting in want.

I crook my finger in a "come hither" gesture. He bends down and tucks me in, pulling the covers right under my chin.

What the...

"What are you doing?" I whisper.

Taking a cue from me, he speaks in a low tone just above a whisper. "I'm leaving. The next time I make love to you will be when we are free of this place." He kisses me. "You have your choices to make. While I can't say that I agree with your choice to stay, I can respect it. You are strong, Vivian."

He kisses me again. Then he sits on the side of my bed and gazes down at me. Only tenderness and love flow from his eyes.

He bends back down, his mouth directly against my ear. My heart skips as he exhales, and his warm breath caresses my skin. I wonder if he knows what this is doing to me.

"I also have choices to make," he whispers into my ear. "The next time I make love to you will be when and if you choose to be mine. Then, and only then, will The Captain get to spend the rest of our lives in his favorite place, buried inside of you."

I cannot believe him. How rude.

For some reason, a huge smile crosses my face. Still, I smack him a few times with my pillow. He's got some balls. He just laid down the gauntlet and let me know that I'm not the only prize to be earned or won. He is a prize, and he knows it.

"Vivian." His tone is serious. "I have a failsafe in place. I know you're a brave girl, but if it gets too hot in here, if you sense danger, I will come back. Then, I will not leave here without you."

I nod. I can't argue with that. "Wait. How will you know if I'm in danger?"

"Trust me." He bends down and kisses me. "Is there anything you want me to do for you on the outside?"

I pull the sheets off of myself in a last attempt. "More pressing is what you can do for me on the inside," I say too loudly. I look over in the direction of Sky and Sapphire. Nothing. I'm not surprised that they are still asleep. After a night in our Chambers, we usually sleep like the dead.

"Vivian. Behave." He covers me up.

I immediately show my disappointment with a frown.

"Only when you are all mine. Believe me, I want nothing but you forever. If I could detach The Captain and send him around inside of you whenever we're apart, I would. That's how much I crave being inside of you. But you know my terms. Life is about choices, and I'm no consolation prize. I..." He floods my face with kisses. "Want..." More kisses, but this time I answer him with kisses of my own. "...you all to myself. I will never share again."

I instantly know what he means. The Chamber.

"I know you had a life that was interrupted when you came here. I will pray daily that I am the one you believe you can't live without, but I want it to be your choice. Now get some sleep, Madam Stubborn."

I gasp at his nickname. "Funny. I love you, too."

"I love you more." He kisses me. "See you in seven weeks." He kisses me again and stands.

Panic starts to build inside of me. I come onto my knees. I don't want him to go. "Will you tell my friends and family that I'm okay?"

"Anything for you, love." He kisses the top of my head. "Now get some sleep."

Without another word, he's gone.

"I knew you loved him," Sapphire says into the darkness.

"Shut up, Sapphire," I say, but not in anger. She understands how I mean it.

"Seriously, Flame," Sapphire says. "You were brave not to go. I'm glad you didn't. I would hate for one of my sisters to live like that...on the run."

The tears start forming as reality hits home. "Thanks. I'm glad I didn't go with him, too, but I wanted to. Now I'm gonna say this in the nicest way I know. Leave me alone so I can cry myself to sleep."

Sapphire laughs softly and leaves me to my weeping. I hope I'm as strong as everyone else thinks I am. Because Dominic is right—life is about living with the consequences of the choices we make, and I just made the mother of all choices.

I survive.

24

LIAM, SINS OF A FATHER

Waiting for my father to come back with information is killing me. He has been helping me search for Vivian for almost a whole year. He knows I'll never give up, and in a surprising show of support, my father has not given up either. He called me to tell me that he has what he hopes is a very promising lead, and that he is coming over. That was three hours ago. I am pacing my room.

When he finally shows up at my doorstep it's just in time, because I am about to lose it. I invite him in and offer him a drink and a seat. I don't miss that he's checking out my place and doesn't approve.

"Nice house," he says. He's trying, at least.

"Thanks. I have a couple of roommates. I'd introduce you to them but they aren't here." I bring my dad a beer and a glass, because he isn't a straight-from-the-bottle kind of guy. "So, you said you have a lead?" I ask, unable to hide the hope in my eyes.

"Actually..." My dad smiles. "I have more than a lead, son. If my sources are correct, I think I found the place where she's being held."

"What? Oh my God, Dad. Are you serious?" A year's worth of pent up energy rushes through me. I blow air out of my mouth. "And she's okay? She's alive?" My hands shake, waiting for my father to confirm what I've been dying to know. I busy them running them through my hair.

"I am not one hundred percent sure if she is there, or if she's alive. What I do know is that a group of young women were taken around the same time as Vivian. If she is a part of this group of women, then yes...she is alive."

"Dad." My sails lose all of their wind. This isn't news. What he's giving me is fragile hope, at best.

What if she isn't one of these girls?

"How can we be sure?" My dad takes a seat on my sofa. I can't sit. I'm too worked up. "What are we supposed to do now?"

"Son, I'm waiting on further information from my source. He says the girls inside of this place aren't using their real names. He's trying to gain more intel, but doesn't have direct access. He believes if she's with this group of girls, they're in Canada...and..."

My dad is interrupted by my doorbell. I glance over at him. I'm not expecting anyone.

I open the door and am face to face with someone I don't know. "May I help you?" I'm six feet even and he's at least three inches taller than me.

"Are you Liam Patrick?" he asks me.

"That depends on who you are."

"My name is Dominic. I'm a friend of Vivian's."

"What the fuck do you mean, 'a friend of Vivian's?' I know all of her friends, and I don't know you." I cross my arms over my chest. I suddenly have a bad feeling about this dude.

"May I come in, please?"

I back up, giving him space to enter my place. I regard him with scrutiny when he passes.

"Dad, this is Dominic...uh, I didn't get your last name."

"Luke. Dominic Luke. But I think that your father and I have met," he says and extends his hand out to shake my father's.

"I'm Nelson Patrick. I don't believe we have. I'm sure I would remember a man of your stature," my dad says, his hand still in our visitor's.

"Oh, but I never forget a face. This was about three years ago. I believe it was in Italy." Dominic finally releases my dad's hand.

"Dad, what is he talking about?"

"I have no idea," my father says. But he does not look me in the eye.

"I remember you spent a lot of time in Europe. That had to be about three years ago, because it was my first year in college. What's this guy talking about? How does he know you, Dad?"

My dad goes pale. "The more important question is, how does he know Vivian?

"He is no friend of Vivian's. I would know, Dad. What is this about?"

"May I?" Dominic gestures toward the sofa.

"Why not?" I say. "Dad, you have anything to add?"

"Let's just hear him out," my father says. I note a slight unease in his voice that wasn't there before. Does he really know this guy?

Dominic takes a seat on my sofa, and I wait to hear what he has to say. "Well, like I said, I'm a friend of Vivian's. I worked at the place where she is being held."

I listen.

"She's alive and well. I was asked to leave two days ago. This is the first place that I came, because Vivian asked me to come here and tell you and her family that she's okay."

"She's okay?" My voice cracks.

Thank God. She's okay.

I can no longer contain my emotions. I run as fast as my legs will carry me to my room and slam the door. This is a private moment.

I fall to my knees.

Thank you so much for keeping her safe, I pray to the heavens. For a year I thought the worst, and now I hear that she's alive. I sit on the edge of my bed and let the unmanly tears that I have come to know too well fall, unchecked.

She is alive and well. Thank God. She is alive and well.

Wait a fucking minute. A thought breaks my silent rejoicing. I hop off of my bed, fling my door open, and make my way down the hall to the bearer of this news. I walk straight up to him.

"If she's your friend, Dominic, let me ask you a question. Why the fuck are you out here while she's still locked up wherever the hell she is? Why didn't you bring her home?"

His face falls into his hands. When he looks up I can see that it's etched with worry.

"I tried. Believe me, I tried. When I was removed from The...place—"

I notice he almost says the name of the place. Hmph. What's he hiding?

"—I broke back inside. To get her out. She started to leave with me, but then she changed her mind. You know her, she is amazingly stubborn."

"Are you fucking kidding me? What are you, two hundred pounds? She weighs a hundred fifteen soaking wet. You throw her over your shoulder and you take her the fuck out of there! Where the fuck is she? I'll go get her myself!" I'm pacing. I'm ready to break this asshole's face for leaving my girl in captivity.

He stands, probably feeling the aggression I have toward him.

"I know you're upset. I broke a few things myself after I left her there, but I had no choice. She stayed because of you, and Maddie, and her family."

"What?"

"The man who's keeping her and the others..."

There goes that pause again. Just spit it out already.

"...he threatened to bring harm to those closest to them if they left before their year was up. She will be released in about seven weeks. She won't leave before then. I wanted to drag her out kicking and screaming, but..."

"But what?"

"She's right. He wouldn't stop at making her life miserable if she broke out. He would hurt her through the people she loves. I had to listen to her. She would hate me for bringing that kind of fate upon her loved ones."

Why should he care if she hates him? Her life is with me and her family, not him. He doesn't know her. Then it hits me. The pain in his eyes. "I get it," I sneer at him. "You think you love her." There's no way Vivian fell for this...this...wannabe exotic, rugged super model. She's mine. I'm the love of her life and she's mine.

"I don't think I love her. I know that I love her, and I'll do anything for her because of that love. Including walk out of her life if she so chooses. No one can blame me for falling for her. If it helps, she never tired of speaking of you."

"And when she chooses me?" I ask, because she already has.

"If that happens, then I will respect her wishes," he says.

Hearing that does help. I do feel better. Of course he loves her. She's the most amazing woman in existence.

"Well, you can love her all you want. As long as you understand that she is mine," I threaten.

He nods in agreement. But I know deep down he has no intention of giving her up without a fight. I'm still not satisfied.

"I need proof that you really know her. Right, Dad?" I glance to my father for reassurance. "He could be lying, making this shit up." My dad nods in my direction. He's suddenly very quiet. Hmm.

"Okay. You want proof?" He lets out a deep breath. "Her name is Vivian Travis. She has dark hair, almost black. Her skin is soft and fair. She has the most striking steel-gray eyes that penetrate your soul."

He gazes at my father and me and can see that we're not convinced. A picture could tell him that.

"Her parents are Edward and Lidia Travis. She has a brother named Shane, who's still in high school. Her dog's name is Growl." He lets out a sigh. "And her best friends are Maddie and you. Before she was taken, she was going to spend the weekend with you guys in some secret location. She also told me that she's in love with you. Listen, I'm not some asshole from off the street. I know Vivian. Come on, Mr. Forrest, tell your son."

"What is he talking about, Dad? Why is he calling you Mr. Forrest? Do you know this guy? Don't lie to me."

My dad stands up and faces me, but not before giving Dominic the most deadly look I've ever seen. Dominic doesn't even flinch under his glare.

"Liam, it is a really long story, but, yes, I do know Dominic. We met three years ago. At The Chamber." My dad worries his forehead with his hand. Then he scratches his head. I can tell he doesn't want to have this conversation with me, but I don't give a fuck. Somebody had better tell me something.

"The Chamber?" I ask.

"When I left your mother and you boys, my life spiraled out of control. Women were throwing themselves at me because of my money. I knew that I had made a mistake leaving your mother. I tried to come back, but she wouldn't have it. I met a gentleman who told me about an exclusive club...completely secret. Members are chosen at random. The membership fee for just one year was in the millions." My father stops talking. He turns his back to me.

"Go on," I say through gritted teeth. I'm starting to get the picture.

He turns back and looks me straight in the eye. "I was one of thirty-five men. In Italy, I got to have sex with these young women five days a week for a year. That's how Dominic knows me. No one uses their real names in The Chamber, so during my year there, I was Dev Forrest."

I'm going to lose my fucking mind. My father just confessed to being a sexual deviant.

"So what the fuck did you come here to tell me, Dad? Lies about where Vivian might be when you knew the whole time?" I start pacing again.

"Son, please. Girls go missing all the time. It never crossed my mind in the beginning. I had my suspicions, but only recently. I had no real knowledge that she was at The Chamber until Dominic showed up. I swear it."

I lose it. I can't believe what I'm hearing. This is worse than her being dead. At least if she were dead, she wouldn't be suffering in some sex club, being passed around like something cheap.

My fucking father was a patron. I take my anger out on my furniture.

My table is the first to bite the dust when I put my foot through it. I send my flat screen crashing to the ground.

"Fuck!" I shout.

My wall is the last to feel my wrath as I put several holes in it with my feet and hands.

My father grabs hold of me, and I crumble in his embrace. The tears don't stop.

Her innocence is lost. Will she even be the same when I get her back?

I realize in a flash. "How. Do. You. Know. Vivian?" I ask Dominic.

He sucks in a deep breath. "I was her personal guard. My job was to make sure that she was unharmed," he says.

"Is that all? Is that all? Did you fuck her, too? Did you get a taste of the beautiful virgin?" I'm enraged. "Answer me. Did you fuck her?"

I take a swipe at him, but my father is still restraining me.

"Let go of me!" I yell. "You're no different than him!" I break free of my father. I'm in Dominic's face now. I want blood—his or my fucking father's. "If you didn't fuck her, you watched while other men fucked her." My voice low and menacing. "Get the fuck out of my house. Both of you."

He doesn't flinch. He takes all of my insults and verbal abuse.

"You have every right to be angry. Trust me. But I can't leave yet. There is more that I must share with you and your father. You think you're suffering? You don't know the meaning of the word." He spits the words at me.

I shove him hard with both hands. His body reacts, but not like I want. I want him on the ground so that I can pounce on his ass. He just steps back on one foot.

"You just want to get your grubby paws on her. She's mine. Just leave so I can pack my shit and go get my girl out of there. She doesn't need you, she has me."

I'm losing it, like a crying toddler. "You probably fucked her, too. I was supposed to be her first, not you, not them...me."

I'm disconsolate. I fall to my knees.

My father tries to comfort me. "Son, I'm sorry. Now that we know that she's in The Chamber, we need to discuss this. You have to pull yourself together. Vivian needs you to be strong." He pulls me to my feet.

"You will help me get her out of there. You owe me. You owe Vivian." I spit the words at my father.

The room is thick with my hate-fueled anger. I turn and try to stare a hole through Dominic.

"Why aren't you gone?" I shout at him.

"You're pissed, I get it, but none of that's gonna help Vivian. She is what's important here, not your fucking ego. Now, I talk."

He steps forward. His face is a mask of composure.

"You and your father would be wise not to try and get her, and not to involve the police. Your father knows firsthand that this would be a suicide mission. The most powerful men in the world frequent The Chamber. They move around constantly, and are highly guarded. The protection goes as high up as the federal government. Nothing aside from killing the man who runs it will shut it down. If you don't kill him, you will spend the rest of your life wishing you had. You and your loved ones will never sleep a sound night again. Your best plan is to wait until Vivian is released, and be thankful to God that you have that."

What? Is he fucking insane?

Everything hurts. Images of swarms of strange men fucking my girl are ripping through my heart. Especially when I close my eyes and I see her with Dominic. He won't come clean, but I can just sense that he has tasted her.

This shouldn't be what I'm focused on. I should be happy that the person who landed on my doorstep isn't asking me to go with him somewhere to identify her dead body. The least of my worries should be her virginity. It's just that I've dreamed about her being mine for so many years. I've coveted her virginity and believed that it would be me she shared herself with the first time.

It shouldn't matter, but it does.

I shouldn't care, but I do.

Look at me. I'm no virgin, and what's worse, I fucked her best friend. Why should she be on a pedestal?

Because I put her there.

I turn to my father. Even after learning that he's worse than I thought he was, he has come through for me since Vivian was taken. He has been here for me.

"Dad, what should we do?"

Unless my dad says we go to Canada, storm the castle and bring the rain to get my girl back, I have seven weeks to wrap my head around the fact that the Vivian who comes back to me may not be the same Vivian who was taken from me. I'd better figure out how to be okay with that soon, or Mr. Exotic Super Model Smoldering Eyes is going to be waiting in the cut to steal her away from me.

My head is not in the right space. I need my dad to make sure this is the right choice. If it were up to me, I would go in there in a blaze of glory, but I'm a hothead, and Vivian is too important for me to make any snap decisions.

"We wait, Liam," Dad says. "That's the safest thing to do. We risk her being harmed if something goes wrong in an attempt to extract her. Besides, Mr. Luke already told us she refused to leave with him when he attempted to rescue her."

Mr. Luke, my balls. He's a fucking rapist. I know he fucked her.

"What about her parents? And Maddie? Shouldn't they at least know that she's okay?" I ask.

"I say we wait on Maddie, and her parents, just in case. We will tell them when we know for sure," my dad says. "They've waited this long. Seven more weeks is nothing. Especially if something goes wrong, and she doesn't come home. We wait, son."

"Mr. Patrick, Liam, I'm heading back to Canada. I have contacts on the inside who will alert me if there is a need to extract her sooner. I informed her should that become necessary, all bets are off. If we can exchange information, I'll be able to keep in contact with you. I know she would want that."

"I can do you one better. The Chamber is near Prince Rupert, B.C. right?" my dad asks.

"Yes, Mr. Patrick. Your intel is very good," Dominic says.

"Our family has a spacious cabin very close to the area," Dad says. "I can arrange for you to stay there. I would like to meet with you to discuss The Chamber's future...if you get my meaning. I have a lot to make up for, and I would say that this is a good place to start."

"I do get your meaning, sir. And we are on the same page. It's high time for The Chamber to cease to exist. Thank you for the use of your cabin."

"I'm going, too!" I shout. I don't want this clown to be alone with my girl again. If anything happens, I want to be there when she is extracted.

My father doesn't respond. Instead he is writing something down on the back of a business card. He hands it to Dominic. "My contact info is on the front, and I wrote the address and the name of the cabin's caretaker for you. He'll be expecting you." He shakes his hand.

"Dad. Did you hear me? I said I'm going."

"Liam, that would be a bad idea. You're too emotional. You serve her best by staying right where you are. You'll never forgive yourself if something happens to her."

Even after so much time, my father knows me well. He knows there's no way I could be that close to her and sit and wait, especially knowing what's happening to her. I would try to get her, and if that could in some way bring her to harm, then it isn't worth it.

Seven weeks.

25

CHOICES

*W*hat a fool.

I let Dominic walk out of here without me. My head is killing me from crying all night.

I must be going insane.

Did I make the right choice by believing Mason's promises to release us after a year and to punish us and the ones we love if we tried to escape? Surely I did the right thing for myself, my mom and dad, Shane, Maddie, Liam...and for Dominic.

Seven weeks is nothing.

Dominic surprised me with his tenacity, his tenderness, and his gift of love.

I thought this was a dream, and when I returned home, Dominic would be this amazing guy who was part of the dream that I'd left behind. He was supposed to be a memory to fantasize about because he wasn't real. He was only a special part of the mysterious Chamber.

My life back home and Dominic would have never been connected because I thought that when I left this place he would remain behind with it. But he has shown me, in no uncertain terms, that he is real and he wants me forever.

Is that what I want?

After last night, I just don't know. It's hard to make a comparison, because my relationship with Liam has been based on friendship. We both desired more, but we were too wimpy to act upon it. Dominic and I started out with a sexual relationship and friendship blossomed out of it.

How can I compare the two?

Now I have to go about life in The Chamber knowing that he is not with me. There will be no falling asleep in my Chamber. No secret rendezvous. I will not pass him in the hallways and see the secret smile behind his eyes that is for me and me alone.

Seven weeks.

It's our day off today. Heartache is exhausting. It's almost one o'clock when I finally drag my lifeless body out of bed. I still can't believe Dominic denied me last night. He knew exactly what he was doing. I miss him already. My Chambermates are gone when I wake up.

I make my way into the kitchen, and find it just as quiet as the rest of the place. Where is everyone? I get my answer when I see the note.

Flame,

We decided to have an impromptu pool party. Nothing big. Get your ass in a suit and meet us in the pool area.

The Girls

I don't have the desire to swim and play. Moreover, I don't want to see any of the guards. Especially Carson. I hate him for not being sympathetic to my needs, but mostly I despise him for not being Dominic. I appreciate that they thought of me, but I skip it.

I grab a peach protein shake out of the fridge and guzzle it, not even bothering to taste it. The world seems dimmer somehow. I make it to my bedchamber and fall back into bed.

Maybe I can sleep away the next seven weeks. I don't even bother with the next scheduled meals. Why eat? Today is all I've got. I know tomorrow is another story. Mason won't approve of my sleeping through his Chamber, but today I can.

Today I can sleep and sulk and pout and refuse myself nutrition, all in the name of sadness.

~

I DON'T KNOW what time it is when my covers are wrenched off of me. I know it's nighttime. I shoot up in alarm. It's too bright in here. I squint. "What the hell!" I yell. Who's waking me up in such a manner?

"We are worried about you."

It's Sunshine. I can tell by her Caribbean accent. I squint in her direction and see that she isn't alone. They are all there, standing around my bed.

"We are not going to let you shrivel up and die, Flame," she says. "You're a fighter. We all are. Now get up so we can get some food in you."

The last thing I want is food. I don't get up, because although the words are sweet, none of them know the loss I feel. Worse, I did it to myself. I let him walk away.

"Please go away so I can die in peace." I pull my pillow over my head.

But my sisters are not taking no for an answer. The six of them begin jumping and flopping onto my bed. I can't ignore them, so I relent. I let them pull me by the arms toward the kitchen. Sunshine has one arm and Sapphire has the other.

"Fine. You guys really suck. You know that, right?"

"Yep. All you have to do is eat and we will leave you alone," Sky chimes in.

"I said 'fine.' Is it okay if I hate each and every one of you right now?" I ask, shooting all six of them a dagger stare when they plop me into a chair in the dining room.

"Yes, ma'am...as long as you eat," Sunshine states.

Someone places a bowl of soup in front of me. Everything is still dim. Even my sisters lack their normal colors. My sense of smell is diminished, but I can't miss a faint hint of bacon. My interest piques.

"Did you guys make bacon?"

"Yes, we did," Raven says and places a plate of smoky meat in front of me.

"Sneaky," I say. They know how much I love it. "Sneaky and shameful." Inside I smile.

My body lightens. These ladies really know me. Tears drip onto my plate. It's all too much. Being here, without my family and friends, Dominic's unexpected exit, and the love of my sisters. In a sudden move, twelve arms embrace me.

We are a family.

I sit with my girls and devour my favorite food. I didn't realize how hungry I am until I eat.

I don't touch the soup, just the bacon.

The girls sit with me and talk among themselves. They include me now and again. I can tell they're trying to act like everything is okay and normal.

"We know how much you miss Tyson, but we need you, too," Raven says. "We have seven weeks in this bitch, and we all have to band together and stay strong. Besides, I'm sure he'll be waiting for you on the outside when you get out."

That thought thrills and scares me. I glance down at my plate, trying not to cry. I have cried so much already. They are right. It was my decision to stay, and I have to be strong.

26

END-OF-THE-YEAR PARTY

*W*e are at the homestretch. Time is flying by, and I'm ever grateful.

My world still feels emptier without Dominic. I miss everything about him. He made me feel important from day one in The Chamber. I hope that he is there when I'm released. I want to see his beautiful face and behold his captivating gaze. There is nothing better than being on the opposite end of his hazel eyes peering into your heart.

The last few weeks are business as usual—five days in my Chamber, two days off. Without Mr. Creepy being here it has lost its eerie feeling.

Mason announces that in the tradition of Chambers past, we are inviting all of the lottery winners for an end-of-Chamber party. Violet's groomer told her that every year during the last month, Mason holds an orgy as a send off.

I'm seriously praying that this isn't true.

When Ivy informs us that she heard the same thing, fear shoots through each of us. The audacity of this is off the charts and one more thing to force my subconscious to absorb.

An orgy. A free-for-all. No Dominic.

Mason decides to host the event on a night that all of the lottery winners are in attendance, basically substituting for a night in The Chamber.

There's no lengthy preparation.

We're all shuttled into the same ballroom where the coming out took place in the buff. The room is breathtaking. Mason has it set up like an opulent sex den. Heavy fabrics in deep purple, lavender, pink, gold, and red fill the room and hang from the ceiling as veiled curtains. The floors are lined with huge pillows in the same hues. Gold dust is everywhere. Tables dripping with grapes, cheese, and wine-filled goblets are sprinkled around the entire area. The music compliments the décor, with heavy trancelike tones.

Stunning.

The lottery winners are eagerly awaiting our arrival. I am nervous. Not because of the men, I know them all. Some of them I have grown close to in the last year. How could I not? The setting is what has my stomach in knots. My Chamber offers me a privacy that is absent in this vast space. At any moment, I will be able to look up and see one of my sisters, and they will be able to see me.

The thought is unsettling.

Seven to thirty-five, without Mr. Creepy and including Mason is a terrible ratio. Mason's nude presence lets me know he has every intention of participating. How will this work, with five men to each one of us? That isn't an orgy...that is something else entirely.

My question is answered in the next few minutes. At least twenty naked women fall in line behind us. A few I recognize, and I'm in shock. Most of our female groomers join us, including Zion. She doesn't look the least bit nervous. Her body is amazing. Roxy is in line, and of course, I don't miss Ivory. I've never seen the rest of the women before. There are now twenty-seven of us—much better.

Fear shoots through me as to how the other women were acquired. I don't have long to ponder before Mason makes an announcement. There's a small stage set up, and Mason steps onto the stage in all of his glory, his erection full, long, and pointing up. He is completely at ease with his body. He hasn't reacquainted me with his cock since my first night in The Chamber, but I know some of my sisters have gotten to know that part of his body very well.

"Welcome. Welcome." He looks out at the sea of naked men, then he scans the room to find us all lined up, awaiting further instructions.

Carson, my new personal guard, is by my side. He hands me a piece jewelry—a bracelet? My eyes give away my confusion. He indicates that I'm supposed to wear it around my upper arm. Oh.

It's a beautiful arm cuff—a snake with large, ruby eyes. I wind it onto my upper arm. The girls are all donning them. The beautiful snake, rope, and flowers cuffs all add to the exotic theme.

"As always, I stand before you sad to see this year come to an end. What a wonderful year in The Chamber it has been!" Mason is over-animated.

He gestures for the men to rise. They do as they are told. Thirty-four very naked, very aroused men stand. Mason reaches for a goblet and gestures for the men to follow. They each grab a goblet from a table near them.

"May tonight be memorable and enjoyable. To The Chamber!" he says with excitement, and takes a draw of the liquid.

The men repeat his toast and take swigs from their goblets. Mason gestures for us to enter. We start out in a single file line, but break from the line to find our first sexual partners. I don't actually pick. I just stop at the first random man I come across. I have had sex with all of them. It's Mr. X.

"Flame," He breathes my name.

Mr. X sits back onto a soft purple pillow, his erection pointing at me. I follow him down to the floor and take his erection into my mouth. I start out licking the tip of his cock, swirling my tongue around and around. I know what he likes. I slowly slide my mouth down the length of his cock, and pull my mouth back up with a sucking motion.

When I feel hands upon my rump, I'm caught-off-guard. I don't look back. I'm singular in my attention to Mr. X. I feel my legs being spread apart, and I continue sucking Mr. X's cock. When I feel a tongue on my sex, I'm taken by surprise. Still, I don't look back.

I suck his cock faster, pulling his length deeper into my mouth. The tongue that is between my legs finds my clitoris and begins sucking, the ache between my legs is increasing.

The excitement stirring between my legs becomes evident in how I suck the cock before me. I take it out on Mr. X, and from the moaning and hip thrusts coming from him, he's enjoying every bit of it. My tongue bathes his length, then I drive him into my mouth and suck without rest until he spills into my mouth. I feel him pull me toward him, causing the person who's pleasuring me to stop. I was so close.

Mr. X pulls me onto his length and I slam him deep inside of me. He brings our third party around in front of me and I see that it was Zion tasting me. What? In an unexpected move, she sits on his face.

The sheer sensory overload turns me on.

His cock is buried inside of me. Zion is grinding her pussy onto his face.

She gazes at me through hooded lids. Her dark auburn hair falls in messy curls around her shoulders. She is so fucking sexy. I don't back away when her lips touch mine. I've never kissed a woman before. Her tongue dances tenderly with mine. She reaches out and touches my breasts, pinching my nipples. Never taking her mouth away from mine, I answer back, my tongue rough in her mouth.

Zion's fingers finds my clitoris and she starts rubbing it with quick movements.

"Fuck, that feels so...fuck."

He eats her pussy and I'm so turned on. She grinds on his face, faster. She mewls and groans, her sex sounds are undoing me. That, and the swell of the cock inside of me cause my breathing and heart rate to climb and climb. I squeeze my pussy around his cock, and I bounce and buck.

My skin flushes and my muscles contract as waves crash into me. I'm falling and tumbling.

"Fuck. This is... Yes!" I shout before I shatter into a million pieces in overwhelmed pleasure. In the seconds that follow, Mr. X fills me with his essence in a series of shudders and growls.

In perhaps the sexiest thing I have ever experienced, Zion comes in front of me. She kisses me and moans into my mouth. Well, damn.

Not bad for my first experience with a chick. I learn quickly that tonight it will not be my last. My next experience with a female comes when Mason has his turn with me.

"My dear Flame. I'm delighted to get to sink my dick back inside of you again."

I don't speak, because I have nothing to say to that. He's up on his knees and he brings me down to mine. He guides my mouth toward his erection. I take him into my mouth.

"I really was sad to have to dismiss Tyson. I know how in love the two of you are, but I had no choice. He is blind when it comes to you. Ahh. You are very talented," he says, complimenting me on my technique.

I move my mouth up and down his length, taking in nearly its entirety. I feel it hit the back of my throat.

"We have company," he says.

I look up and see Sapphire standing in front of us. She bends down and pulls his cock from my mouth and draws it into hers. I don't know what to do with myself. I've never been in this situation. I watch her skillfully lick and suck Mason's cock, and then, surprising myself, I steal it back from her and wrap my lips around it and begin to suck him. Mason is enjoying us fighting over his most cherished body part. He rubs our heads and brings them closer to each other. He wants us to pleasure him at the same time.

We do. We share his cock.

While I work the tip with my tongue, Sapphire licks and sucks his shaft. Then we switch. When Mason has had enough, he aggressively tosses me onto a huge, blood orange pillow. He pulls me back so that I'm on all fours with my back arched and my rump in the air. Mason slams his entire length inside of me. Sapphire appears in front of me. She kisses me, while Mason fucks me blind, in the way only he can. He fucks with a combination of never-ending speed and powerful thrusts. In and out, faster and harder, he sinks his cock inside of me. I explode around him. The insides of my sex contract aggressively.

Sapphire is next. Their encounter is more intimate. She sinks down onto his cock. I watch her grind on him, but he pulls her to his chest and takes her into a passionate kiss. They are not fucking. They are making love. I feel embarrassed even watching.

I step around them and wander through the party, watching the orgy unfold. In one corner, I see a woman lying on her back with three people kissing and fondling her, all the while her sex being pounded by one of the lottery winners. In another area, Ivy's pussy is in Ivory's mouth, while one of the lottery winners' cock is down her throat. So much sex, I can smell it in the air.

It makes me miss Dominic even more. I wish he were here. I miss his Thunderdick. The thought of having to share him makes me reconsider.

In another area, I see one of the pleasure horses has been brought out, and one of the lottery winners is pulling random women to plea-sure themselves while he watches. My girl Sunshine is on the horse right now, working it. Just when I think everyone is in their own little world, completely unaware of my silent observations, someone takes me by the hand. I'm led by another lottery winner to a very private area. This area is draped by jewel-toned blue netting that gives it an exclusivity. I remember this winner. He was always romantic and tender. He had a kinky side, but even when I was tied up, he was gentle with me.

"I think I'm going to miss you most of all, Flame."

I sit on one of the pillows across from him. He hands me a goblet and I take a drink. Warm, delicious liquid slides down my throat. A sweet wine?

"In another world, I would have liked to really get to know you. You're the kind of woman that I would like by my side in life," he says.

I'm confused. "But I have sex with guys in a sex Chamber." Why would he want me by his side?

"Not by choice. I know that you were forced into this. You all were.

I bet you're a college student or something. You probably have a nice boyfriend back home and a bright future ahead of you."

I nod. "I was a virgin before I came here," I tell him.

"If you were mine this would have never happened to you. Perhaps we can keep in touch when you are released? I would like us to get to know each other better."

No thanks, buddy. Why would I choose a man who frequents a place like this? Dominic worked here, but I am the first and only girl he has ever slept with inside of this place. He also told me how dark his life was when he came here. Now that he's found the light, even he knows this place is wrong.

"That might be nice. A girl can never have too many friends," I lie.

I have no intention of getting to know him. At least not the way he means. I really want him to just get on with fucking me so that I can get this evening over with.

After too much talking, Mr. Romance finally gives me what I want. He sinks his cock inside of me over and over until he comes apart at the seams, releasing me from his private room, and wandering off to find his next conquest.

By the end of the night, I'm exhausted. I have been fucked and sucked enough to last a lifetime. All in all, our celebration is a success. When my sisters and I make it to our bedchambers, we are spent.

I collapse into my bed and drift off into la-la land.

27

HOMEWARD BOUND

*T*onight is my final night. I survived The Chamber.

My fellow Chambermaids and our groomers decide to have a special dinner. We whip up a delicious meal of herb-crusted chicken, warm spinach and pecan salad, wild rice, and apple pie.

"Dinner is served," Sky announces, and everyone gathers in the kitchen.

"We set everything up buffet style, so dig in," Violet says.

There's not enough room in the kitchen, so some of us grab our plates and file into the family room. I call it that now because we really are a family. I always wanted a sister, and now I have six.

"Can you believe we get to go home tomorrow?" I ask the girls.

"I am too excited. My stomach hurts," Sunshine says.

"What if tomorrow comes and we find out that Mason lied? What if we don't get to go home?" Raven says what we are all dreading aloud.

"I say we cross that bridge when we get to it. Today, let's celebrate," Sky says.

"I think he'll follow through with his promise, but is it crazy that I want to stay?" Sapphire says.

We wrap her in an embrace. She has fallen for Mason, hard. Damn.

"I'll be okay. I was foolish to believe that there was more between us," Sapphire says. She sighs and brushes her wet eyes with her hand. "I don't want to ruin our celebration. Come on, it's a party," she says.

And celebrate we do. We feast and drink and dance. I'm in the middle of busting some serious moves when Zion pulls me aside. She leads me by the hand down the hall.

"I just want to tell you that I'm really going to miss you. In case I don't get to see you tomorrow, here's my information."

I take the envelope and immediately recognize its familiar lavender hue. "It was you," I say in hushed tones. She was Dominic's ally.

"Of course it was. I had the closest access to you. Besides, I know real love when I see it." Zion takes my hand and squeezes it. "Tonight is my last night here, too. Maybe the three of us can meet up for dinner sometime. That is, if you want to." Zion gazes at me, unsure of what I might say.

"Seriously? I'm so happy for you, Zion. Absolutely. You know you're my girl." We hug.

"My real name is Hailey." She makes a point to whisper in my ear. "You know, Vivian, Dominic is head over heels in love with you. I want you to remember that when you're on the outside," she releases me from her grasp.

I nod my head vigorously at her. It's amazing how much I love hearing my real name. Before my year here, before losing my name, I always thought it was old-fashioned. My friends had names like Miley and Brooke, and I got the old lady name. I love my name now. It means I get my life back.

Zion and I return to the family room to find Mason joining in on the fun. I scoop up my plate and find a spot on the couch. I smile at Mason and he smiles back.

"Ladies, please take a flute of champagne. I have wonderful news," Mason says.

We do as we are told, each of us grabbing champagne that's being passed around on several silver platters. The other girls who were in the kitchen have gathered. I gaze around at the six other amazing young women. All are beautiful, strong survivors.

"As you know, tonight is your last night in The Chamber. As promised, you will all be delivered home first thing in the morning, just about a week shy of your year. Transportation will be waiting at the airport to drive you to your individual homes. Each of you will receive an envelope with further details and bank account information. I hope that your new bank balances are hefty enough to show my gratitude for your service and also enough to buy your silence. Before you accept these envelopes, the guards will pass around a document called an NDA, or nondisclosure agreement. After signing it, you are legally bound to never speak of the details of your stay here to anyone."

"Also, you will be blindfolded until you're safely in the air. This is a formality that I cannot forgo. Anonymity is the only way to keep this place going." He raises his glass. We all raise ours. "You ladies were amazing. To The Chamber."

We all repeat the words and drink.

When the evening winds down, each one of us is eager to sleep so we can return home. The seven of us sit together in the family room like we have done so many nights. This time we hang on to one another and cry tears of sadness, relief, and joy.

We exchange names, addresses, and phone numbers and vow to keep in touch, though I know most of us will want to keep any thought of this place behind us. That may include any people who remind us of it. I'm not sure how I feel about that.

Sky, Sapphire, and I give our final hugs to the other girls and make our way back to our room. There are large manila envelopes on each of our beds. I am the first to rip mine open.

"Oh, my goodness! Oh, my goodness!" I squeal.

"What is it?"

Sky and Sapphire are at my side at once. The three of us stare at the bank statement with the four-million-dollar balance. Knowing you might get an unknown sum of money and seeing the actual amount, in your name, are entirely different animals. There's a note attached that simply says, Thank you.

Sky and Sapphire run to their beds, tear their envelopes open and squeal in unison. The three of us jump up and down in excitement. Somehow, knowing that we are returning home significantly wealthier makes the future feel brighter.

I WAKE EXTRA EARLY. I'm ready to make the move. I've said my goodbyes.

I'm ready to go home.

There's nothing for me to pack. After all, I was brought here in only pajamas. Zion honored my request, leaving a pair of blue jeans and a white tank top out for my trip home.

No more red. One more thing to shed.

Carson, the guard who took Tyson's place, leads me toward the hallway. I glance back one last time at what was my life and home for the past year. All is quiet, and there's not another soul in sight. My roommates were gone before I woke. Carson ushers me into an elevator.

"Sorry, Flame. I gotta put this over your head," he says.

He and I have come a long way from the first night when he entered my Chamber. His treatment of me is significantly more respectful.

I nod as the hood covers my head, leaving me sightless. It smells fresh. I don't care. I get to go home. He could put me in an entire body sack and I wouldn't be fazed as long as my sack-covered body ends up in zip code 89135.

On faith, I follow him as he leads me. I know the exact moment we are no longer in the great walls of The Chamber because it feels like heaven when the fresh air caresses my skin.

It's chilly and delicious and foreign.

I imagine all the steps that I traversed a year ago will happen in reverse., so I'm not surprised by the car ride, followed by the plane.

My emotions are also reversed. On the way here a year ago, I was petrified and willing to die rather than be a tortured prisoner. On my return trip home, I'm optimistic about what my future holds—a future that a year ago I believed was over.

On the private jet, the hood is removed. The windows are covered, ensuring that I have no idea where I have been over the last year. The only details I have are that the ocean was near and the building was castle-esque. What city, state, or country I was in will forever be a mystery.

In a way, Mason made separating myself from this experience easier. With no idea where I was, and no one using their real names, including myself, and no knowledge of what was going on in the world, it kind of makes the whole year seem made up, like a dream. Except, I know it wasn't.

What about the future of The Chamber? Are poor girls being taken from their homes and lives, as I'm returning to mine? What obligation do I have to stop this from happening to anyone else? Where would I even start?

Now I add to that. What do I tell my family? Will my parents believe me? Will they accept the limited information that I can give them? What about Liam and Dominic? When I came to The Chamber, Liam's face was all I saw. He was my strength, and all I wanted to do was return to his waiting arms. I prayed that he would still want me, but after all that has happened, will I still want him?

When the plane touches down after several long and solitary hours, I am wrought with nerves. Somehow, I never anticipated going home being so hard. It's April again in Vegas. It must be some kind of weird joke on Mason's part, sending us home on April Fools' Day. My birthday is nine days away—talk about coming full circle. I'm more than grown up now. I'm aged by experience, not by choice.

I rush down the private jet's steps. The wind catches my hair, gloriously blowing it each and every way. The sun kisses my face. Tears blaze a trail down my cheeks. I'm overcome by this new freedom.

A limo, not a taxi is parked on the tarmac. The driver stands with the door open for me to enter. I don't hesitate. I practically run and throw myself inside.

"First time in Vegas, miss?" the driver asks me.

"Feels like it, but no. Vegas is my home." I can't fight the smile spreading across my face.

We're silent the rest of the ride, which scares me, because I don't want to be left alone with my thoughts. How will I look to my family? The same? Will they know I've changed? Will they care?

My heart wants to leap out of my chest when the limo comes to a stop in front of my house. I'm as nervous as I was during some of my uncertain times in The Chamber.

This is my home. I'm free. The people inside of this house love me unconditionally.

"Your destination, miss," the driver says.

"Yes, thank you. I wish I had cash for a tip. I'm sorry."

"That has been taken care of, miss." He opens his door, preparing to assist me with mine.

"Are you also from Vegas?" I ask him. I don't know why.

He halts his exit from the limo. "No, miss, I'm from California. Is everything okay?" He makes concerned eye contact with me in his rearview mirror.

"Sure."

I quickly avoid his eye contact. I know I can't stay inside this limo anymore, but I can't go inside either. My heart beats like a drum in my chest. I sit in the limo, the air thick, the only sounds are air flowing into and out of my lungs.

Armed only with the black satchel that holds my bank account information, I steel myself.

"Okay. I'm ready."

The driver is at my door at once.

"Thank you," I offer him when I step out.

He doesn't wait for me to walk to the door. He drives away the second his butt hits the seat, leaving me at the curb. I can't say that I blame him.

My legs feel like shaky twigs. If I take another step I'm sure to fall.

So, I stand there, panicking and staring at my house in disbelief. Am I really here? It takes all of the strength I can muster to move forward. I pull my shoulders back, lift my head and walk up the path to my front door.

I ring the bell.

It seems like an hour passes by while I wait for someone to answer. I worry my fingers. Come on.

Shane opens the door and just stands there, staring at me as if I were an apparition. "Mom! Dad!" yells out in shock. I pour myself into his arms. My baby brother towers over me now.

"My God, Shane. What's all the commotion?" I hear my mother approaching. "Lord, Jesus! Eddie! Eddie!" My mom screams at the top of her lungs for my father.

Tears pour down my mother's face as she grabs hold of me and Shane. We fall to our knees, in a sobbing heap.

"Thank you for bringing my baby home!" she cries to the sky.

The last to join in on the reunion is my dad. We finally break our embrace, the three of us wiping tears, and I see my father standing in the hallway.

"Daddy!" I scream and run into his arms. I have never heard my father cry before. I become overwhelmed by the sounds of his heavy sobs. I join him. He suddenly pulls me away from his embrace.

"Let me get a look at you, kid." He examines me. "Are you injured? Were you harmed?" He's serious in his tone and inspection, angry.

"No, Daddy. I'm fine," a sob rips through me.

"Come sit, baby. You must be exhausted. Lidia, get Vivie some water," he says.

My mother leaves and comes back with a glass of water for me. She and Shane sit across from me and my dad on the couch. I take a sip of the cool liquid.

Let the inquisition begin.

"Darling, where have you been?" my mother asks.

Fair question.

I gaze at the faces of my family and realize that telling them where I've been will be harder than anything I have experienced over the past year. Suddenly, I miss my sisters. I send a silent prayer to each of them, that reuniting with their families is an easy task.

I sit up straight and begin to tell them as much as I'm allowed to say. "Umm...the night I was...taken, I thought it was Liam and Maddie. You know, with the birthday surprise and all. I thought they were coming to pretend-kidnap me. It seemed like something they would do." Tears escape my eyes. "Daddy, if I'd known for one minute I was really being kidnapped, I would have screamed this house down, so you could have stopped them. I would have kicked and scratched and bit. But I didn't know!"

My dad wraps his arms around me and strokes my back as I bawl like a baby. When I regain my composure, I sit back up and continue. "They put a hood over my head, and by the time I realized that something wasn't right, it was too late. I was already in the van. So I decided not to cooperate, so they would just kill me and get it over with."

My mom cries out. She holds on to Shane.

"Sorry, Mom. I didn't know what else to do." My poor mom. "They used some kind of chemical to knock me out, and when I woke up I was on a plane. I don't even know if I was in the United States. Today is the first day that I have seen the outside since I've been gone."

"Why did they let you go?" my dad asks.

"If I agreed to follow the rules, they promised that I would only have to stay one year. I never planned to agree to any terms, until they gave me no choice."

"What do you mean, honey?" My mom puts her hand to her mouth.

"They had pictures of all of us. They threatened to hurt you guys. So I stayed and I did what they wanted. Now I am free."

"I'm calling the cops!" My dad jumps up.

"No, Dad. You can't." I follow behind him. "These people are very powerful. This goes high up, and if they find out I said anything, we will spend the rest of our lives looking over our shoulders. Besides, I don't know the captor's real name. I'm safe, I'm home. Please, can't that be enough?"

"Vivie, I don't know about this." My dad stands, trying to decide.

I pull him to sit back down with me. "There's one more thing. They paid me four million dollars for the year that they kept me."

"Why? What did they have you doing?" my mom asks. I can hear the alarm in her voice.

"I'm home safe. Does it matter, Mom?"

"Oh, Edward, our baby. Our baby!" She cries again. I believe she has an idea of what I was asked to do now.

"The cops are gonna want to sit down with you. Once we call them and tell them you are home," my dad reminds me. "What are you gonna say?" he asks.

"I will cross that bridge when I get to it. I need to call Liam and Maddie."

SOMEONE MUST HAVE FORGOTTEN to lock the door, because ten minutes later, I hear Maddie screaming inside my house.

"Where is she?"

She finds me sitting on the couch and tackles me, squealing the whole time.

"I thought you were dead!" She squeezes me again.

Before I know it, Maddie is firing off question after question. I don't get the chance to answer her. I feel the energy shift in the room and my eyes dart toward the entrance. I see Liam. Tears flood my face and I run and fold myself into his arms. I missed him so much. He squeezes me and I fear he'll never let me go.

"Vivian," is all he says. It's a whisper, a prayer.

He kisses my forehead. In my dreams, this went so differently. In my dreams, we couldn't keep our hands to ourselves. In my dreams, there was no Dominic. For a second, I feel guilty.

We all take a seat in my family room.

"So, Vivian, where were you? I want details," Maddie asks, like I was on a date that I didn't tell her about, and not imprisoned and forced into sex slavery. "I mean, a year... Where were you for an entire year?"

I recount a similar story to the one I told my family earlier. I leave out the parts that might send Mason's wrath our way. Fortunately for me, I have no true knowledge of my whereabouts or who took me. I can feel the anger surge through Liam, who is seated to my right.

"We have to involve the police, Vivian," Maddie says. "This is insane. Someone kidnapped you from your bed! What if they come back for you again?"

She asks the question I fear the answer to, but can't voice. If I'm being honest with myself, I know that the thought will probably haunt me for quite some time.

"Maddie, please." I turn my attention to her. "What are we going to tell them? I don't know who took me. I don't know where I was. I don't know how I got there. It's no use. Plus, if I say anything, he might come back for me. I can't risk it!"

"I think Maddie is right, Viv," Liam says from my other side.

One look at my father tells me that he's fighting every instinct not to pick up the phone and make the call. I start to panic. I can't fathom Mason's wrath. I know that he won't stop at anything to make me pay if the police get involved.

I jump up from the couch with alarm bells sounding in my head. "You...you can't! I'll leave. I will walk out this door right now, and I will disappear."

The room is getting so small around me, everything is closing in. I can't breathe. Why are they all standing up and shouting at me?

I can't hear their words. I only see their moving mouths. But I can tell from their strained neck muscles that they are not whispering. Blackness is crowding my sight. The last thing I see is the floor coming up to greet my face.

"Vivian!" I hear my mother. I can tell that she is worried from the shrill tone of her voice. "Honey?"

I open my eyes to my family and friends around me. My head is cradled in my father's arms.

"What happened?" I ask.

"You fainted, baby," my father says.

I start to sit up. Four pairs of hands try to pin me down. "I'm okay," I say. The family room is spinning. "I'm okay. I promise."

My brother comes rushing back with a glass and hands it to me. I take a long draw from it. Mmm. The iced water feels cool going down.

"Listen, we're not gonna involve the cops right now, aside from letting them know that Vivian is home. The most important thing is Vivian. Understand?" My father makes eye contact with everyone.

I rest my back against the couch. Thank you.

Everyone in the room nods.

We sit in silence for an unknown amount of time. I gulp down the iced water while my family and friends stare at me like I've grown a second head.

"I need some fresh air." I stand up.

The room doesn't rotate, but my head feels light. Everyone stands with me.

"I'm fine...I just need a minute." I take cautious steps toward the front door, checking my balance and for signs of another syncopal episode. My legs feel sturdy underneath me.

The front door sounds heavy when I close it behind me. The cool April winds caress my skin, and I feel better immediately. I find comfort in my favorite porch swing.

My reunion with my family is every bit as difficult as I thought it would be. What would I do if my own daughter went missing for a year? I'd want to call the police, too. I'd want the bastards who took her to pay.

Rocking back and forth soothes me. I miss Dominic so much.

It has been too long since I've laid eyes on him. Was he even real? I cry for him. Relief for being home washes over me. Anxiety of what my future holds consumes me. Fear that I might not ever see Dominic again grips me. I think that's the scariest thought of all.

"Can I join you?"

I look up to see Liam's vivid blue eyes staring at me, full of hope. His hands are stuffed in his pockets. He is uncharacteristically unsure of himself. There's a lot of that going around.

I wipe my face. "Sure." I pat the seat beside me. He takes a spot, and we sit in companionable silence, regarding one another.

"Your family wanted me to check on you. I told them I would."

"I just needed a minute. I've been waiting so long to be home, and I'm overwhelmed."

"I'm sure they know that," he says.

We continue to swing in silence, avoiding the elephant that has invaded our space.

"Can I ask you a question?" he asks.

"Sure, anything."

"I had an unexpected visitor a while back."

"Oh, yeah?" I ask.

"Who is Dominic Luke?" His blue eyes hold mine.

"He's a friend." Not a lie. Dominic went to Liam's house after he left, but not my house?

"When he came to my place to tell me you were alive, he seemed to imply that you were...more than friends." His eyes never leave mine.

"It's a complicated story, Liam. He helped me in there when I had no one else." I don't break eye contact with him.

"Do you love him? Because he stood in my living room and told me he loved you."

I can hear his breathing pick up. I try not to react, but Liam knows me like I know myself. Before I was taken, I might have said better than I know myself.

"Why would you ask me that?"

"Because I need to know." Liam halts our motion. "I never stopped searching for you...you were on my mind constantly. This guy...his presence scares me, Viv. I don't want to lose you before you were ever really mine."

I fold in on myself, attempting to make myself as small as possible. I don't want to go here with Liam. A year ago, he and I were ready to profess our love for one another. A year ago, we were prepared to ride off into the sunset as a couple—that was exactly what I wanted then. Now, things are complicated. My love for Liam is still there. I feel the pull and connection, and he is still just as heroic and gorgeous as always.

He has waited for me, searched for me, and fought for me the whole time I was gone, and I know that I owe him an explanation. I take in a long draw of air, and blow it out slowly.

"When I was taken, I wanted to die. I could only see your face. I hated myself for not telling you how I felt. How each night I stayed at your house...I wanted to not sleep, but be yours. You were all I ever needed, all I ever wanted. I felt stupid for being so weak that I didn't tell you how much I loved you."

Liam attempts to interrupt me, but I don't let him. I put my hand to his lips and he kisses my fingertips. A trail of tingles travels down my fingers and my arm. Hmm.

"When you don't know if you are going to live or die, you start to evaluate your life and catalog your regrets. You were my mine, Liam."

He takes my hand. "I don't have to be. I'm right here."

I smile. He's right. He doesn't have to be a regret. I can make a decision right now to let him love me and pick up where we left off. It would be easy, if not for my feelings for Dominic.

"I was so scared in there. I don't know. Dominic was this beacon of light. He rescued me. I guess after spending nearly a year with him, under such dire circumstances, I guess I do love him," I say. I owe him my honesty. I add the word guess to soften the blow, because there is no guessing where my feelings for Dominic are concerned. I love him.

Liam brings my hands up to his lips and kisses them.

"Vivian, I died a thousand deaths when you went missing. I hated myself for being too much of a wuss not to tell you that I loved you. Like a fool, I thought we had forever. Then when I finally get up the courage, you are gone. I never thought I would see you again." In a surprising move, Liam pulls me onto his lap.

"I know what you were asked to do in there, and that doesn't change a fucking thing. I love you so much that it hurts to breathe."

His last words are a whisper, his lips to mine. Urgent, hungry. Tears flow steadily down my cheeks as I give in to what I've wanted for as long as I can remember. To be here in his arms, just like this. This kiss—our first—is tender and animal, lustful and adoring. In a word, it's desperate. My fingers pull greedily through his hair. His hands squeeze my waist. I pant with desire. Could this be home in Liam's arms?

Images of Dominic pop into my head—him smiling down at me, he and I wrapped in each other's arms in my Chamber. I break contact with Liam and slide from his lap.

"What is it? What's wrong?" Liam asks, wiping his lips.

"Nothing. I think I'd better go inside. I'm exhausted. I need to rest."

Liam stands up. "Please don't tell me this is about him. He was your guard in a sex club. He doesn't love you. I do! He watched you fuck other guys!"

"Shhh!" I rush to his side. "My parents don't know anything, Liam! My lord. I know you're frustrated with me after all this time, but Dominic is a part of my life, too! You weren't there…"

He is pissing me off. I know him to be temperamental, but never toward me.

"You don't know how I suffered. This isn't just about you and your wounded heart and how badly you missed me. I fucking suffered. I am forever changed by that. What I need from you is time and understanding." I storm toward my front door.

I can't deal with any more of this reunion shit. I tell Maddie that I will see her tomorrow. She smothers me overdramatically with hugs and kisses. My mom promises to bring me warm tea later. I hug my mom and dad and Shane, and make way down the hall to my room with Growl by my side.

Liam's outburst surprised me. He should be glad I didn't come back with, "He didn't just watch." I had to fight everything in me to not throw that little nugget of truth back at him.

I'm still trying to wrap my head around the fact that I was in Liam's arms and I walked away. Are my feelings for Dominic that strong? Can I let Liam go after all this time?

My life feels so off-kilter.

In The Chamber, my mind was wrapped around a finite time—one year. I could circle a date on a calendar, but my life now is...infinite, filled with nothing but possibilities. Will I choose to be with Liam? Will I be able to go back to school? Will Dominic come back to me? Can I pretend this last year did not exist? The mindless chatter in my brain is going to make me crazy.

My mother knocks and enters my room with tea and ibuprofen.

"Thanks, Mom," I say as I sit up on my bed. She takes a seat on the edge.

"Honey, not one of us knows what you went through in that God-awful place."

I can tell she is trying to be brave for me. Maybe this is where I get my so-called strength.

"I just want you to know that I love you...and if you ever want to talk...I'm always here for you." Her voice breaks on the last word.

I set my tea on my bedside table and my mother and I hold each other. Her tears dampen my shirt.

28

FOUR LITTLE WORDS

I drift off to sleep with the uneasy feeling that something is missing. Dominic. I'm free. He's free. But he's not here and my homecoming doesn't seem real without him.

I don't know how long I am out, but a knock at my door is an answered prayer. "Come in." I sit up in my bed.

My dad pokes his head in. "Honey, sorry to wake you, but you have a visitor. He says his name is Dominic."

I fling the covers off, spring out of bed, and nearly knock my father down when I burst through my door.

"Okay, guess I should have invited him in," my father yells after me.

I pull the door open in haste, and for the first time since my release...I breathe.

I don't know what role Dominic will play in my life. The bottom line is, I want him there.

"Hi," I say around the lump in my throat. My heart stutters before picking up its natural rhythm.

"Hi," he says.

"Hi," I say again. I can feel my father's presence behind me. "Come in."

Dominic crosses my threshold. I look up to the heavens in thanks. He's here.

"Who is our visitor?" my dad asks.

I turn to my father. His eyebrows raise when he gazes at me. Probably because of the huge grin on my face, and the fact that I'm probably blushing a deep red.

"Dad, this is my friend, Dominic. This is my dad, Mr. Travis."

"Eddie will do just fine," my father says, shaking Dominic's hand.

I can see confusion cloud my father's face as he glances between us. We make our way to the sofa. We sit. All of us. On the same sofa.

"Dad, can we have a minute?"

"Sure." He stands. "Nice to meet you, Dominic."

My dad offers his hand again. Dominic takes it, and he leaves. I watch him walk out of the room and wait for the sound of his door closing, and I curl into Dominic's arms. He crushes me into his chest.

"I was so worried."

"About what?" he asks me.

"I thought you weren't coming." I tear up.

"Baby, I'm here. I was never far away. You and your family deserved a proper reunion."

I wipe the moisture from my cheeks. "Always thinking about me." I smile through my tears.

"And only you."

This is the moment I was waiting for. His presence makes everything feel complete. Even though Dominic wasn't a part of my life before I was taken, he belongs in my life now. He pulls me so close to him on the sofa that there is no space between us.

"How are you?" he asks.

"I'm okay...reunions are exhausting."

He gives me a small, reassuring squeeze. I lean into his embrace. Is this home?

"We need to talk," he says.

Immediately my heart sinks into my stomach. My breaths, calm only a few seconds ago, become frantic from his utterance of four little words. We. Need. To. Talk. No good conversation ever starts off with those words.

He's leaving me. He told me inside The Chamber that he wanted me any way he can get me. He made me believe that he wanted to be in my life. We. Need. To. Talk. I think I'm gonna faint again.

"Okay." My voice is weak.

"You want to get some fresh air? Take a walk?" he asks.

"Sure. Let me go tell my mom and dad." Even though I sound like a child, after the ordeal we all suffered this last year, I think it is best to let them know my whereabouts.

Dominic nods, because I'm sure he agrees.

On shaky legs, I make my way to my parents' room.

DOMINIC STANDS when I enter the family room.

We. Need. To. Talk. I'm dreading every word that will come out of his mouth next.

"My dad was not in love with the idea of me leaving the house. He made me bring these." I hold up my cell phone and pepper spray. "The pepper spray is for you." I giggle. "He also wouldn't let me leave without your first and last name. I'm fifteen all over again."

Dominic walks toward me. When he reaches me, he takes my hand in his. My fingers tingle at the contact. "If I was your father I wouldn't want to let you leave my sight, either."

We make our way out my front door. I decide to head toward the neighborhood park. It's close to my house. The sun is setting, and the sky is dusky with pink and purple. I will never tire of it. We walk in silence, hand in hand. This is natural. I wasn't sure how Dominic and I would feel outside of The Chamber.

"So...you wanted to talk about something?" I ask.

"I do."

Okay, spit it out already. "You're leaving me? You came to say goodbye."

He spins me around to face him. "What are you talking about?"

"You said we need to talk! Everyone knows that's code for "this is over" or "I need space." I can't say goodbye to you Dominic and I won't!" I snatch my hand away from his and I run.

If I never hear him say the words, then they don't exist.

The park is in my sight. I don't know if he is behind me. All I hear is the wind whooshing in my ears. I almost make it to the picnic tables. I have no idea what running from him will accomplish. All I know is that I don't want to hear him tell me goodbye.

"Vivian!"

He's right behind me. His words were bound to catch up to me. I don't turn around. I can't face him. "I'm not going anywhere. I told you what I want...how I feel. That's not what I wanted to talk about." His voice is soft, careful.

I turn to face him. "You're not?" Relief floods me.

"No, I'm not going anywhere." He reclaims my hand and we take a seat at one of the picnic tables. "You really thought I was here to say goodbye to you?"

I nod.

"Never." His hand raises my chin and turns my face to his.

He is beautiful.

"I counted every minute until I would see you again. Letting you remain behind was the hardest thing I have ever done in my life, but you are the bravest, strongest person that I know."

This makes me roll my eyes at him. "I don't know why everyone thinks I'm so strong. It was fear that made me stay."

"Only a strong person can make a decision based on logic in the face of fear," he says.

The familiar current running between us is delicious, but a thought crosses my mind. "Why didn't you tell my family that I was safe?"

"When I left you behind, I did as you requested. I sought out Liam first. His father was there. Vivian, this is what I came to tell you. They were on their way to break you out. At the time, we all felt your family would be better off waiting until you showed up here today rather than letting them getting their hopes up. Just in case."

"You didn't think I was coming home?" My eyes open wide.

"Of course not. If I believed that for one minute, I would never have left you inside."

I nod. I'm relieved. I don't care what his reasons for not telling them. I trust him where I am concerned. He has proven himself to me.

"What I wanted to tell you is Liam's father has some very powerful associates and friends, Vivian. Because I never want to lie to you, I have to tell you that I recognized Liam's father."

"What do you mean you recognized him?" I stare at him in confusion.

"He participated in The Chamber three years ago in Italy."

"What?" I'm going to be sick to my stomach. "Does Liam know this?"

"He does now."

"Dominic, I can't believe this." Tears sting my eyes.

"He was meeting with Liam to give him the location of The Chamber," Dominic continues. "I don't think he planned on telling him about his real knowledge of The Chamber, but he also wasn't expecting me to show up, either. Liam was pretty pissed, but his dad managed to bring the focus back to you. They were hell-bent on getting you out. I managed to change their minds because I told them how stubborn you were when I tried to take you from there and how upset you would be at them, but now that you are free..." . He looks into my eyes.

I realize what he's getting at...what we need to talk about. I stand up. "Oh, no! You are not going back there. You can't!"

Dominic is on his feet. "Vivian, please sit. Let me explain."

I don't sit. I pace. Is he insane? "When? When are you going back? Are you staying and working for him again?"

"What? No. Please sit and let me explain."

I take a seat at the table, but I can't be still. My knees bounce with worry. I keep my face buried in my hands. "Talk."

"I'm not sure when I'm going back. By now, the original information that Liam's father had is old. Mason usually moves the second he releases the girls. I'm not going back to work for him. Liam's father is giving me the necessary intel to help me bring down The Chamber. I'm going back to end it and bring Mason to justice."

I turn to face him. "Alone? This is insane. Why you? We just got out."

He grips my face in his hands. "You said something to me the night I left you there. You asked me if the other girls who were taken were less important than you. That stuck with me for weeks. Liam's father created an opportunity for me to make up for my sins and also to make sure no woman suffers at the hands of Mason again. I have to make this right!"

Oh, my God. I feel sick. I pull his hands off of me and walk away, I need space.

"This isn't right, Dominic. Mason took advantage of you. You weren't well when he found you. You said so yourself. You had been in the dark since your mother's murder. First, the government took advantage of you, then Mason. He knew that he could exploit your weakness."

"It still doesn't make it right. It wouldn't be fair for me to ride off into the sunset with the girl and the happy ending, knowing other girls are being taken from their loved ones. Don't you see? It's because of you that I can finally do the right thing. You brought the light with you, and now I know what I must do." He stares at me across the space I've created.

I throw my hands up in defeat. "Dominic, you are good. You never once touched a single girl inside. You are a good person."

I can't lose him.

"Okay, Vivian, you're sort of right, but I still can't let The Chamber continue. It won't be easy. Mason is crafty. He hides very well. He never selects the same location twice. It may take a while to find him. Liam's father and I are assembling a team."

I walk to the table, climb the bench, and sit on top. He joins me and sits so close, we are touching. He is here and he is real and he is leaving me. We sit in silence as the sun drops out of the sky—pinks and purples shift to purple and navy.

"Then I want to help you."

"Too dangerous. As it is, I have to be very careful he doesn't get wind of my plans because that will put you in immediate danger."

"So, you are leaving?"

Dominic's expression softens. He leans forward, and for the first time since our reunion, his lips find mine. Our kiss is desperate. I haven't been touched by him in seven weeks. Desire ignites within me. There is nothing I can do but fan the flames. I climb onto his lap and greedily take more. I crush my mouth to his. Our tongues dance. All I want right now is him.

"I love you," I say.

"I love you more." His arms engulf me.

I feel his love emanate from his every pore. He is the first to break contact, leaving my lips burning.

"We have to stop," he says.

"Why? I don't want to. I want you to walk me back to my house, sneak into my room, and make love to me," I whisper in his ear.

"You know I can't do that, Vivian. I want to more than I want anything else in this world. I want to live inside of you. You are my heart, Vivian, but you have an important decision to make. It wouldn't be fair of me to cloud your mind right now. You had a life before The Chamber that was interrupted. You had a man who loved you before you were taken. He still loves you. I want you to decide with a clear mind. I am not a fool."

Okay. My head is spinning.

"I have something for you." He takes out a familiar lavender envelope and hands it to me.

I note that it is bumpy. I immediately begin to open it, Dominic stops me before I can make any real progress.

"Not now. It'll be too much all at once. Open it when I'm not with you."

I can't imagine living in a world where he is not with me.

"Let's get you back home." He climbs down from the bench and extends his hand out to me.

I shove the lavender envelope inside my back pocket, take his hand, and we walk back.

We avoid our impending separation and talk about trivial things like the weather. I wish I could just tell him right now that I choose him, but he's right. I owe myself this time because of the nature of our relationship. Will I find out that it wasn't real love, or that is it the truest of all? Only time will tell.

He stops at my front porch. I know he's not going to come inside. This is goodbye, for now.

"Know that no matter what you decide, I will not stop until The Chamber is no more," he says.

I nod.

"Also." He takes my hand. "If I sense any danger headed your way, I will take you away from here, no questions asked. Mason paid me well for my services, and I will use that money to bring him down and keep you safe."

I nod again.

There is no way words can compete with the lump in my throat. I can only imagine what would happen to me if Mason ever gets his hands on me again. I can't argue with the plan. Dominic pulls me into his arms and squeezes me tight.

"I love you, Vivian." He kisses me on my lips in sweet farewell. Then, he's gone.

I CAN'T RETRIEVE the lavender envelope from my pocket fast enough. I flop onto my bed. The first thing I check for is the source of the bumpiness. A gasp escapes me when I pour the contents out and find a diamond ring inside. It's hanging on a silver chain. The band is delicate white gold. The diamond is at least a full carat and princess cut with two smaller diamonds adorning each side.

I unclasp the necklace, and carefully pull the ring from the chain, making sure not to kink it. My fingers shake as I work to free the ring from the necklace. The ring fits perfectly. I clasp the chain around my neck for safekeeping and unfold the letter.

My Vivian,

This is a whole new chapter, an unwritten book for both of us. I haven't been in the real world for five years. I never realized how isolating The Chamber can be. Of course, I had more freedom to leave. You, on the other hand, must be looking at the world with a new pair of eyes and experiencing the simple pleasures. Fresh air! The sun!

I know that you had a whole other life before you came to The Chamber. Friends, a possible new boyfriend, a loving family, and college. My point is, Dominic Xander Luke was not part of your past, but he damn sure wants to be part of your future.

I do not want to stress you out, Vivian. My intentions in writing you this letter are to tell you mine. I plan to take a step back, let you work things out, and choose for yourself, but before you do, you need all the facts.

I love you and I will lay the world at your feet.

I love you and I will protect you always.

All of me misses you...and I do mean ALL of me.

I want to spend the rest of my life with you.

Will you marry me? There, I asked the magic question. I don't expect an answer now. Is tomorrow too soon? I'm just kidding. That's what the necklace is for.

On a sadder note, with everything that we have been through, I won't be stopping by, visiting, or wooing you as much as I want to. I don't want to influence your decision. I'm staying at the Aria Hotel, room 832. I don't know how long I'll be in town. I guess until I feel like I know what your answer is.

Remember, you are a very strong woman.

I love you.
Dominic

Tears pour down my cheeks, and I read the letter over and over. Finally, it's one I don't have to destroy.

I fight every desire in my body to pick up the phone and call his room, or get in my car and drive to him.

He's right.

I need distance from them both to ease my confusion. Both of them have told me that they are mine for the taking. This is so strange, considering the fact that Liam was once the only candidate.

I fall asleep with the necklace around my neck, the ring on my finger, and the letter in my hand.

29

PROMISES

*O*ver the next few days, I get used to being home. My mother isn't hovering over me quite as much. My father is allowing me to drive on my own instead of chauffeuring me around. He signed me up for self-defense and shooting lessons.

I haven't talked to Dominic in three days. He didn't lie when he said he would give me space. Whenever I think of him—which is most of the time—I bite my lip and grab hold of my ring that dangles from my necklace, hidden from sight.

Liam and Maddie, on the other hand, I have seen daily. With Maddie, I fall easily back into step. She doesn't ask me much about the events that happened at The Chamber. She told me on my first night home that I can tell her whatever I want, whenever I want, or never.

She is cool like that.

I catch her watching me sometimes. It's like she wants to tell me something, or ask me something, but she never does. When my gaze meets hers, she gives me a brittle smile. I don't pry, though. Like any best friend would do, I figure she'll ask or tell when she is ready. I'm sure my entire family has much more to ask me, and they don't know how much I appreciate them giving me some time.

Things with Liam haven't been as smooth.

I guess he thinks that we should begin where we left off before I was taken, and I wish it were that easy. I'm trying to decide if my old, normal life is what I want.

The other issue is, he wants to talk about what happened to me. I don't. It's like he's trying to convince himself that he's okay with what I went through during my capture.

I also don't miss the undercurrent of anger in him. Not at me, per se. Maybe it's the circumstances or his lack of control over the things that I went through.

He is trying, though. So I will, too.

At lunch yesterday, the four of us went to our favorite spot— Wahoo's—for tacos. Stevyn and Maddie were all over each other, as usual. Liam and I were more discreet. He held my hand and kissed me a couple of times. I kissed him back. I really am trying.

If I could let Dominic fall into the background, like the rest of The Chamber, maybe I could be happy with Liam. Dominic is all I think about.

It's the phone call that sets my future in motion. On my ninth day home, I get an early morning international call. I only know a few people from other countries and they are all my sisters. This call is from Sunshine... Whitney.

We talked for an hour about our return home. She explained that her boyfriend is having a hard time with her disappearance, the circumstances, and the lack of details. She told me he's dealing with some unresolved anger. I told her that I'm experiencing the same thing with Liam.

We ended our call promising to keep in touch and to perhaps visit each other soon. With four million sitting in a bank earning interest, we can visit anytime we want. I love my sister.

It was later, after our phone call, that something she said hit me.

He was dealing with some unresolved anger. Hmmm.

Why are they so angry? They weren't the ones being paraded around for a host of sex-starved men. They weren't the ones who were violated. It was us. I'm sure they missed us and feared the worst, but what about unconditional love and understanding?

That's just it. They'll never understand. We were forever altered in that Chamber. Liam will always feel angry about the things he could've done to save me.

What happens when I want to spend time with one of my sisters or Zion...Hailey? Will I have to lie and tell him they are friends from school or work just to save his ego?

After that phone call, I realize a life with Liam is not what I want or need. He's a part of the old me. It's a wonderful past, but he doesn't know me anymore. It's not his fault or mine that the world shifted on its axis in this way—it just did. Now I can't help but wonder if the reason that Liam and I never were is because we weren't supposed to be.

I don't know how much time I have, so I dress quickly, grab my car keys and head to the Aria Hotel, the location of my love, and I hope I'm not too late. It's ten-thirty a.m. when I leave my car at the valet. I rush inside and grab the first elevator, which moves too slowly. I pace as it ascends.

When you know what you want without a doubt, you want it immediately, like your very life depends on it.

I want Dominic. With Dominic, I can breathe.

He knows me, and he knows everything I have been through. He was there, and still he wants me without judgment. I'll never have to lie about anything or hold back.

When the elevator dings, I exit on the eighth floor. My heart speeds up, and my arms pimple with gooseflesh. Nine days.

What if I waited too long? I stop in my tracks, unclasp my necklace and quickly place the ring on my left ring finger. I don't want there to be any question in his mind about my visit. I place the naked chain back around my neck, so that it stays pristine.

Breathing heavily, and with a hammering heart, I make my way to room 832. I drag my moist hands along my jeans.

The Chamber has indeed changed me. Before, I would never be caught dead in anything but casual wear unless it was a special occasion. This morning, I'm in four-inch heels, skinny jeans, and a low-cut purple blouse. I feel sexy now. I never did before, and the man on the other side of this door is responsible for that. My knuckles sting when I knock. There's no immediate answer. He might be sleeping.

I knock again.

I wait.

And wait.

And wait.

I realize that he's not inside. I'm too late. No! I knock harder. I beat on the door.

Stinging pain shoots through the sides of my fists. I lay my head against the door of the hotel room. This can't be.

He gave up on me. He fucking left me.

I don't know how long I'm leaning against his door when I'm startled by a person with a deep voice clearing his throat. A hotel guest probably called security on the batshit-crazy lady, crying and beating on a door so early in the morning.

Batshit. That was Sunshine's favorite word.

I don't look his way. What's the point?

"Is everything okay, miss?"

My heart skips. I spin around to see Dominic, shirtless and sweaty, and shirtless, sweaty Dominic is something to see. I have an overwhelming desire to lick every inch of him dry. He has a workout towel draped around his glistening, chiseled shoulders. Mmm.

"I thought you left," I wipe at my eyes.

"Never."

Neither of us move.

"You looked pretty sad a minute ago," he says. Our eyes are deadlocked.

"I was pretty sad. I mean, I had something important to show you," I say, overcome by coyness and a foreign, girly feeling that only Dominic has ever brought out of me.

I flash my left hand in front of my face, and squeeze my eyes shut. I squeal in delight when I'm lifted off the ground. Dominic spins me around.

"Are you kidding me? Your answer is yes?" His voice booms in the hall. I nod my head quickly. "Say it, baby! Say it!"

"Yes! I will marry you, Dominic!"

His lips crush into mine.

My whole world goes in and out of focus. This is home.

After being back for nine days, I realized he was the only thing that was missing. We don't have to do anything but sit near each other in complete silence, and I feel like the luckiest girl on earth.

He just does it for me.

The only reason it took nine days for me to admit that to myself is that The Chamber made me question all the choices I've made. The sheer fact I never tried to escape, makes my judgment questionable. I'm glad I came to my senses, though, because right now I'm in heaven.

I try to devour him in the middle of the hallway, I can't get enough of the taste of him.

His suite door opens and shuts behind us. I start coming out of my clothes before he sets me down. Dominic kisses my body, while I work at disrobing. When I unbutton my blouse and it falls past my shoulders, he adores my bare skin with his tongue and lips. He's so fucking sexy.

He kisses my naked stomach. His fingers unclasp my bra and he peppers my breasts with kisses. His increased breathing is killing me. I glance down and see that The Captain is awake. I lick my lips in anticipation. I've missed him, too.

Dominic helps me step out of my black heels and peels my jeans off of my body, kissing every newly exposed area of skin as if they are his gifts that he is unwrapping. It's fitting, since tomorrow is our shared birthday.

He uses his teeth to remove my panties. Shivers rip through my body. I'm dripping wet with want. My chest rises and falls in haste.

Dominic doesn't touch me. He stands back and gazes into my eyes.

"I love you so much. Thank you for this gift of love. I'm the luckiest human alive to get to spend the rest of my life with you in my arms."

I say nothing. My eyes don't leave his.

What he doesn't realize is that I'm the lucky one.

Dominic stalks around me. I'm his prey.

He stops in front of me. He removes his shoes and socks.

A thrill surges through my body.

He slides off his workout shorts and boxers. The Captain springs free, fully awake and alert. I bite the corner of my lip, and my eyes widen. I still can't believe that beast was ever inside me, and will soon be again.

The two of us stand in awe of one another. Feasting.

"Vivian, you have agreed to be my wife."

I nod like a schoolgirl. Every moment with him tells me that I've made the right decision.

"This is sudden. Are you sure it's want you want?"

"You're all that I want, need, and desire," I say. "I know it took me some time. I wanted to be sure that the feelings I have for you were born out of love, and not just our unique circumstances. I owed us both that, but I can't quite breathe without you. I rushed over as soon as I realized that. For me, there's only you."

My eyes never leave his. Pure joy covers his face, and he drops down on one knee. He takes my left hand into his.

"Then I promise to spend the rest of our lives together loving, honoring, cherishing, and protecting you. Our lives together will never be dull because you are my light." He kisses my left hand and admires the ring on my finger.

While my hand is in his, he trails sweet kisses along my arm. Heat follows close behind.

Still on his knees, he kisses me just above my sex. I squirm and fidget. This is salacious torture.

Before I pass out from over-excitement, Dominic scoops me up into his arms and walks me toward the bedroom, his lips never leaving mine. Who would have ever thought that after all I've been through, love would come from it?

I love this man.

He lays me onto the bed. I pant, wanting, waiting. My favorite appendage appears to be doing the same. Dominic climbs onto the bed with me. Hovering. His eyes are hooded with desire.

I tilt my hips up in want, and like an answered prayer he sinks himself deep inside of me.

Eights weeks without him and it's like the first time. My walls resist stretching to fit all of him, and the pain is delicious. He watches me. Analyzing my expressions, he pulls out of me partially before plunging deeper into my sex.

I'm so full of him. It's the most welcome and amazing feeling I'll ever have. Nothing can ever compare to him inside of me.

The next time he pushes deep, I grab hold of his ass and grip him to me. I raise my hips off the bed and grind myself around him until I can't see straight. The building pressure makes me so dizzy, I come apart in a mass of sensations. I shake and shudder and scream out his name. He follows behind me with a final thrust deep within my walls, causing me to convulse again.

We repeat our lovemaking until we are starving and exhausted.

Dominic orders room service, and when it arrives, we sit on the bed naked, eating an assortment of post-coitus fare.

"Our birthday is tomorrow. What do you want to do?" he asks me, his hand absently rubbing my thigh.

"What we're doing right now is good for me. How about you?" I ask. I raise my eyebrows up and down suggestively.

"Spending the day buried inside of you isn't a birthday gift, Vivian. It's a dying wish." My love leans over the food and plants a messy kiss on my face. I try to move back and escape his food-covered advances, but he's too quick for me. The next thing I know, he's buried inside of me again.

Covered in food, we make love until we are numb.

I DON'T REMEMBER when we fell asleep, but I wake with a start. I calm immediately when I realize that I hadn't dreamt my afternoon. I'm wrapped tight in my love's arms.

He wakes to my stares, and floods me with kisses. More accurately, he attacks me. What starts out as good clean fun, full of giggles and cries for the tickling to cease, ends with me straddling him. I'm riding the real Dominic, my very own live pleasure pony. I roll my hips in slow, deliciously agonizing circles.

He looks drunk on me. I move my hips forward and back, my sex completely full of him. I gaze into his eyes through my lashes and increase my pace, going faster and harder. I can't get him deep enough inside me. I take all that I can, as my body flushes with heat and cold. Electricity surges through me, causing my body to jerk and jolt. I ride the wave of the orgasm, quaking with pleasure.

"Dominic. Dominic. Oh, fuck! I love you!"

He follows right behind me.

After, we lay with him still inside of me until we can finally breathe normally again. "Shower?" he asks.

"If I can move."

"Here, I'll help you. Stay where you are." He begins to slide us off the bed. When his feet are on the floor at the edge of the bed I'm still straddling him. He's still throbbing inside of me. Yes.

"Wrap your legs around me."

I do as I'm told, which pushes him deeper inside of me. He stands and we make our way to the bathroom. He turns on the shower, a beautiful walk-in marble stall with no door and a huge seat.

"Do you want me to put you down?" he asks.

I show him my renewed excitement, moving my hips around him. He sits us down on the bench, and I go to work riding him. I lift off of him and slam myself down onto his erection.

"Ahh...this is all I want." I repeat this motion until we are only sensations, moans, and proclamations of love.

I am his Flame. A small part of The Chamber will always be with us. Up and down I ride him until I erupt in an explosion of shivers, contracting around him. He finds his release with me, filling me with warm, delicious fluid.

I can't contain my emotions. Sobs that I can no longer hold escape me. I bury my face into my love's chest and cry as the shower steams and luscious hot water rains down on us.

"Baby, are you okay?"

I nod, but I can't speak. I only sob. My arms grip him as if my very life depends on this moment.

"Vivian, you're scaring me. Are you okay?" He pulls me back so he can see my face.

I stare into his eyes. His face is blurry through my tears. "I'm happy."

He looks relieved. "Oh, thank goodness. You silly, beautiful girl." He floods me with kisses all over my face and neck. "I'm happy, too. The four of us are going to have a fantastic life together."

My right eyebrow raises in question. "Four of us?"

"Of course. You." He kisses my lips. "Me." He kisses me again. "Captain Thunderdick." He floods my face with pecks. "And Fuckingham Palace. Or 'The Palace' for short. You know, everyone loves a palace." He wiggles his hips under me, and I start to come alive with feelings again, especially when I hear his nickname for my sex.

"Oh, no, greedy girl. I need to get you cleaned up, and you need to call your parents so they won't worry. Then you're going to sleep. The Captain is not to be trifled with. I don't want you bruised up. We have a lifetime together, remember?"

I do remember. A lifetime of love. I'm ready for that adventure. Only Dominic can stoke my flame that only lights for him.

30

THE SPIRIT OF LOVE

Our wedding day was beautiful. We didn't have the traditional, yearlong engagement. We couldn't start our lives together soon enough. We waited four months, and only because the planning took that long.

My folks weren't too thrilled about me being engaged. Especially since they always expected me to marry Liam. I definitely broke Liam's heart.

Liam didn't talk to me for a while. Even though we're on better terms these days, deep down, I believe he'll always feel as though I betrayed him. He couldn't make the wedding. He told me he didn't want the vision of me walking down the aisle for anyone but him.

I wept for us after that conversation.

Maddie informed me that he's been dating someone from UNLV for the past couple of months. I really do hope he's happy. He's a good guy, and good guys deserve happiness.

Our day was wonderful—just as we wanted. Our wedding took place in August, in a secluded area on the beach in Malibu. The sky was the bluest I'd ever seen. The wind blew whisper-soft and glorious, just like we like it. The ocean fragrance danced on the breeze and brought with it the calm and serenity that I needed.

It was a small ceremony, just close family and friends. I got to meet Dominic's family from Hawaii. He has two beautiful younger sisters.

Speaking of sisters, all of my sisters made it. They had to—they were my bridesmaids. Maddie was my maid of honor, and Ivy, Sapphire, Sunshine, Sky, Raven, and Violet were all in attendance wearing the most beautiful scarlet red gowns They all looked sexy, even though we had to do some last-minute alterations for one of them to accommodate her six-month pregnant belly, but that's another story.

I will just say this: what happens in The Chamber, doesn't always stay in The Chamber.

My father walked me down the aisle in my snow-white gown with splashes of red in the corseted back and trim along the bottom. My bouquet was red and white roses. I've decided to embrace red. It is a part of me, just as Flame is.

My love was at the altar waiting for me in a white suit with subtle touches of red.

Our vows were simple—to live in the spirit and moment of love. Isn't love what it's all about?

For our honeymoon, we decided to take a private cruise around the Hawaiian Islands first, then the Marshall Islands, New Zealand, and Australia. Who knows where we'll be after that?

I put school on hold indefinitely. At this point, we don't even know where home is for us yet. I guess, like all the other bridges, we'll cross it when we get to it. With our combined nine million dollars in the bank, we don't have to rush back home too soon. Dominic says moving around makes us harder to track, just in case someone decides to come looking for us.

He hasn't given up his quest to bring down The Chamber, but he doesn't discuss the details with me. Instead, he tells me only what I need to know. I know that he's making gains. Something's going down because two months ago I was introduced to Declan, the new man in my life. He's in his mid- to late thirties, I would guess. He's tall, dark-haired, well-built, and all business. Declan is a highly trained military badass who has become my new security and shadow. Wherever I go, he goes. There were even security guards at our wedding who were dressed as wedding guests.

Dominic says that he can't take any chances with my safety until Mason is behind bars. Only then will he feel like he redeemed himself. He says it's the only way that he'll know real peace. It's because of me that he found the light, but The Chamber's existence will always create dark spots in his vision. I don't fight the new added security because I want The Chamber to cease to exist as much as he does. The idea of any woman experiencing what I did haunts my dreams at night. If this is what it takes for my love to see with one hundred percent clarity, then it is worth it to me.

Dominic and I won't go into our future forgetting about our past. He says my embracing that part of us is another demonstration of my strength. I just tell him we can't leave it behind. The Chamber will always be a part of us because that is where we met and fell in love.

EPILOGUE
DOMINIC

I can't believe that out of the darkness someone so unbelievably perfect as Vivian came into my life. A lot has changed in the last year and a half. I'm married. I never in my life thought I would want to be married, but somehow, being in Vivian's presence makes all things possible.

I remember the first time I laid eyes upon her.

My life was at an all-time low, but I became Mason's right-hand man. My disinterest in the women made him trust me more. I hated myself for so many reasons. Mostly, I hated myself for not saving my mother. My father told me over and over that I was just a kid, and that he was thankful to God that the thugs didn't take us both from him that day. In a lot of ways they did, though. I was in the hospital for a week after my mom died. I underwent surgery to remove the bullet that the fuckers left in my shoulder.

I wasn't the same when I was released from the hospital. I went through the motions and barely finished high school. When I enlisted in the marines, my father gave me his blessing. I wasn't fit to be around him or my little sisters. I brought everyone around me down.

My military life went by in a colorless blur. I did what was asked of me without thought or explanation. I didn't care about what happened to me or whether I lived or died. I certainly didn't care about anybody else. I made the perfect government weapon.

By the time Mason found me, I was deadly and highly trained. Nothing and no one mattered, especially me. Then Vivian's image came up on the screen. It was the first time I'd felt anything in a long time. Everything around me came to life. I knew that Vivian was special. The sight of her and the sound of her voice brought me back to life.

I didn't cry when my mother was killed. I was just a kid, and my anger kept me from crying. There was something about Vivian that lit me from within, and I wept for my mother for the first time. I realized that participating in The Chamber in any capacity was wrong.

I never wanted her to come to The Chamber. My plan was to move to Las Vegas, enroll in UNLV, and find a way into her life. I begged Mason to pick someone else, anyone but her. No matter how much I pleaded with Mason, he would not relent. He had to have her, and I hated him for it. Instead of being my boss, he became the enemy.

The thought crossed my mind to take her and not bring her to The Chamber. I'd take her to safety—anywhere where Mason wouldn't be able to find her. But as well as I believed I knew her, she had never laid eyes on me. I knew that would never work. She would always see me as a villain, not a savior. Thinking this way, even now, solidifies why I have to stop Mason. No one else should feel the pain of losing someone they love to him.

I am lost in memories as I sit on the balcony of our cruise ship headed to Sydney, Australia. That's not too far away from Brisbane, Australia, which is the location of this year's Chamber. It's not too close, either. I risk so much bringing Vivian with me, but I can't be far away from her. My intel tells me that Mason is holed up in some fortress. My security is scouting out the location while we travel in post-wedding bliss.

I have two unlikely allies on this journey. Scarlet...Raven, and Lewis Patrick, Liam's father. Scarlett and I crossed paths on more than one occasion during my early research. She has also made it her life's quest to bring down Mason, and we decided that it would be better to work together than jeopardize each other's plans. We both also decided that the less Vivian knows of Scarlet's involvement, the better.

Liam's father, like me, has a lot to atone for. He has a great deal of influence and that has proven to be very helpful in our quest. Between his contacts on the outside, and my knowledge of the security and inner workings of The Chamber, our chances are good.

"Hey. Earth to Dominic."

The sweetest voice breaks my reverie. I open my arms to Vivian, as she walks around me then folds into my lap.

"You were daydreaming," she says.

"It's easy to get mesmerized by this." I gesture toward the beauty and bounty of the ocean before us. "And by you." I smother her with kisses.

"It's gorgeous," she says.

"It pales in comparison to you." I'm not exaggerating. Her beauty brought me to the light. Everything around me is brighter and more detailed because of her. I will do everything in my power to protect her and the world around her.

We don't discuss the details. Vivian has been enjoying what she calls "blissful ignorance." She knows that even during our honeymoon, my plot to find Mason will not halt. She didn't fight the security detail that has accompanied us on every step of our journey. She was relieved when I told her that I even hired someone to keep an eye on her family.

She was brave when she went through the emergency kits. I told her it was important that she familiarize herself with its contents: cash, disposable debit cards, and a list of the locations of our hidden cash in every country we have visited in the past two months. I even had the forethought to have money stashed in a few accounts across Europe. Each kit includes multiple alternate identities and passports, should they become necessary. There are also disposable phones with each other's numbers pre-programmed. I don't plan on us being separated, but I can't take any chances. When dealing with Mason, one can't be too prepared or paranoid. With everything that's at stake, I know that I only have one shot at this. If I fail, Vivian and I will be on the run. So failure is not an option.

"Tell me again," she asks, straddling me.

Our current position has possibilities. "What?" I feign ignorance.

"My Malay nickname."

Her steel-gray eyes hold mine, and I am her prisoner. I will do anything and everything for her.

"Cahaya saya," I say the words. They dance off of my tongue and the truth of them float on the Pacific breeze. "My light."

"I don't know why, but those words sing to my soul," she says. "I learned one for you."

"Really," I say and kiss her perfect lips. Her long, dark hair is blowing in the wind. She doesn't know the things she does to me.

"Stop kissing me so I can tell you." She giggles.

"Okay, fine." I relent. Still, I smother her with a few more kisses.

"Hati saya. My heart. That is what you are and what you have."

"I love it! Maybe I should have those names on our identification. The Sayas. Hati and Cahaya Saya."

Vivian just smiles. She puts on a very brave face, but I know that she is worried. Mason is the cloudy sky in our otherwise perfect days, but not for long. I will be successful, because the future of the woman who holds my cahaya and my hati, is depending on me. No matter what, I won't let her down.

Read Weeping Violet, the next sinfully delicious book in The Seven Chamber Series, and one of my favorites!

WEEPING VIOLET EXCERPT

Chapter One

How can I be afraid and excited at the same time? On one hand, I'm free. Mason kept his promise and let us go. In style, too. I'm sure the private plane and escort to our front doors had more to do with him and his control than it does with concern for us. But here I am, rolling down the road in the back of a luxury sedan on the way to my house. I missed my mother so much while I was gone. I'm almost more afraid to see what my disappearance did to her. She already suffered the loss of my father, and now this. Maybe calling her first would be a better option?

I've been counting the minutes, hours, and days to my release, but I never thought about what it all means for me or for her. *Shit*. What about my best friends Tabitha and Taron...and Logan? What about him? Did he move on and find someone else? Could I blame him if he did? No, I can't. I've been gone a whole year.

The closer we get to my destination, dread and fear replace my excitement. I have to remember my new mantra. I open my journal that has been sitting on my lap this whole ride and I scrawl the ten words that have given me strength since I boarded the plane home. *I am safe. I am strong. I am a survivor.* I close my eyes and take deep breaths; we are close to home.

"Miss, we're here," the driver interrupts my attempts at calming myself down.

I glance up at him and offer a tight smile. My heart is racing and slamming against my chest.

I turn and look at my home. It's small and sweet, just like I remember it, with bright spring flowers and a neat, manicured lawn. I stare down at the words I have written in my journal—my salvation during the last year. I filled it with my fears, my secret wishes, and dreams, and my growing inner strength is revealed between the lines. *I can do this.*

This is it. I am going to hit the reset button. *Home.*

It's time to forever shed the label of Violet the sex slave...the Chambermaid...whatever I was during the last year, and become me again.

Once I ring that doorbell, I step back into my life as Brinley Avery Bishop—college student, daughter, and aspiring actress. *Girlfriend?* Maybe I should follow my agent's advice and dye my naturally blonde locks. I could do a vibrant red, or even a deep brown. The color doesn't matter. The point is, if I look less like *me*, I will feel less like *her.*

My legs are lead as I climb out of the car and make my way up the short path to the front door. With sweaty palms, I reach for the bell. My only thoughts are for the woman on the other side and what her reaction to my arrival is going to be. Mom must be out of her mind. I can't imagine what she suffered—waking up one day to learn that her only daughter is missing. I'm sure by now she believes I'm dead. How else could she mentally survive?

What am I going to say to her about my absence? What will be enough for her? What will be too much for Mason?

Too much time has passed.

Still, I have to do this. This is my home and we are the only family the other has. With shaky hands, I depress the bell and I wait.

It feels like forever.

My chest feels heavy and tight. My body is teeming with nervous energy, so much that my hands tremble. She'll have questions. How will I answer them? Mason was dead serious when he made his threat to us: "Breathe a word of your whereabouts, or what took place here, and you will see me again."

It's not like I even know where I was. He made sure to blindfold me during my arrival and my departure. Mason did his job well. No one used their real name in The Chamber, not even me. So what would I say? There is nothing that I could add that would help anyone locate the place.

What Mason doesn't know is that he has nothing to worry about. All I want to do is forget about my year of being passed around from stranger to stranger as they used my body for their own pleasure. I am the last person who would run around broadcasting what I went through. The sooner I can put it all behind me, the better—but, somehow, I know I will never forget.

When the door flies open my mother and I just stare into each other's green eyes. She looks older. Her eyes lack their usual brightness. Her blonde hair lacks its usual luster. I probably look *too* good. During the last year I was kept in impeccable shape and condition through regular spa treatments, my own personal groomer, and massages. That's another thing I'll have to explain to my mother. Of course, one would expect a kidnapping victim to look beaten or bruised, worse for the wear, not like she just stepped off a photo shoot.

"Brinley." The word is a whisper. She gazes at me like I'm a ghost from her past.

I grab my mother into my arms. She folds into them and we both sob in the doorway. I don't let my mother go for what feels like forever. I don't want to. She is home. Seeing her, holding her, is my only proof that I am home and free.

"Come on. Let's get you inside, honey."

My mother takes my hand and doesn't let it go. I follow her inside on unsteady legs and take a seat on the sofa because I lack the strength to stand at the moment. On my long plane ride home, I thought of all the things I would say to my mother. Somehow, all of those words have evaded me. I feel like a stranger, like a cloned version of myself. All of a sudden, I am a sci-fi experiment. I look like Brinley. I sound like her, too. I even have her memories. But something feels different, because I am not the same. I'm tarnished and forever changed because of The Chamber. How can anyone experience an entire year at the hands of a cunning and sadistic monster and not be ruined and broken? Even the strongest among the seven of us will struggle when she gets home.

I gaze around the house where I grew up, and it pretty much looks the same as it did a year ago. My mother has always preferred a minimalist approach to decor. There's a sofa, a television stand, a small flat-screen television, a bookshelf she made from recycled materials, and her abstract paintings adorn the walls. I remember when she first picked up painting. I teased her and said, "Just because you purchase a blank canvas and acrylic paints, it doesn't make you an artist." But looking around at them now, after a year of missing her and my home, I realize her paintings are masterpieces. They are to me because they're an integral part of our home.

My mom is a hippie who has always believed that a house is meant for eating and sleeping, and living takes place outdoors. Camping, hiking, biking, sightseeing, or gardening—any activity that gives us the opportunity to convene with nature—is what we should spend our valuable time doing.

She returns with a glass of water. I hadn't even noticed that she'd left the room. I take my time sipping my water and tasting it. I savor the simplicity of a drinking a glass of water in *my* home. I glance over at my mother and see that her face is wet with tears. Mine is, too. Suddenly, the water has to compete with the lump that has taken up residency in my throat.

"I can't believe you're here!" she blurts out before taking me into her arms again. There is no coffee table to set my glass on, so I hold onto it and her. We cry big, sorrowful, relief-filled tears onto each other's shoulders. "I am never letting you out of my sight again. Do you hear me?" She breaks our hold and begins checking me in earnest. "Where have you been? Are you okay? Are you hurt?"

"Define 'hurt,'" I say, wiping my eyes.

"Please tell me what happened, Brinley. Where were you?" She wipes her eyes.

I take a deep breath and begin to tell the last story I ever want to repeat. The worst part is that I know this won't be the last time I have to tell it. There will always be questions. The hardest part is figuring out the equal balance of what I can tell her without landing myself on Mason's hit list, while keeping in mind that she's a mother who has been without word from her child for a year.

"I decided to go for a morning run near school," I take a long draw of my water. "I know that I should have listened to Logan. He said it was not safe for me to be running alone, especially in Hollywood. But you know me. You always said 'Stubborn' was my middle name.... Mom, do you happen to have anything stronger than water?" *I need liquid courage before I can keep going.*

"Sure, baby." She pops up and quickly returns with a bottle of Pinot and two wine glasses.

I guess we both need something extra right now. I take my full wine glass and practically down it. It only takes a couple of minutes before the alcohol makes me less anxious.

"Like an idiot, I left my dorm and my friends, and I took off on a run toward the GPO by myself."

"The what?" Mom asks.

"Seriously, Mom? The Griffith Park Observatory. I didn't think anything of it, really. I mean, I always thought the freaks came out at night, you know? But that was the day I learned the freaks never sleep." I take another long draw of my wine and finish it. My mother refills my glass. I don't hesitate to take another sip. "I made it to the GPO in record time. I was feeling that high I get from running. Then I bent down to tie my shoe, and before I could get back to my feet again, I saw three men coming for me. I didn't even have a chance to run, scream, or fight. They were on me before I could process what was happening. They put a cloth to my face and that was it. Lights out for me."

My mother finishes her first glass and pours another. Tears are rolling freely down her cheeks. I can't visibly see her hands shaking, but I hear the bottle clank repeatedly against her wine glass.

I continue. "When I woke up, I was on an airplane."

"Where did they take you?" Her voice catches on a sob.

"I have no idea. I thought for sure I was headed to my death. I had no reason to believe otherwise. I mean, only psychos would kidnap perfect strangers. I just knew I was going to die and we'd never see each other again." I pause and draw in two deep breaths. This is the tricky part. What I say from here on could get me into a lot of trouble if I believe Mason's threat, and I do. "What I learned after I got off the plane ride was that death would have been the easy way out for me, Mom. Death would have meant peace. But when I got off of that plane, I never thought I would know peace again."

My mother tries to stifle her heavy sobs as they rip through her, but I can tell she has never been more scared than this moment, hearing my words. My living nightmare.

"The place I was taken was a sex club for rich and powerful men. I was forced to work there, and...I'm sure you can figure out the rest."

"Oh my god! Oh my god!" My mother pulls me into her arms. Her cries are loud and frightened. "We have to call the police." She squeezes me.

"And tell them what?" I pull away from her so I can look her in the eyes. She needs to understand that calling or telling anyone is not an

option. Especially the police. "The man who took us warned us that if we said anything, he'll come after us. He said we wouldn't be safe anywhere on earth. He will make us suffer. He's a dangerous man. Trust me. The men who take part in his annual chambers will do anything to keep this covered up. Let it be over. Isn't it enough that I'm home?" I beg and plead with her.

My mother grabs my arms and shakes me a little. "You listen here. I don't give a rat's hairy ass about this monster. He took you, kept you for a year, and made you do unspeakable things. He has to pay. He has to be stopped." Her voice is sharper than I've ever heard it.

I jump up from the sofa. I have to get through to her. "This is a losing battle. You don't want this. What if he takes me again? Just drop it, Mom! When I first got there he showed us videos. He watched us for two years before he kidnapped me. He's probably watching me now. I have the money. I just want to forget." Tears are pouring down my cheeks.

I just want her to understand, I don't want to look over my shoulder. I want to live my own life, free of The Chamber. Free of The Monster. I need to work at living my new life. I hit the reset button and now I need to find my new normal.

"I just want to get past this, Mom." I am exhausted.

"What money, Brinley?" she asks.

"Four million dollars," I say. My voice is just above a whisper. I know she is going to freak out. I mean, if I was a mother and my daughter was telling me what I am telling her, I would freak out, too. "I know you have to call the police and tell them I'm home. I know they will want to talk to me and ask me questions. But I can only tell them the bare minimum." I continue to speak in a low, unsure voice. "This is the way it has to be, Mom. It's the only way I can be here with you."

"I can't believe what I'm hearing." My mother jumps up from the sofa and starts pacing. "I don't understand. Why would you have four million dollars?"

I flop back down on the sofa. I bring my knees up to my chest and bury my face into them. At this point, the only way I can speak to my mother is from this position. Discussing any aspect of my time in The Chamber is exactly what I wanted to avoid. It was the most humiliating and embarrassing year of my life. I know that showing up on my mother's doorstep, after being gone for a year with no word or communication, an explanation can't be avoided.

"I don't know, Mom. We *are* talking about a crazy person here. He kidnapped seven of us, made us have sex with a bunch of rich guys for a year, then paid us millions for it. Crazy is not meant to be understood. Crazy seems to have the power to do whatever it wants." I knew this would be difficult for her. How can I expect anyone to understand what I went through? I know—with the exception of the six other girls, my sisters—no one ever will. I'm not happy that I was paid, but I'm not going to give the money back. It won't change what happened to me, or to any of us. I left a sex chamber a millionaire.

The worst part of all of this is how confused I feel. When I first arrived at The Chamber I wanted to die—to curl myself into a tiny ball and fade away to nothing. But an experience like that changes you. The Chamber was nothing like I expected it to be. I wasn't chained to a wall. I wasn't kept in some dank, dark cell. I wasn't beaten or drugged.

It was quite the opposite. I made friends with the other girls. I had massages and manicures and movie nights. I had my own personal trainer and groomer. The only time I felt like I was in hell was when I had to perform sex acts with strangers who, by the end of the year, weren't even strangers to me anymore. All of this knowledge, coupled with the money, makes me even more confused, and makes my experience even harder to fathom. Anyone I tell the full details of my story to would think I'm crazy, too. The first question that will spring forth in their minds will be, "Why did you stay?" As if I had a choice.

Personally, I don't know why Mason is worried about us telling anyone. I never want anyone to really know what happened within those vast walls.

What would I say, anyway? *Well, Mom, I had sex with thirty-five different men. Thirty-seven if you include the times that Mason had his turn with me, or the times I fell asleep in my Chamber, and my personal guard, Gabe, came to visit me.* Why should I feel guilty about the money? I know it won't buy me my sanity, but that much money will help me start my new life—especially when I don't even know who I am anymore.

My mother watches me with concern in her green eyes. I hope she can see *me*. I'm the same little girl who loved acting and making up stories since I was in grade school. I'm the same girl who wanted to finish college and travel to New York with my boyfriend, Logan, and attend Juilliard. And even though I am not quite as hippie as she is, I hope she still recognizes the me who saw the beauty in the mountains, the trees, and the ocean. I am praying that as she gazes at me with confusion and concern, *I* still exist in her eyes, because I may need her help to find myself along the way.

When my mother scoots toward me on the sofa, I am surprised and relieved when she grabs me into the most loving and protective embrace I have ever felt. We both sob again in each other's arms. She may never understand what happened to me, but she loves me, regardless.

"We will get through this together, baby," she promises. I am so overcome, I can only nod. There are no words.

Mom calls the police and she agrees with me that I can tell them whatever I feel they need to know to keep us safe. I don't mention the money to them, fearing it will raise too many questions that I cannot answer.

I'm beyond exhausted; fortunately I manage to get by only sharing the bare minimum with the officers—the location from where I was snatched, the fact that everyone in the place I was kept used a fake name, that I only saw the outside for the first time today. I told them that I traveled a great distance by plane, but have no idea where I was being kept for the entire year. My mother sobbed quietly while I spoke to the officers, who could only tell me how lucky I am to be alive. I see a look on my mother's face that worries me. It's a combination of fear, pity, and sadness. She tries to mask it, but I catch a glimpse before she can turn away.

One of the officers gave us his card in case I remember more. If only they knew just how much I remember. They also gave my mother some information on places I can go if I need emotional help. And just like that, they were gone. I hope I don't receive any more visits from the police. I am willing to bury any memories of the last year. If I am lucky, my name and case will get filed away under unsolved crimes.

My room looks just like it did before I moved into the dorm two years ago. I feel like I'm back in my last year of high school. My walls are plastered with the heartthrobs of that time and my many photo collages from high school. I was really into pastels my senior year. My room looks like an Easter basket exploded all over the walls and floors.

All of my belongings from AMDA, the American Musical and Dramatic Academy, are back in place in my room. Damn, I had a sweet spot in the bungalows, too. I'll bet my friends and teachers all think I'm dead. Whatever. I'm too tired to think about my life. I hope my mom calls Logan for me, if he is even still in Los Angeles. It was bad enough just popping up on her doorstep after all this time. I can't do that to him. That thought frightens me. At least if she calls him first and gives him time to process the fact that I'm home, he won't have to stare at me like a ghost come back to life when he sees me. As much as I can't wait to see Logan, I fear the look in his eyes.

What if he has moved on? He could have a whole new life, complete with a girlfriend, by now. *What if he has a girlfriend?* I can't be upset with him if he does. It's been a year. *Snap out of it, Brinley. If he moved on there is nothing you can do.*

Today I will sleep and recharge. Tomorrow...life.

When I stare down at my bed, my stomach becomes queasy. The light purple comforter thrusts me back to The Chamber and my life as Violet. I run into my bathroom and deposit what little I have in my stomach into the toilet. Closing the lid, I sit on top of it and run cool water into the sink. I don't fight the tears that stream down my face. I have grown accustomed to crying this past year. *You will be okay, Brin-*

ley. It is just a color. It doesn't define you. It never did. You are a survivor. You wouldn't be here if you weren't. I grab a towel, dampen it, and wipe my face. I gather myself, walk back to my room, and remove the comforter. I drop it in a heap in the hall outside of my room and shut the door on any memory it might force me to recall of Violet.

I pull a quilt from my closet, wrap up in it, and lie on my bed. Right away, I feel the pull of sleep. My body is spent from a very emotional reunion. I am almost out when my mother knocks on the door.

"Honey. Sorry to disturb you, but I saved these for you. I knew you would come home to me."

I glance up and see that she has a stack of journals.

"I planned to give them to you for your birthday last year. I know how much it helped you to write in them when Dad died. I just thought maybe..."

I sit up in my bed and take the journals from her hands. She plants a kiss on my forehead. After everything, being home still doesn't feel real. I think I'm numb. I stack the journals on my bedside table. "Thanks, Mom. I think I can use them." She's right, and she knows me well. When my father died a year after he was stricken with cancer, my journals were the only thing that kept me sane. I let it all out on paper—the anger, the fear, the pain. I did the same in The Chamber.

"Would you rather talk to a professional?" she asks.

"How about I try these first, Mom?"

"Okay, baby. What do you want me to do with the comforter? Was it dirty?"

"Throw it away. I don't like purple anymore."

"Will do. Let me know if you need anything." She heads for my door. "I love you."

"Love you, too, Mom."

I think I'm asleep before she closes the door.

Chapter Two

One by one, we are named—branded like cattle. We're all given names of colors or objects that represent a color. Raven, Sunshine, Flame... The Monster has literally stripped us down to nothing, destroying our souls and essence.

My heart is beating in my throat as he makes his way down the line toward me. There is no escape. I can only stand here and suffer my fate. I watch in horror as five antique bookcases slide open along the circular wall, revealing hidden staircases. Five girls slip into the darkness and the bookcases close behind them.

Then there are two—me and the dark-haired girl standing to my right. I can feel her fear because I share it. Mason, The Monster, wants to have fun with us. He flashes us his serpent-sized erection, and I almost pass out. He calls us his "two virgins."

Mason named the other girl Flame. She and I are led to another area. With every step we take, I'm closer to having a full-blown panic attack. She must be just as scared. The only thing keeping me from collapsing is the picture of my mom that Mason showed me and what he told me would happen to her if I don't cooperate with him. He has me, and he knows it. I would never sacrifice my mother for a very slim chance to escape.

We follow a blonde named Ivory down a series of corridors and tunnels. Her white stilettos clack loudly against the stone floor. I look around at my surroundings and see that we are in a castle-like structure with high ceilings and stone walls and floors. With each echoing step, my head aches more and more. We turn the corner, and come to a door with a sign that says: DEFLOWERING CHAMBER.

Shit. Ivory ushers Flame and I through the door. There are naked guards on either side of the entrance. Their erections are at attention, for us, I assume. It doesn't seem like we will have a choice about what happens next. I want to die. I don't want to do this. I don't deserve what is about to happen. Neither of us do. Tears fall heavily down my face. I have never been a fighter.

The room is stark white. The only color accent comes from the blood-red and lavender pillowcases on top of two of the three beds.

Tyson and Gabe, two guards who have also flashed us their enormous erections, come into the room. Tyson leads Flame to one bed, and Gabe takes me. I don't fight or try to run. I should, but where would I go? I do as I am told. Before I have a chance to prepare, Gabe removes my clothes and lays me down on the bed with the lavender pillows. His tongue begins to sweep over my sex. He takes his hands and pushes my legs as far apart as they will go. I squeeze my eyes closed as tight as I can. If I hold my breath maybe I can make myself pass out, or better yet just stop breathing entirely. Relentlessly, he sucks and licks until I feel something come over me. Heat floods between my legs as his tongue pushes forcefully inside of me.

I lose my train of thought and focus only on the feeling down there. An unwelcome moan escapes my lips naturally. I am a woman with hormones, and with every lick and suck, my body betrays me. When his lips latch on to my clitoris, I come undone. The intensity of his relentless sucking is unnerving. I scream out and my body explodes with violent, uncontrollable shaking. Gabe doesn't stop. He is unyielding with his punishment. He drives his fingers inside of me. I try to scoot my body back away from him, but my efforts are pointless. I feel my innocence tear away from me as he continues to thrust his fingers inside me and devour me with his tongue until I come apart again.

He stops. "You are fucking amazing. I will take extra special care of you this year," he says before walking away.

"My, my, Violet. Your personal guard sure did warm you up for me." I open my eyes and see Mason, The Monster. His dark hair, nearly black eyes, and fair skin symbolize pure evil to me. He looks to be in his thirties, and for the briefest second, I wonder what makes a man decide to kidnap women and run a place like this. It doesn't matter what his motivation is. I hate everything about him. To me, he will always be a monster.

He is completely naked and I see that the large snake between his legs is prepared to strike. I dare a peek at the other bed and see that Flame is busy with her guard. Mason doesn't give me another second to react or prepare. He flips me over onto my stomach and pulls me up onto my knees, causing my back to arch with his exaggerated pull. My breath escapes me when he slams the entire length of his erection into me. He isn't patient, he isn't kind—he is a wild animal, a real monster. He pounds into me relentlessly—impaling and filling me inside over and over. I am distracted suddenly by the sound of screaming. It is loud and horrific. I seek out Flame, but she is not screaming. She looks like she's enjoying herself. *Where are the screams coming from?* Someone is utterly terrified for her life and needs help...

"Brinley. Brinley! Wake up." Someone calls me from a distance.

I feel arms around me. I thrash, trying to break free of the binding arms so I can help the screaming girl.

"Brinley, it's okay. You're home. You're safe."

I open my eyes to Logan, and realize the screams are mine. I've had my first nightmare.

"Oh my god, Logan!" I cry out and fold into his arms. I break down into heavy sobs. His hold is strong and protective. "I was back there all over again."

"You're safe, babe. I promise."

He rubs my back and it is immediately soothing. It's the first touch from a man I've welcomed in a year. I'm so relieved it was a nightmare and I'm waking up to Logan's strong embrace. It felt so real.

"When did you get here?" I ask.

"Your mom called me after you went to sleep. I couldn't wait for you to wake up, so I have been here for a few hours."

"Doing what?"

"Watching you sleep."

I gaze up at him and see that his blue eyes are red-rimmed.

"I thought I lost you forever. I died a little every day that you were gone." He squeezes me.

I hope he's right. I really hope that I am back. I don't know how much of me I left behind.

"Are you thirsty? I can get you water or juice," he offers.

I panic. "No. Don't leave me. Please." I feel the remnants from my dream tugging at me. My entire core is shaking.

"Never." He kisses the top of my head.

I fall onto my side and Logan follows suit, holding me. "Where's my mom?"

"She went to the store to get food for you."

"But I'm not hungry."

He kisses me on my cheek. "Well it'll be here when you get hungry."

I'm afraid to fall asleep again. I don't want to go back there. Can a person die from sleeplessness? I am willing to try. I never want to sleep again.

Chapter Three

I wake with a start. I fell asleep again without knowing it. No nightmare. No dreams at all. It was a glorious, dreamless sleep. Logan's body is entwined with mine. I have no idea what time it is, and I don't care. I'm home. My mother is safe, and Logan is by my side. Though, once he finds out what I went through over the last year, I wonder how many sleeps I can expect him to hold me through.

With my free arm, I shift myself and roll over so I'm facing him. Logan Wright. I used to joke that we'd see one day if he was, in fact, Mr. Right.

We were going on our second year of dating when I was taken. Logan and I met at USC. He was a film student and needed a blonde actress who didn't require payment for a short he was filming. Through mutual friends, the news traveled over to me at my performing arts college, and I jumped at the opportunity. He takes filmmaking very seriously. He was all business when we met, but I was immediately attracted to him. When I first saw him, I thought he was another actor with his clear blue eyes, dark brown hair, and tall, athletic build.

Having so much in common, we easily fell into dating. He isn't from L.A. like me. He's from Denver. But he was born to live by the ocean. Our courtship wouldn't be called a fairy tale, but I always loved that there was no competition between us. We both only wanted the best for each other. Before I was taken we had even begun discussing a future together. He was getting ready to graduate from USC, and I only had one year left. He was already accepted into NYU's prestigious graduate screenwriting program, and I planned on moving to New York as well—so we naturally began speaking about the idea of marriage. We both decided that we would wait to become more serious after college.

Most guys would run for the hills from a girl who believes in abstinence, but not Logan. He always felt the same way about it as me. "Too much instant gratification in the world and not enough sacrifice," he would say, especially when we would get cornered by some of our less understanding college friends who thought we were insane prudes. So the odds of meeting a guy who was into film and the arts and wanted to wait until he got married to have sex...I thought we were perfect for each other. It felt like fate to have found my *Mr. Right*.

With one hand, I brush his brown hair from his face. It's longer than I remember. He is sleeping so peacefully, like an angel. I wish we could stay just like this. In this moment, he most likely still loves me. Right now, he is happy about my unexpected return. Once he wakes up, he will learn I'm not the pure love of his life that I was before I was taken. I love him so much, but I fear that my love won't be enough. He is beautiful with his fair skin and soft, full lips. I wonder briefly if our kids would be brunettes like him, or blonde like me. I'm sure now I will never know.

Logan's eyes open and a sweet smile crosses his face. "Hey."

"Hey." I smile back at him. I can pretend for now that everything between us is okay and that the last year did not happen.

He stretches. "You okay? Any more bad dreams?"

"Nope. Not with you around." I give him a smile that is equal parts gratitude and relief.

"Good." He plants a kiss on my cheek. "Are you hungry yet?" He jumps out of my bed.

It's in this moment that I already know something is wrong. He hasn't questioned me about where I've been. *He already knows.* My mother let the cat out of the bag. "Logan. Can I ask you a question?" I come up onto my knees.

"Anything." He sits on the edge of the bed.

"Did my mother tell you what happened to me and where I've been this whole time?" I almost don't want to know the answer, but I have to know how to proceed with him. I'm tense and nervous bubbles fill my stomach as I await his answer.

He clears his throat. "She told me everything you told her. What you told the police."

"And?" I let the word drag out.

His brows furrow with confusion. "And what, Brinley?"

"You're still here?" I ask, my brows matching his.

He leans forward, takes my hand, and pulls me closer to him. "Listen..."

I can't bring myself to look at him. Fear of the words is causing my skin to crawl and my heart to race.

"I need you to look at me." He guides my chin gently with his hand toward him. I drag my eyes to his reluctantly, doing what I can to hide the hope in them.

"When your mother told me what you had to endure, I wanted blood. I still want nothing more than for someone to pay for what happened to you. But, Brinley, not you. You shouldn't have to pay. You have suffered enough. I loved you before you were taken. Nothing has changed."

I can't stop the waterfall that springs from my eyes.

"Do you want to talk about it?" he asks me.

I shake my head no.

"Then we won't talk about it." Logan wraps me in his strong embrace.

I wipe my eyes, nodding my head in agreement. "I just want to forget about everything. I know that I'll never be that lucky." I pull out of his embrace. I do my best to clean my face up with my quilt and I force a smile.

"I'd rather hear about you. I missed you so much, Logan. Tell me what I missed," I ask, wiping my eyes again, this time with the back of my hand.

I'm sure this is not what he really wants to talk about. How could he not want me to tell him all about the last year of my life? I am thankful to him for giving me some time. He loves me enough to give me what I need right now.

"Well, I graduated last May. My final film did very well. So well, in fact, that I landed a job with Bluest Moon Productions. I'm in the editing room, but it's all good. I want to learn every aspect of the filming process." He sighs, rubbing my back.

"Keep talking," I say because the silence is deafening. "Tell me more about working for a big film company. I'm so proud of you." *I am.* He has stayed focused on his dreams. But more than that, I'm happy to keep the conversation off of me. It keeps me out of my head. I know that I will have to talk about things eventually, but I just got home. I have forever to face what I will never forget.

"It's amazing, babe. Everything I ever wanted. I'm learning so much."

I'm a little surprised that Logan is this happy. We always planned to leave L.A. and head to New York together. New York was as much his dream as it was mine. We had it all planned out. He would go immediately following graduation and I would follow him a year later when I graduated. *If,* of course, I was accepted into Juilliard. It is now my belief that we are not the only ones in charge of our destinies, no matter how much as we plan our lives out. If we were, the last year of my life would never have happened. Being home now feels like waking up from a coma or being abducted by aliens for a year, only to be dropped out of the sky and back into my normal life. It feels familiar and strange at the same time. I missed an entire year of Logan's life. I have questions. *Why no NYU? Does he have a girlfriend?*

"What is it, Brin?" he asks.

"Nothing," I lie. I don't want to ask because I'm not sure I want the answer.

"You can ask or tell me anything. Just talk to me, please."

"It's just…" I look at him briefly and then away. "Getting on with Bluest Moon Productions is an amazing accomplishment, but what about your dream to go to NYU?"

He is silent as he stares into my eyes. "I couldn't go."

"Why? You were already accepted. What happened?"

"Some psycho kidnapped my girl off the fucking street, and everything in my life changed."

I drop my head to my lap. My tears fall with ease. I hear the anger in his voice.

"I'm sorry, babe. I know you're not ready to talk about what happened. Just know that I couldn't leave. I felt like as long as I stayed here, you would find your way back to me…you would come home. I was lost without you, and since New York was our dream, I just couldn't do it." He rubs my back.

"I thought about you every day, every minute," I cry out. "Thinking about you was the only thing that kept me strong, but, honestly, it also scared me to death." I cry harder. He pulls me back into his arms. "I was worried that you would find someone else. Or worse, that if I did make it out of there, you wouldn't want me anymore because of the things that were done to me."

He pulls me up and is gentle at the task of turning my face to his. "Brinley. There is only you. There will only ever be you for me. I will never stop loving you." Tears leak from his red-rimmed eyes as he weeps for me. "I love you."

"I love you ,too."

He continues. "No amount of time, no kidnapping, or rapist assholes will change that," he promises me.

Hearing the word "rapist" is like being slapped in the face. It accurately describes what I went through, but the use of that word also confuses me, because in spite of everything that happened to me, I was treated very well for the most part. *We will see if his promises hold true. I still don't know how much crazy I brought back with me.* After a year, I am no doubt changed, and only time will tell how and how much.

For now I can revel in the knowledge that, in this moment, he loves me.

Continue Reading Weeping Violet

AFTERWORD

Did you love Stolen Flame? Be sure to review it on Amazon and let other romance readers know what you thought!

💋 Dionne

MAILING LIST

Did you enjoy Broken Sky be sure to join my mailing list and get the inside scoop on new releases, and have access to unreleased short stories about the characters you love!

D.W. MARSHALL'S DARK HEARTS

Want to talk with other romance lovers? Join my Facebook Group, D.W. Marshall's Dark Hearts.

ALSO BY D.W. MARSHALL

The Seven Chambers Series

Stolen Flame

Weeping Violet

Shattered Sapphire

Poisoned Ivy

Eclipsed Sunshine

Broken Sky

Cruel Obsessions Series

Twisted Soul

Coming Soon Twisted Heart

The Men of the Seven Chambers Series

Dominic

The Escorts Series

ABOUT THE AUTHOR

D.W. Marshall is a graduate of Tuskegee University. She is a native of California, but grew up in Las Vegas. If you opened her purse you'd find too many pens for one person, lip balm, and the dreaded receipts that never seem to go away.

D.W. loves to read dark *and* sweet romance, fantasy, YA, thrillers, and lives in Las Vegas with her husband, two sons, niece, and her one-eyed Bichon, named Sadie.

www.dwmarshallbooks.com

ACKNOWLEDGMENTS

This book started with a dream, was published during a tough time in my life, and like my main character, Flame, I made it through, but not on my own. My family and closest friends have been with me for the long ride, and for that I thank them. For having to listen to me talk about my characters as if they were real people or patiently listening to me explain the details of a new story idea, I say thank you.

I never imagined when I went into this that becoming an author would take so much effort and hard work. I thought if I had a great story to tell and wrote it down, then bled my ideas all over the page, magically everyone would find my books in the sea of books and love reading my words as much as I loved writing them. Boy, was I wrong. It has been said that it takes a village to raise a child, and I'd like to add that it also takes one to produce a book.

My villagers are Danielle Acee and Danylle Salinas from The Authors' Assistant. I would be lost without them. They keep me on task, keep me organized, edit my work beautifully, marketing, and most importantly: keeping me on task, did I say that already? It bears repeating, because the ideas never stop coming. Which is something else I'm thankful for.

Lastly, my readers are rock stars. Thank you so much for the messages that you send me, telling me what you loved about one of my books, or asking me when the next one of coming out. You are fuel to my flame.